W9-CIF-040

Old Devotions

Also by Ursula Perrin

*Ghosts*
*Heart Failures*
*Unheard Music*

# Old
# Devotions

# Ursula
# Perrin

THE DIAL PRESS
NEW YORK

Published by
The Dial Press
1 Dag Hammarskjold Plaza
New York, New York 10017

Grateful acknowledgment is made to the
following for permission to reprint from
previously published material: Little, Brown and
Company: Excerpt from "March Elegy" from
*Poems of Akhmatova*, Selected, Translated and
Introduced by Stanley Kunitz with Max
Hayward. Copyright © 1972 by Stanley Kunitz
and Max Hayward. First appeared in the
*Iowa Review*.

Copyright © 1983 by
Ursula Perrin

All rights reserved.

Manufactured in the
United States of America

First printing

Design by
Francesca Belanger

Library of Congress Cataloging in Publication Data
Perrin, Ursula.
    Old devotions.
    I. Title.
PS3566.E694404    1983    813'.54    82-9663
ISBN 0-385-27656-7

*For Richard Kot . . .*
*editor, scholar, friend*

I have enough treasures from the past
to last me longer than I need, or want.
You know as well as I . . . malevolent memory
won't let go of half of them.

*Anna Akhmatova*
*"March Elegy"*

# I

Home
Again

# 1

When I got back to New York from Leningrad, I found that my newly rented apartment was gone—burned out by the fool on the floor below me, who had fallen asleep while puffing on his hookah. He was dead, a canvas-covered bundle of charred bits, and his apartment and mine were one large blackened hole in the gut of the five-story building. Two days after the fire the NYFD called me to say they had rescued out of the swirling, stinking ruins, my mother's silver tea service, which (in order to thwart thieves) I kept in a secret cabinet of the cool, tile-lined bathroom, and a silver-framed portrait of my ex-lover David, the frame intact, the blackened picture nothing much but a gleam where his smile used to be and one dark, steady eye that stared at me with sad reprobation.

What were my emotions at this disaster? Shock, of course, and curiously, relief. My past had been irrevocably reduced to ash. I was, despite the trip to Russia, at one of those dead ends of the imagination, a cul-de-sac of the heart, spirit, and guts. It was as if life, gently pointing, had led me down certain streets and byways and then, shrugging, showed me a high blank wall. I was bored with the kind of boredom that starts in a vague feeling of listlessness and then insinuates itself into your bloodstream until, like the victim of a tropical disease —sleeping sickness or the one you get in riverbeds from snails —you lie there in the morning wondering what there is to get up for, and when a woman you like calls, you think: *Oh, no, not her again,* and when a man you like calls (and you envision going to bed with him), it seems like too much trouble. That,

3

my friend, is the kind of boredom of which I speak. Anyway, with my apartment and belongings now a heap of rubble, I had nowhere to stay and I thought how lucky I was to have two excellent friends to call upon: my old friend Morgan Whiteside and my boss at WJVB-TV, Joan Thistle.

I didn't, however, much want to stay at the Thistles'. In the first place the Thistle house is smelly and messy—they have a senile dog that Joan is too tenderhearted to dispatch ("I refuse to practice dog euthanasia"), and the dog, Clarabelle, who is blind and incontinent, wanders peeing from room to room. At the Thistles' the guest room sheets always have curious stains on them, and the wastebaskets are full of other people's crumpled Kleenexes and cigarette butts; the bathroom walls are speckled with mold, the bathtub bottom has long strands of Lorelei hair on it, and there is only one limp towel hanging by an ear from the towel bar. The main problem with going to the Thistles', however, is not the house but the fact that Joan and Stuart, after twenty-three years of married life together, openly began to dislike each other all of a sudden a year ago last July. I know this happens frequently, but it makes me impatient with marriage as an institution, and I certainly have no desire to be what I have so often been lately when in their company—a poorly regarded referee, a marriage counselor on the cheap.

At the Whitesides', on the other hand, the guest room is neat, the sheets have been recently changed, the towels are rough and fresh, the children are tolerably well behaved and stay out of your way, there are no cats, the dog is amiable but only indifferently so, and the whole picture is one of domestic happiness and conjugal bliss, a rose-covered cottage straight out of Charles Dickens. Of course, usually when I am asked to stay at the Whitesides', Douglas Whiteside is out of town (it's not that Douglas and I dislike each other, we are only uncomfortable together), so in truth all this Currier and Ives felicity may very well be a sham. This doesn't in the least perturb me. For the several days of my visit I would rather conspire in a pleasant deception than take on an honest mess of trouble. I like my protected status as Eternal Guest.

Thus, humming to myself (*vye-cherny zvon, vye-cherny zvon,* an old Russian song), I dialed Morgan's New Jersey number.

"Come out here?" Morgan said to me on the telephone. "Stay with us? Oh, but you can't. We are going to move, Isabel. I mean immediately, like tomorrow. The bed linens won't be unpacked. The beds won't even be put together. I can't wait till you see our new house. You are just going to die!"

*No doubt,* I thought ungraciously, but until then I still needed a place to stay. And how irritating it is to go on a long trip, to come home with a head full of wondrous images and a suitcase full of photographs only to find that your friend is distracted. Her life, at however petty a pace, has crept on; she doesn't want to look at your slides of St. Basil's, she wants to talk about real estate.

"The kitchen, Isabel, the kitchen is, well, *huge,* and there's a family room at the other side of the kitchen separated by a whatchamacallit, serving bar? and out back there are these divine little gardens all laid out in brick-edged beds, and out in front, near the pool—did I say we had a pool?—there's a rose garden. I've always wanted a rose garden. And the bedrooms! Guess how many bedrooms we've got! Seven!"

"Terrific," said laconic Isabel. "Now you and Douglas can have live-in lovers."

"I can," she said, "he can't. He is not allowed any such thing."

"That's not fair," I said.

"Life isn't fair," she said cheerfully.

"Obviously," I said dryly, "if you have seven bedrooms and your poor friend here has none."

Silence. I examined my fingernails and waited for the guilt level to elevate. At length she said meekly, "Where are you now?"

5

I said (stiffly, coldly—the rejected friend), "At the West-bury Hotel."

"But it's nice there. Isn't it?"

"Yeah, but it's expensive. I'm running out of money."

"Can't David give you some? Isabel? Are you there?"

"About David. You see . . ."

"Wait a minute. *What?*" This was directed not at me but toward some plaintively screaming child in the background. I heard over or between her fingers wrapped around the receiver, "Yes, all *right,* I'm coming," and then her voice careened back toward me: "Isabel, I can't talk to you now, I've got to take Tess to swim team practice. God, your timing is always so off. What were you saying about David? Did he go on the trip with you?"

"No."

"You went alone?"

"Yes, you see David and I are no longer, uh . . ."

"Oh, no, you don't mean it! You fool, he is such a sweet guy. He is perfect for you. Honestly, just when I thought you were all taken care of. And I don't know another free soul, Isabel, I mean, my house isn't exactly the ark, you know. Besides, I have other friends who need male attention."

"Now just one second here," I said, letting my voice project a little frost. "Did I even ask? All I asked you for was a place to stay, not a bunkmate, remember? And if that's going to be such a horrendous difficulty, I'll call my friend Joan Thistle. No doubt I can stay with *her* for a couple of days."

Palpable relief crept along the telephone wires from out of north central New Jersey. "Oh, well, good then. But just to make sure you have got someplace, I'll call you later." She hung up, leaving me to look, appalled, at the heavy green drapes of the hotel room windows. They were pulled back and fastened with brass rosettes and reminded me of two old Russian peasant women snidely smiling, showing gold incisors. Lord. The Thistles. I just wasn't up to it. Once more, in case I had missed a little something or other, I unlatched my canvas mailbag-type purse and unzipped the compartment that held my pretty blue and gold-stamped bankbook. Hmm. Eighty-two twenty-four. Well.

"Joan?"

"Mrs. Thistle is not here at present. She is on location at the Brooklyn Botanical Garden and not currently expected. This is her assistant, Sandy Plotkin, speaking. Who shall I say is calling?"

Sandy Plotkin, eh? Leave for a brief respite and someone else snags your job. No. Joan wouldn't let anyone else have my job, she'd said so before I left. That would be the very end, losing one's lover, apartment, belongings, and job all in the same month.

"Hello? Hello?" Already Sandy Plotkin had adopted the imperious tone used by office underlings.

"Hi, Sandy, this is Isabel. How are you?"

Sulky silence. "Very well, thank you. What is it you want?"

"Joan. She's not there?"

"No. They're shooting today. I'll tell her you called."

"Ask her to call me, please. I'm at the Westbury Hotel."

"Very well."

"Oh, and Sandy."

"What?"

"I'll be back to work on Monday."

"Swell," she said sourly and hung up. Relieved, I went to the window and looked out. Down below, Madison Avenue glinted with small silvery automobiles. So. I still had my job. Often I wished I still had David. On my trip I had missed him. I had dropped him for his own good. I know that is hard to believe, but it is so. The telephone rang. The hotel room phone had a trilling ring, like the laugh of a woman who has had one drink too many.

"Okay," Morgan said, "what's the story? Are you going to Joan's?"

"No."

"Ha. Thought not. She's always such a terrific friend until

the crunch comes. Someday I want you to remember how really good I was to you. Listen to this: I have got you a place to stay."

# 2

Morgan Whiteside (then Morgan O'Malley) was my college roommate. If, on that warm, hazy Connecticut Valley September day so many years ago, a giant computer had been asked to select two obviously incompatible freshman types, it would have punched out O'Malley and Schliemann. Our only similarity was this: We had vast personal reservoirs of energy which we applied in totally different directions. Putting Morgan and me together was like combining nitro and glycerine, and that first day of the Smith College semester, standing there in the doorway of that tiny, dingy dormitory room, I thought I was going to hate her. She had already taken possession of our twelve-by-eight space. Displayed on the striped ticking of the bottom bunk mattress was a jumble of athletic equipment—three rackets (two tennis, one squash), three field hockey sticks, a bulky pair of shin guards, and a pair of ladies' white figure skates, surmounted all by a large leather saddle against the pommel of which foppishly leaned—as if with folded arms—a riding crop, and on either side of which stood two staunch pairs of riding boots, one pair caramel colored and worn, the other viciously blood red and brand new, both with toes snottily upturned. She, Morgan, sat cross-legged on the floor in sneakers, knee socks, plaid skirt, and girl's school gym shirt, meditatively plucking at the strings of a lacrosse stick.

"Hi," she said, looking up. She was thin and tanned, and her black hair was pulled into that little knot at the nape of the neck that horsewomen affect. "Howareya? I'm Morgan O'Malley. You must be my roomie."

"Yes," I said.

"They sent me your name on a card."

"Yes," I said. Oh, I knew her type all right. St. Tim's or Madeira, Daddy taught her to ride, Mummy's a drunken bitch, etc., etc.

"Isabel, isn't it?"

"Yes."

"Where're you from, Isabel?"

"New York."

"City? God. You're not Jewish, are you?"

I turned and fled, hoping to find someone, anyone, who could change my room. Was it too late for a tuition refund? Could I still get into another equally fine institution? Pounding of sneakered feet behind me and a voice caroling down a corridor full of open doors and trunks spilling flimsy things and girls giddily embracing and curious wide-eyed faces flying by—"Isabel, Izz-a-bell, hey, *Izzy*." She was a swift runner. Came a tug at the rolled-up sleeve of my blue button-down-collar shirt. "Listen! Hey, stop, will ya! Look, I don't care, really. I mean, it's fine with me, whatever you are. I'm almost a Catholic myself. My father used to be a Catholic, you see, when I was a child. Would you like the bottom bunk? I'm an excellent climber."

"I bet," I said.

"You can have the desk at the window, too, if you want."

"Thanks," I said. I turned and sarcastically looked at her. She had thin black brows and her dark eyes were positively beaming, and she looked at me now with her hands folded over the butt of the lacrosse stick, as in an old nineteenth-century "view" a traveler surveying the rushing waters in a gorge below leans on his staff. I saw she probably didn't have an idea in her head. I saw that I would have to endure a year full of conversation about how the Greens beat the Blues because of a tricky goal that the right wing made in the last minute of the second half, and I saw that, instead of a picture of a boy, she would keep a photo of a horse on her bureau and that all year long our room would reek of sweat and straw and dung, and my only extravagant hope was that she might flunk out or maybe get pregnant. No, of that latter not a chance. The horsey type never gets prematurely pregnant, she's seen it all at the stud farm, and besides, she is saving herself for Mr. Right, who has enough clipped coupons to support a meadow and stable.

"Come on," she said, straightening and earnestly offering me one thin brown hand. "What do you say? Let's get on with it. Why don't you just unpack, and we'll go play tennis."

I guess I grimaced.

"See, I didn't mean that quite the way it sounded. I've never met any Jews at all, and actually I was kind of hoping you might be it."

"Actually," I said, "not quite."

"What?" she said.

"Skip it," I said.

"Because," she said, "my dad always says that life should be a learning experience."

"What," I asked, "does your father do?"

"He's a horse trainer. Nor for the track, for shows. He teaches dressage."

"Oh."

"So why don't we just get you settled in? Got any more bags? No? You don't play tennis at all? I'll teach you. Actually I think I'm a terribly gifted athlete, if you really want to know. If I don't find someone to marry before I get out of this place"— such honesty—"I might teach phys. ed. But hopefully I'll pretty soon latch on to Mr. Right. You know? Someone with enough money to support horses? You see, I come from a long line of horse trainers. My great-grandfather O'Malley was a horse trainer back in Ireland, from whence he came because of the famine. That was in 1850. He started the American branch of the O'Malleys. What does your dad do?"

Let me see, what was it that my dad did? I'd been grappling with this problem for years. He read a lot—Goethe,

Schiller, Lessing, that whole crowd. He mourned the fate of the modern world. Mornings he worked on his book and in the afternoon he trotted over to Carl Schurz Park to look for his friend Herr Fried so that they could knuckle down to a tough game of chess. Actually, as Morgan would say, he didn't do very much. I said, however, answering her question, "He's currently writing a book." Currently. My gosh, he'd been working on the damn thing ever since I'd been in diapers.

"No kidding! Wow, a scholar. Are you going to be a scholar, too?"

I shuddered. No, my dear Morgan, the very last thing I wanted to be was a scholar. I'd lived with one my whole life. The very last thing I wanted for myself was a room full of books and scribbled-over, crumpled-up papers and the odor of cigarette smoke and stale ideas. I wanted to live, I wanted to travel and see the world and talk to people, and be bright and witty and not too serious. I was sick to death of serious people and how everything had declined since 1933 and the Death of the Weimar Republic.

It turned out, against all possible odds, that we grew to like each other. Besides our roaringly high rates of metabolism we had this in common: We were both broke. I had gone to a seedy, failing girls' day school in New York City where I had been one of two scholarship girls and not often left to forget it. When the school expired my sophomore year in college, I laughed out loud. It turned out that all along the headmistress, a lavender-haired seventy-two-year-old tyrant named Miss Constance Blanchard, had been embezzling from the school's endowment. Morgan hadn't gone to Madeira but to a seedy girls' boarding school in Maryland where, between bouts of alcoholism, her father was the riding instructor. She hadn't (she said) had a mother.

"Really," I said. "How interesting. Now there's a new kind of religion for you."

But on that, our very first day together, she wasn't yet hardened to the crudities of my New York City-style humor and she blushed and dropped her head, and I was embarrassed. I'd expected a crack in return and when I didn't get one, I said, "Hey, I'm sorry," and started unpacking my bags. Snap, click of locks, silence. At length she said, still staring floorward, "Do you know any boys? Because if you do, can you fix me up? I mean, somehow or other I've neglected to meet any. I mean— God! They don't have boys in Maryland and it turns out that everybody around here is going out this weekend, with boys."

I knowingly pursed my lips and looked thoughtful, but in fact there wasn't a whole lot I could say. There was Michael-back-home, of course, and although he wasn't awfully important in my life, I wasn't inclined to share. So I merely smiled sardonically and said something consoling like "Soon you'll catch on" or "It's fun staying home on weekends once you get used to it."

"And by the way," I said, "I'm not exactly Jewish."

"No?" she said, looking up. "What are you?"

I looked at the wall. It was covered with blotchy blue paper. I had read somewhere that blue is the favorite color of schizophrenics. What was it I was? My father used to smile at me fondly and shake his head. "Hy-britt figure," he would say, meaning "hybrid vigor" but rolling his German *r*'s so that they made thunderous echoes, as if all the Hell's Angels had been let loose on wheels in a rollerdrome. On my mother's side of the family arbor there were many Germans, a couple of Danes, and one lone Swede whose black brows and gray eyes reappeared like a flu virus every other generation. I think of these *Volk* all in a lump; they were all solidly, stolidly Evangelical Lutheran, all seemed to have the same large jaw and sternly compressed thin lips, and all—except the Swede—came from an area not exceeding one hundred kilometers in circumference, the Baltic bend in the Scandinavian peninsula, so that while the men often traveled thousands of miles by water (they were sailors mainly, and fishermen), mentally they never ventured far from the dull dunes and insipid coastlines of their ancestral villages.

When my mother took my father home with her for the

first time, back to the tiny Baltic village where she'd been born, my tall silver-haired grandfather took his pipe out of his mouth, looked down at my father, and said, "How do you do?" Then he put his pipe back into his mouth and said nothing at all, sat down, and rocked stiffly in his wicker rocker until it was time to walk to the train station—my parents were taking the evening express back to Berlin. Silently, the three of them walked to the station together down the cobblestoned street, the crevices of the laid stones traced with seaside sand. At the station my grandfather shook hands with my father-to-be. He took his pipe out of his mouth.

"It's remarkable," he said to my mother.

"What, Papa?" she asked.

"The fuss people make over Jews. Except for his hair"—my father had red . . . no, *orange* hair—"he seems like anyone else."

My grandfather had never laid eyes on a Jew before, and while I'd like to applaud his reasonableness and common sense, let me simply state that he didn't know what he was talking about—my father was never, *never* like anyone else.

My father's family were also German, with a couple of far-off Russians peeping out of the topmost branches of the family foliage, as well as one suppressed French Catholic, the scandalous, fashionable red-haired woman who was my grandmother. The Schliemann-Grossbart family were mainly renegade Jewish and decidedly upwardly mobile. In the course of the nineteenth century they doffed the outward accoutrements of their religion faster than a bunch of cons on the run shuck their stripes after hotfooting it over the Big House wall. By 1910 they were thoroughly bourgeois—solid business-professional types with lots of pretensions and no real talents. They objected to my mother not because she wasn't kosher but because she was too countrified, lower class, undereducated. She couldn't speak French fluently. She blushed when she was spoken to and all by herself had read her way through the German classics, an old set which she had borrowed from the village pastor. She was déclassé—for years no one in the Family spoke to her, and behind her back they called her the Slav or the Hun.

Given all this genetic variety, little Isabel should have developed into an enticing exotic. Not to be. When, later that fall at an Amherst Chi Psi party I was voted Miss All-American Girl, I knew instantly what it meant: Miss Bland Blend, Miss Pass Her By in the Crowd. Firm chin, short nose, rosy cheeks, light brown hair, blue-gray eyes—there was nothing, absolutely nothing that excited the imagination. With men I have always gotten by on my smarts. I am not beautiful, I am not sexy, I am nearsighted and I am smart. I have always been smart. I was the smartest girl in the first grade and for years afterward pleased my parents enormously, for they both wanted me to be smart and someday get my Ph.D. Now you understand, don't you, how hard it was for me to answer Morgan's question: "What are you?" I didn't know. But I coolly lifted my chin and said with what I hoped was an appropriate amount of sophisticated disdain, "Intellectually, my dear Morgan, I am a European."

"Oh, yeah?" she said. "Then what the fuck were you so hot about?"

My turn to be surprised. Had she learned this crude word in Maryland, at the Willow Hill School for Girls? Indeed she had, along with much, much more.

# 3

Exchange of information began that very night. Turned out that though neither one of us had had much real experience, Morgan had indeed been to a stud farm, and her clear voice fell upon the confused dark of our room (it was very late) like the sure tolling of a bright morning bell. She was chipper and matter-of-fact about it all.

"No, no, no," she said. "That's not *it*, Iz. God, where'd you get your information?"

I had read it in a book.

"Oh, ha, what kind of book, *Ripley's Believe It or Not?*"

Very funny. No, I had read it in Dr. Lucretia T. Higginbotham's *Sex for Teen-age Girls*. My mother had given me the book on my twelfth birthday. She had told me several times that it would be better not to get pregnant before I was married. "Safely married" I think was the phrase she used. Long before I was twelve, starting at about age one, she used to deliver a musical message in German, a little song about a boy and a rose:

> *Sah ein Knab ein Röslein stehn,*
> *Röslein auf der Heiden.*
>
> (A boy saw a little rose,
> A rose of the meadow.)

The boy proceeded, as boys will, to break the rose in two: get it? Had Morgan's father talked to her about sex?

The bunk bed lurched, our little double-decker tug, steaming so bravely through the foggy dark. "What?" she said.

"Your father," I said. "Didn't he ever talk to you about sex?"

Actually (she said) he wasn't much of a talker. But he had taken her to this stud farm, where, after a while, she had gotten the main idea. And (she went on, her voice regaining confidence) she couldn't believe I had gone out with a boy, a New York City boy, for a whole year and never noticed anything. Didn't we dance?

"No. He didn't dance."

Hadn't we ever Made Out?

Not much. For one thing there was no place to go. Michael

was my age exactly and couldn't yet apply for a driver's license. We never stayed long at my parents' apartment because as soon as we appeared, my father popped out of his study like a cork shot out of a kid's toy gun. My impression was he'd been leaning against his study door with his ear glued to it, listening for the sound of my key in the front door lock. Don't get the wrong idea: He had no interest whatsoever in playing duenna. He was waiting for Michael.

"Aha!" he'd boom at him. "Today I haff for you a most interesting historical problem!" With his glasses up on his long forehead, his eyes squinted almost shut, the book two inches away from his nose, and a stubby forefinger scudding along under a line of type, he'd hum to himself—"nnnnnn"—reading until he came to the line he wanted to quote.

"Kee-rist," I'd say out of the corner of my mouth, and Michael would give me a look—he was very strict, he never allowed me to swear or smoke on the street.

Michael was tall, thin, and curly-haired, a bright, bookish boy who was "unfortunately," as my father would say to me later, smiling apologetically, a Roman Catholic. In all other ways my father thought Michael was perfect, and he spent a lot of time looking up obscure historical facts so that he could bombard him with ridiculous questions. And did he, after the initial quiz period, tactfully retreat to his study? No, he brought his books, papers, cigarettes, files, clippings, pencils and pens, everything but the enormous old-fashioned black and gold typewriter right out into the living room, where he sat in the center of his clutter and smoked and hummed and rustled pages and tapped his pencil (eyes half-shut) while we sat on the sofa boiling, a discreet foot apart, pretending to watch TV, and as if we were both identically straitjacketed, kept our arms furiously pinioned across our chests.

Michael's place was even worse. He lived on the fourth floor of a cold-water flat on Third Avenue with his mother, sometime father, and four younger siblings. If we made an appearance, Mrs. Mahoney, bedraggled and relieved, would immediately kick off her men's bedroom slippers and start pulling curlers out of her hair, she was so sure we wouldn't mind if she just ran out for a bit to get some things from the store.

"Aw, Ma!" Michael would groan.

"Aw, ga'wan now, it'll be good for yous two, good practice," she'd say, winking at me. She was trying to show us the "ultimate truth" about sex without giving us too much chance (what with Lillian, Thomas, Maureen, and Peter all crawling, skipping, running, and climbing around the crowded apartment) to find out how you got to the ultimate, or even just a dear little bypath along the way.

So we'd spent most of the year we went out together taking walks and holding hands, going to museums, riding subways and buses, sitting in cold parks on damp nights until eventually, my last couple of weeks at home (Michael wasn't going away, he'd gotten a full scholarship to Columbia), our good-night kiss had extended into lengthy elevator rides up and down and up and down my parents' apartment building on East Eighty-third Street. On our very last night together his hands had gotten mighty high up on my rib cage, but it had rained, and I had on my raincoat that had two breast pockets whose flaps were decorated with large round wooden buttons. My mother had picked the coat out. Was it any wonder, then, that I'd never noticed anything but the elevator vertically ascending?

Which, as Morgan explained to me that night, "is also called tumescence and that's how you get from A to B, Iz! Otherwise—think about it, kiddo—it would be pretty darn tricky to pull off, wouldn't it?" She said all of this con brio, with a kind of ain't-nature-grand vivacity. She was in many respects a marvelous teacher, enthusiasm being a primary ingredient of effective pedagogy, and in any case fairly soon after that there was ample opportunity for actual experience and observation, for Morgan quickly got to know lots of boys, some of whom she kindly passed on to me and Monique and Matilda and even sad Sophie Schlosser.

In the next two years Morgan taught me other things as

well: how to ski, how to play tennis, how to drink at Amherst fraternity parties, and in all that time we had only one area of major disagreement—the Problem People she collected, those dogs who congregated in our room every night after dinner for Morgan's advice and encouragement, those hopeless, shapeless girls she adopted to shape up: little Monique, a wise, bratty Parisian, who honestly thought you could get pregnant by French-kissing; Matilda Chessley of the dirigible tits—even with a bra she looked braless; and horrible Sophie Schlosser of the overweight Schlossers, a giant, lank-haired, pit-faced slob of a girl who lumbered when she walked and smelled either of stale Roquefort cheese or dead fish.

Sophie had begun to haunt our room, which was tiny to begin with and with Sophie in it, it was as malodorous and jam-packed as the Sixth Avenue IND any July weekday at 5:30. I had politely advised her *never* to sit on my bed, since her weight made the bedsprings uncurl and furthermore she was almost never without a greasy nutritional supplement which she carried around in the same old dirty gray cardigan pocket. And there was something else wrong with Sophie. Something seemed out of whack, not exactly a screw loose, but certainly a couple of wires that had missed their electrode terminals. She had this funny, humble, slavish way of looking at Morgan that one day, quite suddenly, she transferred to me.

"How come?" I said to Morgan. "I've been nothing but mean to her. Why is it I'm getting this wet-eyed look all of a sudden? And this morning? Going to chapel? She touched me! Jesus, the *nerve*. Don't laugh, Morgo, I know she did it on purpose. She brushed up against me as I went out the downstairs door. Come on, you better tell me. I know you said something to her."

"She was upset that you didn't like her. I told her that of course you liked her."

"You told her that? A blatant lie?"

"I couldn't hurt her, Isabel. I told her you just had trouble in locating the center of your emotions, that you merely assumed a sophisticated, worldly, sarcastic exterior as a kind of cover-up for feelings of anomie and all that stuff."

"Oh, *shit,* you don't even know what anomie is!"

"There you go again, Isabel, putting on your little intellectually arrogant act. But we're on to you. We know it's all a defense. We have you all figured out."

"Really! Who's this 'we' we're talking about?"

She held her Psychology II text up in front of her face and giggled. "Why, Sophie and I," she said.

Morgan was kidding, but Sophie was not. Sophie had a midterm A in psychology and thought she had my very essence all nailed down between two vectors on her abnormal personality graph. She had divined that I was much in need of some kind of solace.

"Don't you see?" Morgan said. "This will be terrific for Sophie. She'll get her mind off herself."

"And onto me. Say, that *is* terrific. I wonder what form this help is going to take."

I soon found out. When I charged out the door in the morning, ten minutes late for my first class, there was Sophie, lumbering silently along beside me, her long face slightly pink with exertion and wrapped as if she had a toothache in her father's orange-and-black Princeton scarf. When I went into dinner at night, there was Sophie next to me at the dinner table, in her stained gym shirt and spotty gray cardigan, with a mouldy green wrap skirt tied over her gym shorts. She ate exactly what I ate. If I said uh-uh to mashed potatoes, so did she. She never asked for seconds unless I passed up my plate. I began to lose weight; Sophie seemed to be getting fatter. At night, instead of holing up comfortably in my own snug little room, I walked a mile to the libe to study, but when I got back at ten, there was Sophie, waiting for me.

"Can't you close the damn door?" I said to Morgan. "Just don't let her in."

"If I don't let her in, she just stands out in the hall, breathing."

"This is all your fault. You better think of some way of getting rid of her."

"How? She's formed a very strong attachment."

I had an unwholesome feeling about this attachment. Furthermore, paranoia had set in: I was sure everyone had begun associating me with this lump, as in "Hey, guys, if you send out for pizza, for God's sake don't ask Soph-and-Iz."

After three weeks of this I went to the dean's office and put in a request for instant transfer to another dormitory that had only single rooms and was as far across campus as I could get. Sophie wrote me love notes for a while in the form of poems she copied out of an anthology, and then she disappeared—left college—but she surfaced in another decade. I saw her one night on TV. She had lost eighty-five pounds and had dyed her hair pale green. She had written a work of fiction—sex, money, power, and status at a New York TV station. The book had been number one on *The New York Times* Best Seller List for seventy-six weeks straight. The talk-show cohost was beside himself. Leaning toward her, in an ecstasy of hyperbolic invention, he had just uttered the word *elemental* when I flicked off the tube. I tried to read the damn book, but I couldn't get past page eight—my anomie again, I guess. From time to time old Soph—she has changed her name now, to Sophia VON Schlosser—pops up in mags like *People*. She favors diamond-encrusted hoop earrings that hang down to her shoulders, and she has a dress ("gown" is what it was called by the interviewer) that is made entirely of egret feathers, for the wearing of which she was publicly chastised by the central committee of the Sierra Club. In a word *"O tempora, o mores,"* she has become a culture symbol.

I know I'd be more generous about Sophie, even glad for her (this ugly duckling transformed into show bird), but my second novel came out just a week after her book. My novel sold 1,175 copies, and although I sent Morgan a free copy, I don't think she's read it, because she's never mentioned it. I'm sure she's read Sophie's book, because she has slipped more than once and referred, laughing, to Sophie's "gross prose." At least she knows the difference. And who was it that taught her the difference? Who do you think?

Okay. On balance I'd have to admit that, while Morgan and I learned from each other, what I passed on to her was more in line with the usual stuff: in conjunction with the college I tried to teach her something about music and art and literature. She was, to my surprise, a talented pupil. There is a gift for reading and listening and seeing just as there is for writing, composing, and painting, and Morgan had those gifts, the gifts of an editor and critic. What she didn't have—this surprised me—was much confidence in her intellectual ability, but I worked on her, developing her sense of language and form until (my greatest achievement), in the spring of our junior year, she was, by unanimous vote, made editor of the literary magazine. I was fantastically pleased. I had done it. I had turned little Cinder-Morgan the stable girl into my alter ego, the editor. I had major plans for us. Together we would rise to the top of the publishing pyramid; we would eventually form our own small quality house. I saw in my mind's eye the rough-faced stock, elegant print, and well-known colophon—perhaps a little steed with tossing mane—of O'Malley and Schliemann. We would publish my books, of course, but those of other great authors as well. The whole world over, our house would be known for its elegance and good taste. Is it any wonder that as soon as graduation was over, I was traumatically hurt and disappointed?

As soon as graduation was over and the wooden folding chairs were just being pushed aside on the grass of the Quad and we had found each other in the crowd and (slowly melting under those heavy black gowns that hot, humid June day) had hugged and kissed each other, knocking our mortarboards askew, it hurt me that after all my care and enthusiasm and pride in her, in that moment after graduation (her father had turned up for the event, very pink-and-white–looking, clean-shaven, smelling of wintergreen, in a well-pressed glen plaid suit, almost wholly sober) when the wooden chairs were being clapped together by the grounds crew and hands were still being shaken and congratulations exchanged, and fathers were wiping their brows with large white handkerchiefs, and my mother, somewhere behind me, cheeks mottled with pink, in a rose silk print dress too tight across the bosom, was dabbing at her throat with a lace-trimmed hanky and saying in her high, clear, German-accented voice, "Vonderfull!" and my father was standing some ten feet off, orange-ruffed head modestly bowed, hands clasped behind him in the same pose Beethoven used to strike when walking through the German woods, and I was with half an ear listening to Morgan and hoping at the same time that my father, who was smiling cherubically, would say nothing about hy-britt figure, and hoping also that nobody would notice that my parents weren't standing together, it hurt me that she would say, "Honestly, Isabel. Will you listen to me? Or look, then. Just look!" She waved one thin brown hand in front of my face. The blinding spot of glare almost undid me. I grabbed her hand and held it a foot away. A small, shapely diamond stared at me, then winked. I said, feeling weak, "Douglas?"

"Of course!" she said. "Who else would it be? Didn't it take him forever to catch on?" She was almost dancing up and down next to me, and lurking somewhere in the background I sensed rather than saw a lengthy shadow. "Douglas? Douglas, come here, I want you to meet Isabel."

I prepared myself for another of Morgan's afflictions. For several months she'd dated a boy who was totally deaf, and they'd walked around campus together, hands flying. There was the Japanese exchange student who was three inches shorter than she; the Dartmouth man who was six feet four and unbelievably handsome but had a terrible speech impediment; the man from Harvard who couldn't decide whether he loved Morgan or his roommate; and the harassed Amherst English professor who used to call for her in a battered station wagon with all sorts of smeared kids climbing out of the back windows: his wife had run off with a junior art instructor and he had custody of all six children. Generous Morgan, she loved them all, took care of them all.

"Isabel, this is Douglas! Douglas—this is my best friend, Isabel."

I slowly lifted my eyes. He seemed to be having some trouble in lowering his. He would have preferred, I guess, to go on looking at the roof tiles of Martha Wilson House. He was tall and thin with a long, narrow head. His flat cheeks with their high bones were balanced by a nose that would have made an admirable and chancy ski slope for a very advanced homunculus skier—just past the bridge there was a lump in the cartilage before it plunged straight down, thrills aplenty for my teeny downhiller. His mouth saved this awfully New England-looking Puritan's face from total austerity: either from quirk of nature or force of habit, it was slightly crooked, giving ye olde New England mask a wry look. His ears were so large and stuck out so far that the whole coastline image was reinforced: they reminded me of the sails of a sloop when spread out to either side, as in running before the wind.

I knew at once, of course, that the credentials would be impeccable: lots of Lodges and Lymans, a family tree heavily weighted on the duty-bound, civic-minded, ethical cultural side, leavened with the usual sprinkling of New England eccentrics. (You know: the maiden aunt who as a girl is not quite pretty enough. By some unfortunate genetic crossover she gets the craggy features and she learns while still at Winsor to wear long hoop earrings and chunky silver jewelry and black stockings and skimps her dull, mouse-brown hair back into a knot and, when she is safely past marrying age, has disastrous affairs with young artists and writers and leaves her fortune to the Boston Symphony. And there is usually a bachelor brother as well, who travels a lot and never marries, and he also falls in love with young artists and writers and becomes an authority on something obscure (say Chinese coins or jade), and when he dies, he leaves his fortune to his prep school.

As for money, when Douglas's name was pronounced, a golden mote struck me in the eye and I heard in the background the soft musical clink of silver coins falling into some great-grandfather's cashbox. In a word, *rich*, but the kind of *old* rich that is all modesty and unpretentiousness: ancient clapboard houses in outlying Boston suburbs where the grass can be let go (no need for gardeners) and no one buys antiques, they own them, and paintings are bought only when the stock market is off and then put into storage. That kind of rich. Like dull. The lid of the cashbox coming down smartly on itchy fingers.

His hair was a pale silvery blond; his eyebrows—startling —black and wiry and thick; and his gray eyes so pale and deep-set that he seemed to be viewing the vulgar plebs below, very far below, from some utterly serene, impenetrable, fortified place on an utterly unapproachable mountain. When (on that warm June day) Douglas Whiteside condescended to look down at me, he didn't smile, only curtly nodded, and—oh, yes—his eyes briefly changed color. While gazing upward they'd reflected blue sky, but when he came at last to fix a small portion of his attention on me, his eyes turned perfectly blank, as if reflecting nothing. He frowned. I, too, frowned. I looked down and child-ishly wiped my palms on the gown. He put his hands in his pants pockets and removed his gaze upward again, back to those astonishing roof tiles.

By the end of these first three minutes I knew exactly what Morgan had chosen. Along with Douglas Whiteside (Exeter, Harvard) she had picked a totally conventional life with a clap-board house and a large garden (peonies, phlox, a back-door arbor for Concord grapes), big shaggy dogs, good private schools, ski vacations on a budget, and worries about fulfilling the life cycle: getting the kids into Harvard. I saw that she had—already? so soon?—settled down. *Well, good luck, Morgo*, I thought. *And good-bye publishing house.* I saw that marriage to Douglas Whiteside wouldn't leave much room for anything else. I saw that he was cold-natured and that he would be a lot of work and that Morgan would spend her entire life trying to make him happy. She would dedicate herself to warming up this cold fish and would probably fail. She would endlessly scintillate while he looked on, not amused. She would offer love, warmth, and affection and for thanks get a Puritan's sneer. I saw that she had, indeed, fixed herself up with another problem, New England version, and she would be more or less stuck with him, as they say at the end of fairy tales, for ever after.

I figured then that he was probably going to law school and that he'd end up with an old established Boston law firm. He ended up in New Jersey as the headmaster of a private school. And despite his looking like old Boston money, the Whitesides never seemed well-to-do or even exactly "comfortable." The big new house surprised me.

I don't think Morgan has changed a whole lot since college. She rides and plays tennis and gardens and collects people with problems. She has turned out to be a good cook and a good housekeeper. She reads a lot—mainly, she says, between car pools—and she gives parties and raises the children. Her house is always full of flowers. I guess a lot of what she does strikes me as an awful waste of human intelligence, but maybe most of the things we do in life are exactly that. I'm sure a low-grade moron could fill my shoes at WJVB-TV. It's not what I would do if I had the time or the money or the emotions.

# 4

"This will work out perfectly, Isabel. You can stay at the Allens'. You remember the Allens, don't you? Margaret's the artist and Jerry's in oil—not paints, the stuff they ship on tankers. He's not home overly much—he's away right now, as a matter of fact. Her kids are away, too, so you see, you won't be an inconvenience, and while you're there, Isabel, you might even be a help to Margaret."

"Me? How?"

"Well, you're a writer and you know a lot about people and maybe you could sit down and talk to her. Find out what's going on."

"Oh, Morgan, why on earth would she talk to me? She's only met me once—I'm practically a stranger."

"That's exactly why. People often talk to strangers when they can't talk to their best friends."

"What nonsense! She certainly is not going to start confiding in me in the privacy of her living room."

"Isabel, I have such *faith* in you. She just might! And you do have this bond, you are both artistic. And I sense that she desperately needs a friend."

"How about you, why can't you be her friend? Besides, let me explain right now that I am kind of tired and out of it, and under no circumstances, Morgan—are you listening?— under no circumstances do I need or want to get involved with another one of your Problems."

"Did I say she was a Problem? I just feel she needs a little . . . empathy."

"What's wrong with her?"

"I don't know. I could guess, but I don't want to go into it over the phone. There was a man in town named Paul Caron— wait a minute . . . What? No, you can't, Sarah. Cannot, no, ma'am, uh-uh, forget it. Absolutely not . . . Isabel? Hi, listen, I can't talk right now, there are kids and cartons all over the place. See what you can—gently—find out. Be—you know— perceptive. She seems so unhappy. Did I tell you how many bedrooms we've got?"

"Yes, you told me."

"Oh. You're hurt, aren't you? Because I am shipping you out."

"Me? No, I'm not one bit hurt, I understand perfectly.

Don't worry, Margaret and I will get along just fine. I'll do a rush psychoanalysis and report my findings back to you."

"Right!" Morgan said. "Only of course you are going to be subtle and not too obvious."

"Yeah."

"Because Margaret is . . ."

"I know. Very reserved."

"Must go! Good luck! See you soon!"

In the background I could hear a dog barking, there was a scream, then a crash and then Morgan's voice barreled out, "Oh, no! Oh, *shit*, Eddie, look what you've done!" and I hung up.

So, late on Saturday afternoon I took the train to Summerville, New Jersey, and from the Summerville station took a cab to the Allens' house. My driver, an old grizzled black man, drove slowly, ruminatively down the very center of the road, as if he didn't expect to meet oncoming traffic, and indeed there was none, none at all. Not a car, not a dog, not a child, not a gardener. The Allens lived on the "old" side of town, that part of Summerville built up before and just after the Civil War by businessmen from New York who wanted a quiet mountaintop retreat for their Victorian families. Behind rhododendron and hydrangeas large frame and shingle houses watched us serenely from high up on grassy knolls, complacently girdled by old-fashioned porches, and always, somewhere off in each deeply blue-shaded background stood a distant carriage house with cupola and weathervane.

It was unearthly quiet, and a golden late-summer daylight flashed in and out at the tops of the tall trees that made an *allée* of the road, and the birds sang faintly very far away. It was a sleepy, dreamy time of day, and it could have been a hundred years ago, and the gently rumbling taxi could have been a creaking barouche, and there could have been the ringing clip-clop of horses' hooves. Every time I come to Summerville, I have the infernal feeling that I am a million miles from New

York City. The sleepy, languid, humid air and the monotonous murmur of ancient insects never seem to change, and even the people in Summerville seem culturally distant to me.

Last time I was here, three years ago, I had just been divorced, and there was at the dinner party I went to as Morgan's guest (imagine it, at this point in our century) a kind of general intake of breath at my predicament. None of the people there had been divorced. No one—so went the pious conversation—had ever seen marijuana, and I had the sneaking suspicion that even the children had been conceived through knotholes in bundling boards or perhaps by immaculate conception. It seemed to me there was something unallowedly fake about all this tribal innocence. If I had been an anthropologist, I would have set about taking notes, as if these Summervillites were a lost colony of Stone Agers from one of the more remote Philippine islands. I am not an anthropologist, I am a writer and journalist, and I was thoroughly bored by the town, where the most exciting thing to do each day was to get up and wait for the sunrise. You know: silver-gray lightening of sky, first pink streak on horizon, orange ball rising through tree branches, etc., etc. Seen one, you've seen 'em all. I prefer human nature to Mother Nature, I like all my bags mixed, and I like conversation at the dinner table with a mordant dash of honest reactions. They talked at this, my last dinner party in Summerville, carefully about the stock market and carefully about the country club; no malevolent gossip, only whether The Club (it was always referred to reverently, as if in capital letters) would this year have a balanced budget. Astonishing, isn't it? Thirty miles west of New York City there yet exists a town where almost everyone is named Williams, Wilton, Whiteside, or something else equally Anglo-Saxon from before 1880 and the Great Immigration.

But not all of life gets to be lived in a time warp. I know perfectly well that a good part of the decorum is fake. After this last dinner party, one of these Summerville husbands, an utter paragon of domesticity, called me at my New York apartment and suggested tea for two—so much for Victoriana in the late twentieth century.

I suppose I took it as a bad omen that when the cab driver pulled around the Allens' gravel drive to the front of the wide wooden porch, the house looked deserted. It was a large brown shingle house with a stone tower on one side and, to balance this conceit (the tower resembled a silo), a wing on the other side that was oval in shape and reminded me of the prow of the old Staten Island Ferry. It was the kind of late Victorian house that used to be called "commodious," with the kind of interior space that wanders away from you in the receding perspectives of a dream, so that as in a puzzle or labyrinth you come upon baffling stairways and meandering hallways and unexpected rooms, and the fact that all the doors are open, another and another and another always beckoning, makes the space still more difficult to define.

At the upper windows, shades had been pulled down against the August sun, which gave the house a watchful look, as if it were slyly pretending to be asleep. The old black man (Mr. Carson was his name) carried my suitcase up the porch steps. I thanked him and paid him and trilled the old-fashioned doorbell—one of those rusty metal things you twist. It gave a little echoing *plink* somewhere in the depths of the house. I shaded my eyes and tried to peer past the vestibule, but the wide double doors were hung with sheer white curtains. Behind these curtains nothing moved. No one, it seemed, was coming to answer my ring. I turned the outer door handle—it opened easily. The inner door, too, swung open at a touch. Standing there in the silent hall, I thought for a moment that I must have the wrong house, but no, I was certain of the address, and in any case it was too late, Mr. Carson and his taxi had gone, leaving behind them an umber cloud of dust that was already lethargically settling, as if the driveway itself had taken offense at being disturbed and had sent up this feeble puff in protest. *Well, Isabel,* I thought, *here you are.*

I closed the doors behind me. The instant I did so the hovering summer light and air were shut out, and I stood in the large dark-paneled hall in a cool, timeless gloom. There was a tall, dim, gold-framed mirror over a marble-topped table, a mirror that seemed to have its own flecked version of things, and over the wide staircase with its heavy carved mahogany banister, a pretty Gothic window that was so covered over with foliage it let through only a trembling spatter of light. I tried calling out—no answer. The closed-up air of the house seemed to muffle sound. I looked vaguely again at the mirror and this time saw a scrap of folded paper stuck into the bottom of the heavy gold frame: *ISABEL,* it said on it, in pencil.

*Isabel* (it said inside), *Sorry to hear of yr. troubles. Yr. rm. up and to right. Back soon. Margaret.*

I took my suitcase by its strap—broad-shouldered Isabel! —and strode up the carpeted stairs. I glanced over the banister but couldn't make out much except that it didn't seem at all the house of an artist. I had had in my mind a scheme of museum white walls and shiny wood floors, but the floors were stained dark or carpeted, the walls covered with dark, figured paper, and there were no paintings.

All in all the house made me uneasy. She was an artist, wasn't she? Then where were her paintings? Upstairs, too, all the windows were draped, and it wasn't until I threw up the shades in the guest room that I saw how pretty it was. The wallpaper was abloom with yellow roses, there was a comfortable chaise for reading, and the large, ornately carved Victorian bed was covered with a white crocheted spread. In the long dusty mirror over the dresser I grimaced at myself: I looked shiny-faced and slightly comic, a prim, tart-tongued lady— Henrietta Stackpole?—out of some Henry James novel. The house was very still, not the tick of a clock or the buzz of an appliance, nothing, as if my own ticking life had suddenly paused, and in this silence, this missed beat, I could remember at last how tired I was.

I pulled back the bedspread and lay down. A week ago I

had been in Russia. When I closed my eyes, images of Russia hurtled by: I was still in St. Petersburg (no—Leningrad), where translucent planes of time intersect. At the ancient Peter and Paul Fortress, the old czarist prison (now a museum), photographs of the cells' last pre-Revolutionary occupants showed bearded, mustachioed men who looked like the young executives I knew at WJVB-TV, and in another more vertiginous time warp, the glum crowds that surged down the Nevsky Prospekt, past elegant monuments of eighteenth-century architecture (while the Beatles blared from second-story windows), wore the beehive hairdos and vulgar miniskirts of another even more remote era—New York in the decadent 1960s. By Tuesday I had been in London, on Thursday arrived at Kennedy Airport; now it was Saturday again and I was in nineteenth-century New Jersey.

It seemed suddenly good to be where life had a quieter rhythm, a southern slowness of tempo. Outside in the leafy treetops birds indolently sang and sheer white curtains floated soothingly at the windows—immemorial sheer white curtains out of lazy childhood summers, when the days were so blissfully long you went to bed while it was still light and you lay there sleepily watching the curtains, floating like gauzy seraphs at the windows, watched them occasionally vigilantly stir, flutter, whisper in agitation, then, as you shut your eyes, fall (all is well) into peaceful silence again.

# 5

My father looks directly at me with a smile half-puzzled, half-expectant, as if there is something he wants me to understand. It is the same smile he used to wear when nobody laughed after he'd told a joke—because of his harsh accent he always garbled the punch line. He wears baggy brown pinstripe pants and a brown cardigan sweater with a button missing. My mother is at the window, looking out at the lake, and although even in dream-time it is summer, she has on her old, heavy green tweed suit and she holds a cup of coffee in her hands. I am in the dream and I am not, as if my parents were solid, living presences and I a ghost-observer, still, I *feel* the scene intensely, and not least of all because there is in it a distinct reversal of my childhood attachments—my mother (whom I adored) stands with her back to me, and for my father (who was always such an embarrassment) I feel a quiet sympathy. It is all strange and sad, strange and sad, and I have had this dream several times before.

Or is it a dream? It seems something more—the event resembles a visitation. They always arrive together, my ghostly progenitors, gliding silently, wordlessly into my consciousness—and I sense there is something they want me to know that is beyond speech. This in itself is puzzling, for my parents were nothing if not discursive, and my earliest memories of them are aural—the sound of their voices beyond a door which is reassuringly left half-open but is also, irritatingly, half-shut.

My parents met, courted, and married in Berlin in the early 1930s. The Weimar Republic was already on the skids, but they seemed not to know it. Who was this Hitler? They couldn't take him seriously; they thought he was funny, a nobody, uneducated, a hick from Austria who didn't speak grammatical German. They voted for the Republic, loved the Bauhaus and the International Style, bought Breuer chairs and Kandinsky prints. Later, all the years I spent growing up in New York City, while I sat at the dinner table moodily picking at cold boiled potatoes (my mother was a listless cook), they talked about that time and place as if Weimar were an Atlantis, its chrome, steel, and glass gleaming, immaculate still, only sunk beneath heaps of World War II rubble instead of leagues of green water. Brecht, Weill, Max Reinhardt, Grosz, Gropius, Emil Nolde, Lotte Lenya, Käthe Kollwitz, Nabokov, too, had lived in "their" Berlin. And Weimar, my father told me once, meant more than architecture and art and literature. It meant toleration, democracy, hope. It might have been, he said dreamily, the Enlightenment come true, the Germany of Goethe and Lessing's *Nathan der Weise.* He loved this Germany—the one that had never existed—and as blind as any lover, he reconstructed her features (iron jaw, mailed fist) into the sweet smile and mild eye of Goodness Led Astray, the Tender Maiden Gone Wrong straight out of nineteenth-century novels. Seduced by a wily, evil magician, his Germany had betrayed him—had broken his heart. For both my parents time had stopped, a cracked clock, in January 1933.

I hated endlessly hearing about it, their dead world, this long-gone time and place of which almost nothing remained but a ghastly afterglow. It had nothing to do with me, was as distant from me as my chewing gum and raspberry-scented dime-store lipstick and charm bracelets and plaid skirts were from them. I thought their conversations were boring. It was all just so much talk. In self-defense I'd flick on our small-screen TV.

"What stupid people," my mother would say, looking up from her book to regard briefly one of those family-type sitcoms I enjoyed. She would readjust the reading lamp that beamed down on Thomas Mann and frown in irritation. What I thought to myself was, *Read and talk, read and talk, that's all you do.* Sports were for kids, games for children; my parents never gave parties, they never had people to dinner. They didn't seem to need people—they had each other.

On weekdays and holidays I would wake up to the vigorous rhythm of their voices in the kitchen, talking from before breakfast until after I went to bed at night, two sturdy rosebushes whose glossy foliage and red-tipped branches interwined, thorns and all, leaning on each other, weighing each other down, holding each other up. My mother's voice was clear, with a beautiful crystalline laugh—odd, because she couldn't sing.

When she tried, the notes came out off-key in a husky, embarrassed little murmur. My father's voice was deep and harsh, but when he sang (this wasn't often) golden musical phrases emerged, as if rough bark had been peeled back from the living grain of tender wood. History, politics, music, poetry, art—they talked about and disagreed on everything. My father's fist would make the china jump. My mother's voice would ring out: *"Unsinn!"* When I was little, long before I knew anything about sex, I thought that marriage was a lifetime dialogue, a conversation that undulated like a landscape unrolling in a train's grimy window. There were hills, dells, plains, woods, lakes, and sometimes even strange, burned-out places, but the scenery always improved if you waited awhile.

"Ach, Isabel, Isabel," my mother would say, when I was a kid and she thought I was being too "smart." "Who will marry you? You cannot have always The Last Word. I hope you find someday a man with whom you can talk. Above all, remember this—you must talk to each other."

*Each other.* Another catchphrase of my mother's. Fate had made my parents intelligent but poor; sentenced them to a lifetime of tailor-made wool suits (annually darned and recut); given them good jewelry and no place to wear it. The jewelry was hidden in the lining of my mother's fur coat when they came to this country—refugees! They lived for a year on two gold bracelets and a diamond pendant. In time, the silver got hocked, the Breuer chairs fell apart, the Kandinsky prints disappeared from the walls. What was it they had? Each other!

I believed her, wanted to believe her. Like any other child, I thought they would be married forever. I was nineteen when they separated and twenty when they got divorced, and although I was a senior in college, I felt childishly abandoned and betrayed.

Summerville perches on the top of a mountain ridge, but this late afternoon the breeze had died away and the air in the room, although sweet-scented, was intensely humid, full of a

southern lassitude. I got up and washed my face and lethargically brushed my hair. Far away downstairs I heard a door
slam, and then a telephone rang, once. Alas, my hostess was
home, it was time for me to go to work: Isabel the Spy. I felt
glum about the delicate assignment Morgan had given me: to
prize out the state of Margaret Allen's feelings. In the course of
my brief telephone conversation with Morgan she'd given me
only a couple of clues. I had caught from her tone of voice
that possibly, probably, this fellow—Paul Caron—had had
some intimate connection with Margaret Allen. There was such
acid in Morgan's voice when she'd said, "Jerry's in oil," that I
had an image of Jerry Allen bobbing up from a vat, grinning
and glistening from head to toe. When Morgan had added sarcastically, "He isn't home overly much," the picture was fairly
complete. Obviously the Allen marriage wasn't functioning
well, but that was nothing terribly new—I'd caught large hints
of that myself, three years ago.

Morgan had taken me to a local gallery that was having a
show of Margaret's paintings. I had thought the paintings well
done, but they'd made me uneasy. Her colors were all neutral:
grays, black, startling flashes of white that gaped open-mouthed
on the canvas. The shapes were tilted on end or precariously
piled up, outlined with paint laid on so thickly it glittered menacingly. Looking at the paintings, I felt a terrible anxiety. Later
that night at dinner Margaret had said dryly, "It was my first
show in a very long time, since before the children were born."
She had seemed that evening brittle, cold, ungiving, because (I
felt) she had nothing to give. I had an impression of someone
operating on the very last of an emotional reserve. Still, I'd
found her attractive. I felt in her personality a kind of black
depth with an occasional flash or sparkle, like a deep river that
has frozen over, become thick black ice upon the surface of
which (it is so shining, so smooth) you can see the twinkling
lights of many stars.

My guess was that Margaret Allen deserved a lover. I remembered Jerry Allen calling me in New York—this paragon

of domesticity. I'd said to him coldly, "But you're married."
He'd said (shades of my mother), "True. But Margaret doesn't
talk to me anymore." I'd hung up abruptly, thinking, *Jerk. How
trite can you get?*

Going down Margaret's carpeted staircase, I wondered if I
could get her to talk to me.

# 6

"Hello," she said. "Did you have a nap? I went up to see you,
but your door was closed."

The living room drapes were pulled; I couldn't immediately see her. My feeling as I stood in the hall, looking into the
dim, greenish, over-furnished living room, was that I was about
to step into a forest pond of uncertain depth. The green wallpaper was first to emerge—it was imprinted with pale fernlike
tracings—and then chairs and tables slowly materialized, all
Victorian, all with arms and legs so excessively curved and
carved they seemed to be writhing in motionless agony. And
where was Margaret Allen? In a bay-windowed niche stood a
sofa of tufted rose silk with a heart-shaped back and bow legs.
She lay on this sofa with her hands at her waist and her head
resting against the sofa arm at a peculiar angle, as if her neck
were broken. She was dressed to match the decor in Victorian
white. Her feet were crossed. She wore high-heeled white sandals. She was smoking. The air smelled of roses and smoke.

"Are you all settled in upstairs? Is there anything you
need?"

Everything was fine, I told her, there was nothing at all I
needed.

She sat up and put out her cigarette in a silver bowl full of
red roses. "Then wouldn't you like a glass of wine or sherry?

36

Everything's out on the hall table—there's Scotch, gin, tonic, whatever. Just help yourself."

I filled a glass with white wine and came back to a fringed chair near the sofa, a bandy-legged little thing that seemed to brace itself for my touch. I have always wanted to be thin-boned and fragile, but centuries of Pomeranian peasants have contributed to the making of this body, and I am stuck with it.

Margaret, however, was very slender, and her long neck, set off by a high lace collar, seemed too delicate to hold up the heavy roll of chestnut hair it carried. Her skin was dead white, her long, narrow eyes a dark blue.

We sat there tentatively smiling at each other, not quite knowing how to begin. In fact, I was myself honestly curious about Margaret—she seemed one of the most private, odd, and inviolable people I'd ever met.

"You're so kind to take me in," I said. "I truthfully didn't expect you to remember me."

"Of course I remember you," she said. "For one thing Morgan talks about you a great deal. And then—you probably don't remember—we were at dinner together one night, two or three years ago. You came with Morgan—Douglas was out of town. I believe you sat next to my husband at the table and you wore black." She smiled. "A black velvet dress?" She had a thin, bony, prominent nose and a way of holding her head back and high up on her long neck, so that her expression seemed to match that of the house: it was watchful, as if those dark blue eyes were observing me from some fixed point far off in space.

"Why, that's remarkable. It was a black velvet jumper."

"With a white satin blouse."

"Amazing. Do you have total recall?"

"Oh, no," she said. "I have a good visual memory, but I have very selective recall." She bent forward and plucked a rusty-looking marigold from a small bowl of flowers on the marble-topped coffee table. "There's some I've forgotten and more I'd like to forget. But we did have a long talk that night, you and I. Don't you remember?"

"I remember that we talked, but I don't remember the subject."

She ran her thumbnail over the dry flower head. Brown petals fell on her white skirt and she brushed them off with the side of her ringless hand. "We talked about the state of our arts," she said dryly, "and we talked about Summerville. You said it was a nice place to visit but you wouldn't care to live here." I smiled—she went on, "We talked about Gloria Steinem and Betty Friedan and we talked about Morgan."

"A switch," I said.

"Oh, do you think so?" she asked, tilting her head so that the heavy hairdo seemed in danger. "I've always thought that Morgan did just what she wanted. You were her college roommate, weren't you?"

"For two years. Then it got to be a bit much."

She looked at me curiously. "What did?"

"The mess." She burst out laughing and sat back against the sofa. "I didn't mean her housekeeping," I said. "It was the people we finally had to split up on. She had this horrid way of involving herself in people's lives, of trying to steer them, you know, of generally interfering and lending a hand. There were Sophie's problems and Monique's problems and Matilda's problems. They began to absorb too much of my time and most of hers. The sad part of it was, she's very bright."

Margaret looked amused. "Of course Morgan's bright. But why say it that way? Why is it sad?"

"Because she never worked at being bright, she's never done anything with it."

"Oh, but you're wrong, no one does more than Morgan. She does everything. She sets us all going as if we were those little mechanical bugs, the ladybugs and beetles you buy in Woolworth's at Christmas for stocking gifts, the kind you wind up with a key. Without her we'd be a crowd of deadly bores. She's the eternal hostess, the eternal friend."

I thought about this for a moment, but there is something stern in me that resists the idea of a life dedicated to organizing social occasions and good works. "She's marvelous at all that," I said, "but there's so much more she could have done. I'd always thought we'd do something in publishing together, though, of course, the minute I laid eyes on Douglas Whiteside, I pretty much knew how her life was going to turn out." I smiled to lighten what I'd just said. I didn't want her to think I disliked Douglas. "He's so awfully conventional, you know, in that upper-class New England sort of way."

Margaret gave me a strict, examining look, head held back, eyes darkly narrowed. "But he's also an excellent teacher. He taught my daughter, Cathy, last year, and he managed to do something for her, opened up a kind of imaginative world. She was never much of a history student before, and suddenly she was fascinated—reading books that weren't required, going to museums. I'm grateful to him for that."

"Yes."

"Since he's become head of the school . . . that was"—she lifted her head, thinking—"four years ago, he's raised academic standards and brought in some fine new teachers. I don't believe you'll find anyone in town that people respect more than Douglas."

"I'm sure that's true," I said, "but that wasn't my point. I was talking about Douglas and Morgan together."

She was silent a moment and then said, looking down, "I suppose I know what you mean. Once Morgan gave a surprise birthday party for Douglas, and we all came dressed as circus characters. He was embarrassed."

I laughed. I could see sober Douglas—life is real! life is earnest!—surrounded by a bunch of people in lipstick and whiteface. "She tries so hard to brighten him up, and he rejects it all on the grounds that it's bad for his character."

"But you do think," Margaret said, looking down at her skirt, "that Douglas loves her?"

I thought it a startling question. "Oh, of course, in his own way. You think he doesn't?"

"No, but you seemed to imply something like that."

"I didn't mean to. God, I certainly hope he loves her—she deserves it."

Margaret's smile came and went, quick as a fox. "We don't all get what we deserve. Do you know—this is interesting to me, though perhaps it won't be to you—I feel there's a kind of person who never experiences real love, passionate love, I mean. Lately I read somewhere that in a relationship, I mean in a lovers' relationship, the persons involved are often terribly frightened. Some people never fall in love because they're too frightened, or they enter a relationship hopefully and then suddenly break it off, just when they find themselves becoming intimate."

I wondered why she was telling me this. It didn't seem to be a confession—that wasn't her mode. I felt she used words not so much expressively but as a kind of camouflage, and her meticulous diction, so precisely thought out, was like a light, beautifully engraved armor behind which she waited and watched and measured. She seemed now to expect some sort of answer from me, and I was looking past her at the heavily draped bay window, summoning up a wary thought or two, when her telephone rang.

She shook her head and got up, gave her full skirts a hitch, and left the room. I heard her pick up the telephone in the hall. "Hello?" she said, and then quickly, "Just a minute." I heard a door off the hall open and close. Obviously she hadn't wanted me to hear the conversation. I wondered who it was—a child? husband? Paul Caron? I thought distractedly about what she'd said and wondered how—or if—it connected to her life. It seemed strange to think of fear in connection with love. Didn't one, instead, think of trust and security? I am, always have been, an observer of other people's passions. I suppose I knew about love first and best from Morgan. She'd been in and out of love for most of the four years we'd spent at college, and in the spring of our senior year she'd met Douglas. One May night before final exams we were studying together in her room. She seemed restless; her thoughts were scattered. I was reading a checklist to her: "The Brontës, Emily, Anne, Charlotte . . . Did you actually manage to finish *Wuthering Heights*? I somehow couldn't get through it, it all seemed completely implausible. Why would anyone love that grotesque boor?" Morgan was standing at the window, smoking. Her black hair was lank, her skin was oily and broken out. She said suddenly, irrelevantly, "I'm in love with Douglas Whiteside." She sat down on the edge of the desk and looked morosely at the floor, one arm held across her ribs as if she were about to be ill. I said, "Cheer up, you've been in love before. It will pass." "No," she said, "it's not like that," and she squashed out her cigarette in a saucer.

Margaret came back into the room, skirts whispering. She was frowning so severely that her face looked knotted between the eyebrows. She dropped down upon the tufted sofa and said, looking up, white face composed, "I'm sorry. That was my husband. He's missed his plane and won't be here for dinner. What was it we were talking about?"

"Morgan and Douglas. And love."

She turned her head slightly, but I saw an odd smile begin as a flicker in her eyes, then move on to her mouth, where it lay—barely quivering—along her thin upper lip. I saw for the first time that she was a beautiful woman. In this century the standards of beauty have declined to look-alike *Playboy* playmates with snubbed noses and silicone breasts, bleached mops of hair and large, orthodontically improved teeth, but there has always been a kind of beauty that depends as well on intelligence and that, finally, is far more dangerous, because it is endlessly elusive. Margaret's teeth were not perfect, and she was, under the sheer pleats and lace of her blouse, not particularly endowed. She sat with an arm up along the heart-shaped curve of the sofa's back, mysteriously smiling.

"Oh, love," she said, lifting her beautiful eyes—the smile had become wistful. "Isn't it boring to be a woman and think so much about love?"

For a while after that we talked about other things. I told her about the high price of blue jeans in Russia and the low price of vodka and how lemons were sold on street corners, drawn furtively out of shawls in dark doorways as if they were lumps of gold. I told her about our Intourist guide, who was pretty and divorced and lonely and spoke six languages and had had an affair with the doctor in our group. Margaret looked indifferent and shrugged, and when I began to talk about something I'd thought she'd be interested in—the art collection in the Hermitage, that fantastic French art that is kept in a hot, stuffy third-floor garret, all those joyful thumping Matisses confined like great beating butterflies in a small airless glass jar—she waved her hand as if a bothersome insect had just flown by.

"Oh, the Hermitage!" she said. "Oh, God, I imagine your friend—what's his name? the art collector—loved the Hermitage." There was something mocking in her voice I didn't understand, and at the same time I understood clearly now that she knew quite a lot about my private life.

"You mean David?"

"That's right, David. And before David you were married to a man named Walter. Morgan didn't like Walter. She is awfully pleased with David."

"Isn't everyone? But no, he didn't go to Russia with me. We're not seeing each other anymore."

"No? Oh, poor Morgan. Now she will have to worry about you all over again. And he sounded so nice."

I said sarcastically, "For a small fee I might arrange a meeting. He adores artists."

She stood up with a brisk rustle. "Oh, I'm not an artist anymore. I've given up painting."

"You don't paint at all?"

"No."

A pain like a draught of cold air encircled my heart. I hadn't written anything for two years, but when I thought of giving up entirely, I felt dizzy and nauseous and a white space began to spin all around me, as if I were falling off the edge of everything. I said, "I don't see how it's possible just to stop. How long has it been since you stopped painting?"

She looked impatient. "A year. Now I have got to do

something about dinner. Did Morgan tell you I'm having people over tonight? Nothing fancy or formal, we're all old friends."

I stood up, too. There was a round, lace-covered table next to the sofa, and she bent and put on the table lamp. Instantly the room fell away into blackness, and a gold pool of lamplight illuminated the bowl of red roses and a nest of photographs: snapshots of children, an old view of hills and a lake. I took up the brown-tinted landscape and studied it.

She said, "The lake is the Sacandaga, in the Adirondacks. Do you know the area?"

I put the photograph down. "No. Is that where you're from?"

"Near there." A buzzer went off naggingly in the kitchen. She said, "Time to go to work. Please don't offer to help. I honestly prefer cooking alone."

She nodded at me dismissingly, then turned and went down the hall. Her long white dress made a pale receding glimmer.

# 7

Outside Margaret Allen's house the sky had faded away behind the treetops, and the birds had fallen into silence among the black leaves. In the warm twilight I dressed slowly, moving about the guest room without putting on any lights. It was that ambiguous hour when the room is in shadow but a soft white light lingers and your face in the long mahogany-framed mirror is quite a different face, a face carved out of darkness, hollows beneath the cheekbones, deeply shaded eyes. Leaning into the mirror again, pressing my palms against the cool marble dresser top, I thought that it had been five years since I'd last seen

Douglas. I wondered if he'd changed much. Had he gotten fat? Bald? Stooped? Lined?

We would avoid each other tonight, we always had, and be very polite and very cool when it was required that we speak to each other. Morgan would tease us both. Sometime in the evening she would tell me (her hand on my arm) how much he admired my intellect. Sometime in the evening we would both get refills at the bar, and he would say ironically (looking down at me with cool gray eyes), "Well, Isabel. We are anticipating another book." I disliked talking about my books, and the sarcastic way he said this embarrassed and hurt me.

I wanted him to be kind to me, or at least not sarcastic, and he was always cool. Any friendship of long standing resembles a marriage in that there are ego trade-offs and accommodations; on the other hand there are sometimes ties between friends that are stronger than the ties between spouses. Was he jealous of my friendship with Morgan? Perhaps he thought I made Morgan restless—a little pinprick reminder of life outside Summerville. And maybe I even engendered a tingle of guilt: there was that time long ago when Morgan and I had had dreams and ambitions and plans—he had come between. We had avoided each other for so long that avoidance had become a pattern, and after all these years I was myself too shy to go up to him and put out my hand and say, "Hi! Let's sit down somewhere and get to know each other. I've known you for years and we've never said more than fifty words to each other. I feel you dislike me. I feel you think me pretentious and cynical. Perhaps I'm not what you think, but—what is it you think I am? I sense that you are deeply, remarkably intelligent" (no, I'd never say that) "but why is it after all these years we can't have a simple conversation? You see, you make me feel dreadful, a self I don't want to be . . . a tart-tongued 'lady journalist.' "

I peered into the mirror. The Isabel who regarded me was not my usual strict self but a hazy, grave, gentler Isabel in sepia tones from another old photograph album. She had mystery and depth and large luminous eyes that were full of suppressed passion, like those of an early Victorian heroine. Someday, I thought, it would be fun to write a book with a passionate heroine. She would be an unreliable narrator with warped perceptions. She would be shortsighted—all for love! The book would be full of dreams, portents, storms, tossing branches, the kind of novel my parents used to make fun of. I leaned into the mirror, squinting, searching that face for signs of what I wanted it to become, and then I shrugged and straightened up. Sometimes when I look in the mirror, behind the Isabel I see and the one I would like to become, I catch a glimpse—a frightening glimpse—of another face watching me watch myself. This, too, is an Isabel, but I can never quite make out her features—she has tired, loveless eyes, looks at me mockingly, and is always highly amused.

# 8

Skinny little Trina Pratt came right in, black hair flying, and said, "How are you, Isabel? It's nice to see you again. Did Margaret tell you I'd been divorced and"—her blues eyes flashed angrily—"remarried? Ralph, this is Isabel, she's an old friend of Morgan's. I'll have white wine with soda, Ralph, and lots of ice."

Trina had on an embroidered Mexican dress that drooped off her thin, sloping shoulders. She wore flat strapped brown leather sandals and had a Band-Aid around one big toe. She nudged me into the living room and said, not much lowering her voice, which was high and shrill, "Ralph has custody of his three kids, and I have three, so we have six all together. Frankly it's awful. His kids hate me and my kids despise him."

Thus began the evening, and how bumpily, bumpily did it coast downhill from this glittering apex. It was hot. There was consequently much drinking, and a sulky, surly, bad-tempered feeling in the air that everyone ascribed to the humidity.

"So you live in New York!" Ralph Pratt said, putting a large wineglass into Trina's outstretched hand. "What do you do about muggers, Isabel? What do you do about lunch? Ha, ha."

He was a short black-haired man with shiny pink skin, a little blob of a nose, and a mustache with waxed pointed ends. He kept touching the mustache tenderly, as if it were a boil that hurt. He wore a candy-pink alligator shirt, and pink and green plaid pants.

"I do get into town once in a while," Ralph said. "What do you like for lunch, Isabel? Caravelle? Lutèce?"

"Lutèce!" Trina cried. "Tell her about the chili we had last night. Tell her where you took me on my birthday."

"Excuse me," I said, trying to inch away, "I think I need a refill."

"It was a steak house on Route Ten," Trina said, turning slightly so that she blocked my path. "There were wagon wheels on the walls and there was a worm in my salad. We had a crab-meat cocktail and we were both very ill later that night. Lutèce! He's all mouth, believe me."

"You've been to Lutèce, sweetie," Ralph said coldly.

"The night he proposed!" Trina cried. "Can you believe it? I can't. I can't believe I fell for that old stuff."

"Oh, pu-leeze," Lily Webber said. The Webbers had come in and were standing in the hall, talking to Margaret. "Ah cain't believe you all are at it again. How are you, Isabel? Why on earth would anyone leave New York for this?"

Politely I smiled.

"Her house burned down," Ralph said. "She had nowhere to go. I told her she could move in with us if she wanted."

"Yeah," Trina said, "right. Ask her which kid she'd like to bunk with."

"Was it a ba-yud far?" Lily asked. Lily was from North

Carolina, a small, amber-eyed, white-skinned redhead. Her white sundress showed off a thin little chest rippled like a piece of painted corrugated tin. Her fiery hair was glorious.

"Pardon?" I said. "Oh, the fire. Yes, it was."

"She lost everything," Trina said.

"Mah goodness," Lily said evenly and sat down in a Lincoln rocker. "Was anyone hurt?"

"Well," I began, "the man downstairs," but Lily's eyes slid around me to her husband, who without saying a word had floated smiling to the bar, where he was pouring himself a tumbler full of straight gin.

"Jehosophat," Lily said, "dew y'all see tha-ut in his hand? Cain't somebody talk to him? He's killin' himself. He's killin' me." Donald Webber turned and dreamily smiled. He was a tall, thin, hunched man with misty, unfocused blue eyes.

"Whatd'ya say, Don?" Ralph said in a booming voice. "Kind of a stiff drink, isn't it?"

Donald Webber blinked and looked around as if coming up from under water. "Where's Morgan?" he said.

"God knows," Margaret said.

"She went to the airport to pick up Douglas," Trina said.

"Hey, Mags," Ralph said, "when's chow? We're all nigh unto getting skunked, if you know what I mean."

"You are, we're not," Trina said. "I told you not to have another drink before you left the house."

"I wasn't thinking about myself," Ralph said, indicating Donald Webber with a meaningful tilt of his head.

"Well, that's new and different," Trina said.

"We'll sit down at nine thirty," Margaret said. "The Whitesides should be here by then."

"Meanwhile, Isabel," Trina said and patted the rose silk seat of the sofa, "come over here and sit next to me and I'll tell you the story of my life."

By the time she had reached puberty, I was dizzy with boredom and a craving for sleep. How easy it would be to sneak upstairs. Everyone would think I was only depressed or fatigued or sick. I was so intent on inventing a magical exit line that I almost missed the next interesting item. Trina had stood up and was pulling me along with her toward the dining room.

"You understand," she said in a lowered voice, "that much of this is clearly the Whitesides' fault."

"What is?" I asked, confused.

"Because, you see, Morgan has this habit of taking up people who need help, only this time she went too far, if you know what I mean."

"Not exactly," I said. "Who is it we're talking about? I seem to have . . ."

"Why, Paul Caron," Trina said. "Everyone knows that . . ."

We were standing next to the dining room table, and now Margaret came swinging through the door from the kitchen, carrying a large white china soup tureen. Margaret gave us a sharp look, and Trina, for the very first time that evening, smiled a blazing, ingenuous smile.

The dinner was delicious—cold spinach soup and a pasta and seafood salad—but the drinking continued, and the mood at the table was ominous. Trina Pratt had just opened a business of her own, a crafts shop called The Glad Hand that sold pottery, quilts, rag rugs, and baskets. She and Ralph had disagreed about the store. He wanted her to stay home, "with his kids," Trina said, putting her hand up to her mouth but not whispering, "only the kids don't need a nursemaid, he does."

Lily Webber didn't talk to her husband at all but talked about him as if he were somewhere else or perhaps had died— and perhaps he *had* died. He gave the impression, sitting there stiffly upright at the end of the table, that he was the freak at some carny sideshow, a kind of curiosity who relied on his barker—Lily—to point out his interesting features. For one thing, Lily said, amused, he had totaled seven cars.

"Then before the Mercedes we had the Volvo wagon and the '52 MG. I was right proud of that car, the MG, it was bee-youtiful to look at, but one night after the Christmas dance at the Club, Donal' hit the stone wall at the side of the drahvway, went ovah the stone wall, honey, it was unbelievable."

One of Lily's small white hands lay on the table, and I asked about an antique ring she had on.

"This ol' thing?" she said. "It was his mother's ring, it's just peridot. She died and ah got all the old lady's jewelry. She must be turnin' over in her grave, thinkin' about that no-good Lily Gilbert wearin' all her stuff. We grew up in the same town, Donal' and me. His momma was a Yankee, but his poppa owned the family ironworks. When we got married, my friends all said, 'Lily, it's the coup of the year. Ol' Miz Webber is gonna jes' die over this.' See, my daddy was a car dealer and besides that, he was a Catholic. And she did. Miz Webber died not six months after our weddin'!"

Lily raised her head and laughed, showing small white even teeth. "Down home in those days people really took on if you happened to be a Catholic."

Trina said from across the table, "It's all so stupid. People still take on. My father's Dutch and my mother's Italian and the families hate each other."

"Oh, what the hell," Ralph said, "families always hate each other. My first wife was Presbyterian and I was a Presbyterian and our families hated each other."

Trina snickered. "Maybe it wasn't the families, only you."

Ralph Pratt leaned across Lily Webber and asked me if I'd heard the story of the rabbi, the priest, and the Presybterian minister who were all out in a rowboat.

"Many times," I said.

"Oh," he said, looking perplexed. He stared at his plate for a moment and then went on eating his pasta. Ralph reminded me of the little girl I knew when I was in the fifth grade who was invited to all the birthday parties because she was stupid and never, never guessed the secret word and would always be taken home in tears. It was so satisfying to the rest of us.

"Oh, my God," Trina said, "I really literally hate summer dinner parties. We all drink way too much and Sundays are just shot. How the hell am I going to play tennis tomorrow, my head's big as a watermelon. Honestly, Isabel, I wish I lived in New York. Do they drink this much in New York? I'll bet they don't. I'd love New York except that it's full of such scrungy people."

I longed to be back in New York among scrungy people. I wondered where David was. Was he up in Boston? He didn't drink much, only a little wine, and Walter, my ex-husband, had been a closet Lutheran from Wisconsin. He, too, drank wine and an occasional Molson's.

"Oh, shut up, Ralph," Trina said now from across the table. "Do you always have to make a total ass of yourself?"

"Trina, my dear," Ralph said, "will you kindly fuck off?" Trina picked up a crust of French bread and threw it across the table at him. Ralph stared at it for a moment—it had landed on his gold-rimmed dinner plate and sat in a glazed pool of pimento-flecked salad oil. Then he stood up and removed his water goblet from the table.

"Woo-ee," Lily said, "here it comes."

"He wouldn't dare!" Trina said. "Ralph? Ralph!"

And then a door somewhere opened and a fresh little breeze wafted across the room, and at once the room, which despite the lit candles and mirrors and glow of silver and flash of crystal had had a murky, sullen feel about it, full of oppressive air that wasn't just August humidity but crosscurrents and glum remarks, came to good-humored life. The candles flickered in the draught, guttered, then blazed up higher, and Donald Webber blissfully smiled, and Ralph Pratt, a sparkle of perspiration on his pink brow, held his goblet up in the air and cried, "About time! Where have you two been?" Lily and Trina raised their hands and clapped, and Morgan said, "You all, I'm so sorry to be late. Isabel, you brave thing. All alone with this pack of wolves."

She came around the table to kiss me. She had on a long, bright green tube of a dress. Her black hair had been cut short and swung sleekly down from a white part, and as she bent her cheek to mine her earrings, triple-hooped earrings, chimed, and her bracelets, a whole armful of them, jingled.

At the other end of the table Douglas Whiteside nodded coldly to me and sat down next to Margaret.

"Oh, Margaret," Morgan said, "your table's beautiful. Your flowers are fantastic. Listen, everyone!" She put her hands on my shoulders and lightly squeezed. "Right after dinner Isabel is going to tell us all about Russia. I want to hear everything, all about the Kremlin and Leningrad and everything. I've always wanted to go to Russia."

"Nonsense," Douglas Whiteside said, "you hate to travel."

"It's true," Morgan said, walking around the table to her chair, patting a shoulder or an arm as she passed by, "I do hate to travel. I hate packing and unpacking." She looked across the table at me and smiled.

"A toast, a toast," Ralph Pratt said. He put his goblet down on the table and struck it with a fork, and the musical ringing sound of the delicate crystal made everyone cheer, "To all of us!"

# 9

Margaret, Morgan, and I sat on the Allens' screened porch, sipping black coffee. The men had stayed on at the table; large puffs of yellow cigar smoke floated out of the double doors to the porch, lazily circled the white lath ceiling, and were dispersed by the slow groaning rotation of the Casablanca fan. In the living room Trina and Lily were having an earnest conversation about tennis. Morgan—who shared my wicker sofa—and Margaret, sitting across from us in a rocker, were talking softly about their children.

"Now, of course, kids think they know everything," Morgan said.

Margaret smiled and shook her head. She had put on long garnet earrings for the evening, and when she turned her head, they glowed and trembled.

"The thing I can't figure out," Morgan said, "is how much my daughter really knows. Once I asked Sarah—this was, oh, maybe four years ago, when she was eleven—and she just snapped at me, 'Oh, Mom, I know all that, for heaven's sake.' All *what*, I wanted to ask her. You're eleven and you know it all? Since then, every time I've brought it up, she just glares or leaves the room. I can't decide if she knows more than I think or less. You can teach a kid about sex, all the anatomy and what goes where, but that isn't it, really."

Margaret said, "Is Sarah still going out with the Dixon boy?"

"No, it's a new boy every couple of weeks, which is fine with me, except that she seems so"—Morgan shrugged—"I don't know. Unhappy. Well." She shrugged again. "Did Cathy get off to college all right?"

Margaret rocked, lifting her feet and neatly putting them down together. "Oh, yes. She went off with a trunk, a large suitcase, her cello, her stereo, all her albums, and her entire paperback collection of Henry James."

"Incredible, isn't it?" Morgan said. "I went to college with practically nothing. And why is it they're all reading Henry James? I couldn't wait to graduate so I could *stop* reading Henry James. Sarah's been reading *The Turn of the Screw* this summer. I hadn't read it since freshman year, so I picked it up and zipped through it. Then I remembered that I'd never believed it, not even back then. I kept asking myself, what is he getting at? *How* were those kids corrupted? You know me and my dirty mind. I wanted to know the sordid details."

"That's the charm of the book," I said. "He leaves it to the evils of your imagination."

"Yeah, but I had this feeling he thought a few dirty words

were the ultimate in corruption. Ha! Henry should be a fly on my wall. And that poor dopey little governess and all that stuff about contamination."

I said, "That was the point, wasn't it? She was really the innocent. The teacher got taught."

"Really!" Morgan said. "Well, she didn't seem to get taught a whole lot."

"I always thought it was just a ghost story," Margaret said.

"See that," I said. "You weren't an English major at Smith College."

"I didn't go to college," she said. "When I was seventeen, I went to the Art Students League. When I was eighteen, I met Jerry."

"Where did you meet him?" I asked.

"At a second-hand furniture shop on Second Avenue. I had a room on East Tenth Street I was trying to furnish. Jerry was buying a bed. He told me I was just his girl friend's size and asked me to lie down on the bed with him so that he could decide if they would both fit. I was so surprised by his brashness I did it. I'd never met anyone that forward before." She smiled and looked down at the floor. "We lay there for a moment facing each other and he kept saying, 'Perfect, perfect.'" She smiled. "Yet another ghost story," she said. "All the characters in the story are dead."

"Well, I have a ghost story to tell, too," Morgan said, "only it happened just a few weeks ago. In fact, Iz, I was so upset I tried to call you—I forgot you were away until about the fifth time I dialed. Then moving put the whole thing out of my mind. Now, just sitting here thinking about it bothers me all over again, isn't that odd?"

I asked her what had happened. She raised her thin black brows. "I went to a nursery to get some plants, and I thought I saw your mother. Isn't that weird? I mean, if I were going to see a ghost, why wouldn't I see *my* mother?"

"Because," I said logically, "your mother's not dead."

"Wrong," Morgan said. "My mother died at the beginning

of July, while you were away. So figure that one out. Well I knew, of course, the woman couldn't really be your mother, but it was someone who looked a whole lot like her. Exactly like her." She looked at me apologetically. "I always liked your mother so much."

I said, "She liked you, too."

"A funny feeling stayed with me for days. Later I decided maybe I was just transposing. Maybe I was trying to deal with my own mother's death, and it got mixed up. Because, as you know, I wasn't exactly fond of my mother. Still, I got a trip to Paris out of it—her death, I mean. Ghosts. Goodness, I don't believe in ghosts."

I said that I didn't exactly believe in ghosts, but something my mother had said a long time ago stuck with me, how as you got older your head was full of people no longer alive. I had myself acquired a long list of ghosts. Three of my closer friends were dead, my mother was dead, and my father was probably dead. I supposed that as one got older the list got sadder and longer until, when you were very old, all the people you knew and loved existed only phantasmagorically, in your head. My mother told me once that when her grandmother, my great-grandmother, was very old, she used to walk down to the sea. She would plod along the sand, muttering, talking to her eleven dead brothers and sisters, whose voices she said she heard in the murmur of the waves.

"It's catching," Morgan said, tilting her head toward the dining room, where the men were still talking. I heard Douglas's voice, a deep rumble. Morgan leaned over the edge of the sofa into the doorway. "Oh, Douglas Whiteside, will you please shut up? We are here to enjoy ourselves, not to listen to a bunch of morbid stories about your dead friends."

"Hear, hear," said Ralph Pratt, leaning back in his chair and looking at us from the dining room table. "Good for you, Morgo! Let's have some wine and song! Notice, everyone, that I left out 'women' just to please Trina. Enough of this boring, melancholy crapola! Let's live! Nothing exciting has happened in this town since Paul Caron died."

There was a sudden silence, as if, from out of the black sky just over the rooftop, we'd all heard a clap of feathered wings. Then Margaret Allen gave an abrupt laugh and stood up. Douglas stood up, too.

"Time to go home," he said. Cigarettes were stubbed out, drinks put down. Margaret stood at the front door saying good night, looking tall, frail, severe. Douglas nodded good night to me and went out to the porch. He stood with his long back toward me watching a moth beat upon the porch light's globe. After all, we'd avoided each other for the evening, and I hadn't noticed until then that his hair wasn't silvery blond anymore, it was gray.

# 10

I woke up at three A.M. with a crashing headache; got up; took an aspirin; drank a glass of cold water; thought about my life. My life was going by—so fast!—and at the same time it was somehow stuck, but I didn't know where or even *what* the snag was. For a time David had helped, and then it all went to hell. Just before I left for Russia, David had looked at me solemnly and said, "Can a hybrid achieve wholeness?"

I had liked David awfully much. The first night we went out together, we'd talked through the second act of a play and straight on through to the next night's double feature at the Thalia. We talked in bars and restaurants and in his car and in a Circle Line tour boat. We talked in taxis, his hotel room at the Algonquin, at my place, and sometimes half through the night. Other things worked pretty well, too.

*Then why not David?* I asked myself. I knew he loved me. He'd never leave me, and I wouldn't have my mother's tough life. This was certainly something to consider—financial security hadn't exactly been a constant in the Schliemann household. Whenever the word *money* ominously appeared in domestic conversation, my father would give in to a terrific fit of yawning, head-scratching, ear-pulling. Glassy-eyed with boredom, he would slump into the fidgets, waiting for the conversation to loop up and back into his domain: ideas!

My father was an historian, and when I was ten, he gave up his job teaching college girls in order to devote himself full time to his book, *A History of Modern Germany* (A.D. 800–1933). Soon we were broke. My mother got a job.

She would get up half an hour early every morning and run to the bakery so that he'd have fresh poppy seed rolls for breakfast. At night, after work, she shopped at the market, cooked dinner, cleaned up the kitchen, ironed his shirts, and by 9:30 had dropped into bed. My father would say, *"Teufel!* What's wrong with your mother? She has so little *Energie.* I think she needs a checkup."

I thought she needed another husband. Why had she picked him when she could have had anyone? It was obvious that men adored her. She was twenty pounds overweight, most of it in the bust, but she had a kind of rosy bloom that she kept until her last illness. When we walked down Lexington Avenue together, any male of her acquaintance would reverentially lift his hat and, hat pressed to heart, give an old-fashioned European half-bow. She would flush and twinkle and smile and say in her high, clear, German-accented voice, "Oh, Herr Braun, how are you today?" so sweetly and earnestly that right there, while I stood impatiently on one foot then the other, Herr Braun would mournfully explain (the deep brown of his doggy eyes begging, just begging for a crumb of her lavish affections) the details of his wife's latest operation or his trip—*"Wunderschön!"*—to the Catskill Mountains.

Why had she married my father, this gnome of a man who

seemed to stumble when he walked, whose ties were always spotted, whose shoelaces dragged, whose pockets bulged with books, pencils, notepads, scraps of paper, whose mind (under wiry orange hair) was a vat bubbling over with wholly irrelevant information? For most of their lives together she ran after him with whisk brooms, raincoats, scarves, gloves, galoshes. Standing there at the door before he went out, scolding, buttoning up, brushing off, she always seemed to me like the mother of an amiable but inept three-year-old. She thought he was a genius. I wasn't so sure. He was always lost in thought. He could get lost anywhere, and once, for twenty absentminded minutes, he'd been lost in our building's elevator: he was certain that we were 11 B, and we weren't.

Luckily, except for our summer trip upstate, he seldom drove. Once a year, though, at the first blue hint of ruffled spring, my mother insisted that we drive to Rockaway Beach so that she could see the ocean. As my father pulled up near the boardwalk he would sigh and say, "Thalassa, Thalassa," making it sound like a curse. It was never balmy April, of course, or tender May, but wild, unruly March when my mother conceived this desire to renew her primordial contact with the steel-gray Atlantic. It was all wind and stinging swoops of sand hitting you in the face, and flapping, faded sheets of last July's Sunday comics.

My mother, in her green tweed Sunday suit, with a sad-eyed fox fur slung around her neck and one hand clamped to a flat veiled hat, marched stoutly ahead, only inclined somewhat f'ard, tilted against the wind, like an old-fashioned figurehead cleaving the brine. Next came my father, lost in thought, hands clasped behind his back, bald spot gleaming, his necktie whipping back over his left shoulder. He would look up occasionally, bemused, when the wind got particularly fierce, as if startled to find himself not at home in his study.

Last of all, twenty yards down the glittering strand, came truculent Isabel, listing badly to starboard (sand in shoes), angrily chomping and snapping her Dubble Bubble gum and wishing to God they had let her stay home with her book, knowing perfectly well that before she saw home again, one of two things, possibly both, would happen: They would get lost in Brooklyn, or her father would have an accident. And then there would be the dreadful humiliation of getting out of the car and standing huddled against the fender while her father, as cheerful and innocent as ever, tried to "pacify" that angry young fellow with the flaring nostrils and greasy hair who (cold as it was) wore no coat and had his shirt sleeves rolled up to his brown biceps, which displayed in blue ink (left arm) an anchor and (right arm) a naked lady with large-nippled breasts. Just because for one brief moment my father's attention and beat-up Plymouth had wandered out of one lane and halfway into another on the Belt Parkway. Lost in thought.

While I was at Miss Blanchard's School, whenever (out of dire necessity) we had to traverse the streets of New York together (my father and I), I would walk slightly ahead or loll slightly behind, pretending a vital interest in a window full of ham hocks or fish steaks, so that if someone I knew saw us, that awful catty Victoria Furbelow, for example, she wouldn't necessarily make a connection. At thirteen I developed a terrible crush on the father of a friend of mine who was tall and blond and well-groomed and used to come with his wife (a dumpy woman with gray hair) to chaperone our school dances. He was a kind man and danced with each of his daughter's friends, but when it came my turn, I blushed and ran away to the girls' room, where I stayed all evening long, weeping behind my glasses.

What was it I wanted? I wanted a deft, competent, well-groomed father. My father had a precisely contrary vision of himself. He wanted to carve a niche for himself in the German tradition of the absentminded professor. He wanted to be, had made himself into a scruffy, shabby, shambling, dusty, ash-sprinkled, frock-coated, spectacled nineteenth-century scholar. He wasn't merely out of place, he was out of time.

You see, it wasn't that I didn't love him. It was just that

again and again he betrayed our hopes, let us down with a crash, and again and again it was my mother who shrugged and picked up the pieces. Then, after twenty years in this country, he made one small concession to the American Way of Life: He got divorced.

My mother died four years after that, in great pain and all alone. She left me the silver tea service and a manila envelope full of my ancestors' photographs. Everything else—the jewelry, books, prints, porcelain—had long since been sold. Along with the photographs she had enclosed a family tree drawn in shaky blue ball-point pen.

"You'll want this," she whispered from her hospital bed, "someday for your children." It didn't seem relevant at the time. It didn't seem to make much difference in my life. Whoever got me would have to take me as is. What's done is done. We are what we are. I was twenty-four and had already decided I wouldn't have children. I told her this, and she said, her eyes flicking wide in shock, "But you'll fall in love and you'll want to have children." Then she closed her eyes and after a moment asked, "How is Morgan's little girl?"

Sometimes, late on a soggy black August night, a small breeze, the titillating promise of relief, will unfurl among the treetops. This night I had no such luck. It was stifling. I went to the bedroom window and threw it open. Not much help. The air was heavier outside than in, and there was no breeze. A thick chemical blackness hung over New Jersey, and even the insects sounded sluggish, drugged. I thought how Morgan and I were such opposite types it was amazing we'd ever remained friends. I don't believe in trying to solve other people's problems—I consider it meddlesome. I didn't in the least blame Margaret for maintaining her "reserve." For a moment there in the afternoon's conversation I'd almost felt she was prying at me and I'd resented it.

Then my head began to pound and I felt a flush rise up from the lace of my nightgown. It was as if my blood, muscles, body had figured things out before my brain. In my head Margaret Allen said again with a little one-cornered smile, "Oh, poor Morgan, now she will have to worry about you all over again." In my head I could clearly hear Morgan saying to Margaret on the telephone, "Do let Isabel stay with you, Margaret. And talk to her. See if you can find out what's wrong with her, what's *really* wrong. See if you can *help* her."

I stood at the window for some time. So that was it. We were to spy each other out. Morgan had assigned us—Margaret and me—delicate, duplicate assignments. After all these years, along with Matilda Chessley and sad Sophie Schlosser, I had become another one of Morgan's Problems.

# 11

Sunday morning—cooler, bluer—and Morgan sitting behind the wheel of her big gold station wagon looking too small to drive it, as if somehow she'd shriveled overnight. She had on huge square navy-blue sunglasses which slid too far down on her small straight nose and diminished the rest of her face, making it look drained. Her white pleated tennis shorts were two sizes too big and lumpily cinched in at the waist with a thin red belt, and the white T-shirt she wore was stretched out at the neck and faintly yellow under the arms—it must have belonged to Douglas. As if to counteract this lack of fashion, she had pinned a red enamel heart the size of a half-dollar over what one supposed was her left breast, although under the baggy T-shirt it was hard to tell.

"What's the heart for?" I asked, getting in. We were driving downtown together to have breakfast at a diner.

She said, "It kind of pulls the outfit together, don't you think?"

"Actually . . ." I said.

"Don't," she said in a choked voice. "Don't say one unpleasant word. I am feeling just lousy. I am so hideously disorganized. I can't find a thing, and neither can anyone else. Sarah can't find the bracelet her last boyfriend gave her, and Eddie . . . *Eddie* unloaded all the cartons full of my good china and broke a teacup looking for his catcher's mitt. Why couldn't he have broken a saucer? No one ever breaks saucers—I've got all these saucers and no teacups. And Douglas! You notice how, in the middle of the whole thing, he flew to Boston to see his dying grandmother? Whom he loathes? Then he gets to the new house, which he had so conveniently avoided having anything to do with, and he comes on like the star of the show finally making an entrance, the kids all knocking themselves out to show him everything—'Hey, Dad, look at this neat kitchen, it's got two sinks' "—she said in a tiny, mimicking voice—" 'and here's your new study, Dad.' I could have brained him. Then he gets instantly angry because he can't find a history text that came in the mail the day we moved that he's supposed to review for some journal or other. Oh, God, oh, God, I hate them all. I am totally sick of this rotten, *rotten* family. They are the most ludicrously selfish bunch of people I have ever come across. Worst of all, I suppose the kids are my fault, since I am their mother, but God knows who's to blame for Douglas. I know, I *know* that they think of me as the house genie and I am supposed to fix everything and know where everything is, but I get tired of it. Sometimes, Isabel"—she took her hand off the steering wheel and patted my leg just above the knee—"I wish I were an old maid like you. Furthermore, it's all my fault. I was the one who wanted to move. We were perfectly happy in the other house. Small as it was. Crowded as it was. *Ugly* as it was."

I laughed. She went on mournfully, "Oh, it's funny how I can play tennis all day and feel marvelous, but whatever it is about moving, it's exhausting. Or maybe it's my reaction to a bunch of cartons. Psychologically they make me feel faint, and I withdraw. It reminds me of . . . well, ho hum, you've heard this all before. When I was small, sob, sob."

I laughed again. Who else but Morgan could put this kind of double whammy on you, giving you a satirical version of her blatantly awful life, then proceeding to nail you with a throb-throated, laughter-through-tears Dickensian paragraph recalling her early childhood? In truth her childhood had been worse than she'd ever let on. There were more than a couple of times when she'd gone hungry, and a Willow Hill classmate of Morgan's who had been at Smith with us recounted once, over a beer at Rahar's, the full story of Morgan's packing to leave Willow Hill and getting three sturdy senior girls to help her carry her father (who was dead drunk) into the back of the horse van, which had no horse in it, only two cots for those times when they were truly down and out.

And here was Morgan (I looked out of the car window), living in suburban Summerville, according to a recent survey in *The Wall Street Journal* the ninth richest (per capita) town in the entire U.S.A. Gliding past the window, the town looked utterly complacent, the two rows of three-story brick buildings on Main Street sleepily facing each other, as if they were going to be there forever, which was no doubt true, since (so Morgan had told me) the town's ardent preservationists were dedicated to keeping everything just the way it was circa 1880, the whole town with the look of an early grade-B Ronald Reagan-type western movie set, a memorial in false-front architecture.

Luckily the Great Day Diner was only what it appeared to be, an old-fashioned, silver-colored trolley-car diner with a hand-lettered sign in the window promising: All Baking Done on Premasis, and a rich smell of real coffee as you strolled in the smeared glass door.

We sat down—Morgan softly groaning—in a booth, an old red vinyl number whose slash marks were adhesive-taped shut. She took off her sunglasses, groaned again, covered her face with her hands. There were blue-brown marks under her eyes, as if she, too, had had a bad headache at three A.M.

"Dammit," Morgan said, her dark eyes peeping at me over her hand which had slipped down to cover her nose and mouth, as if she expected to be very ill. "We ought to quit drinking. Why is it we all drink so much? I have the worst headache, and I've got to play tennis in an hour. It must have been the heat that made us all so thirsty. You don't like them, do you?"

"Who?" I asked, startled. I was thinking about my coffee: black, rich, steaming, five hundred caffeine-charged volts.

"The Webbers and the Pratts."

"Well, I haven't given it much thought."

"I know, I know, they did seem awful. It was sort of an awful evening." She sighed. Her hand fell to the table. "Currently everyone seems to be having such a hard go. I guess we're all very self-absorbed. It's the time of life. People get pressed on all sides—aging parents, troublesome kids."

I said, "It would have been nice to have a little conversation. Don't folks out here read *The New York Times?* We might have been in Ashtabula, wherever that is."

"I don't *believe* you. We sat right out on Margaret's porch talking about Henry James. How intelligent can you get?"

"Henry would have died," I said. "He would have left long before dinner. By the way, you did miss one glorious moment— Trina threw a piece of bread at Ralph."

"Really?" Morgan grinned.

"Really. Now that I think about it, maybe in a way I did enjoy it. At least there were some genuine signs of life. Last time I thought you were all just a bunch of robots out here."

The waitress appeared. She was young and pale with sleep in the corners of her eyes, and she had a messy pile of red-blond hair pinned up with black bobby pins under her grayish waitress cap. "You want coffee, ladies?" she asked. "We got some nice fresh doughnuts, too, home baked."

We voted for glazed doughnuts, and the waitress sauntered off to the kitchen, bottom swaying under her limp apron ties. At the other end of the diner an elderly couple dressed up for church was eating breakfast. The old woman was so small you couldn't see much of her over the back of the booth, though every once in a while a large yellow-brimmed straw hat would appear, then dip down again, as if the hat were gently riding out to sea on tidal swells. The old man seemed to be staring at us, then I saw that he was blind, or almost blind. He talked in a nonstop stream, his voice coming out in a high, billowing treble amplified by some sort of voice box. Throat cancer, I thought. My mother had died of breast cancer. When I was little, I used to sit on my mother's lap and contentedly watch her bosom rise and fall, like a soft but firm vanilla-scented soufflé.

"Sometimes," Morgan said softly, chin in hand, looking out the window, "I get tired of worrying about everyone's feelings. I worry about how Douglas is feeling and how Eddie is feeling and Sarah and Tess. Who put me in charge of everyone's feelings? Sometimes I think how much easier life would be if I were a thing like a robot and had no feelings, no feelings at all."

If you are in Summerville on any Sunday between mid-March and mid-October, the entire town looks dressed for tennis. Outside, a man in flashing sunglasses and tennis whites drove by in a highly polished Mercedes convertible. A kid in tennis whites went by on a bicycle with his racquet laid across the handlebars and his blond hair streaming. The town had, anyway, a kind of unreal gloss, as if it had been dipped in lacquer and put under a bell jar. Life seemed so contained, well cared for, orderly, beautiful. Maybe that's why the dinner party had surprised me, everyone letting their bobcats out of the bag that way.

I said, "Did you know Margaret's given up painting?"
Morgan looked up. "No. Has she really?"
I nodded. The waitress appeared with two thick-lipped mugs of coffee—slop, slosh—a paper plate with glazed doughnuts, two chipped china plates, and—ah, well-mannered Summerville—forks.

"Go on," Morgan said, "*mange*. I'm not really hungry. Tell me what *else* you found out."

"That's it," I said. "That's all I found out."

"That's all? Didn't she say anything about her, uh, love life?"

"No."

"God, Isabel, you're no help."

"You should have told me the guy was dead, Morgan."

"What?" she said blankly.

"This Paul Caron. You should have told me that he'd died. I might have said something terrible to her. And what's with her husband? Does he always miss planes on weekends?"

"Basically, it pains me to say this, but Jerry's a shit. Really. I don't say that about just anyone, either."

"Last time I came out? He called me in New York the next day."

"Don't take it to heart, he's called just about everybody. I used to have to wear brass knuckles when we'd go there for dinner. It's gotten so that I feel kind of sorry for Jerry, he tries so hard. Still, he's treated Margaret very badly."

"Why doesn't she leave him?"

"I'm not sure. Money, I guess. It's hard to support two households unless you're very well off. Actually, I know this is going to sound strange since she's a good friend of mine, but I don't know much about Margaret." Morgan put her hand up against her face, sheltering her eyes from the sun that streamed in through the grimy diner window. "It takes a long time to really know people out here anyway. People move to town, buy a house, join a club—nobody cares too much who they are or where they're from as long as they play a good game of tennis and pay their club dues. There's a feeling against asking too many questions. One doesn't. Eventually most people fit in or move on. Even so, I know less about Margaret than I do about most of my other friends. Part of it, I think, is that she's really not interested in the past, she's interested in what's in front of her, whatever she's working on. And she's interested in the future. She once told me that she wanted to leave tracks of some kind, like dinosaur tracks, she said. It sort of depressed me. I never have time to think of my future. I feel sometimes as if I'm just hurtling toward something, but what is it?" She looked perplexed and shrugged. "Anyway, if they did have an affair—I mean Margaret and Paul—she's never said anything about it. Something happened, though. She is so unhappy."

"Last night after you left, Margaret said she thought you must be the last happy woman."

Morgan smiled wanly. "That was last night. Try me this morning. Just since yesterday I've lost my looks and with that gone, well . . . what's left? Sometimes I think I must be a really boring person and a great disappointment to Douglas. Maybe he should have married someone intellectual or artistic."

"Oh, really," I said. "As I recall, you didn't drag him squealing to the altar. Say, it's not December first, is it?"

"What?" She frowned at me but then got it and smiled. In college, every year around December first, we'd prepare ourselves for what we used to call Morgan's C.A.S.—her Christmas Anxiety Syndrome. One year, first week in December, she broke her ankle ice skating, and another year she got mononucleosis on December 5, and they shipped her home. The dean's office didn't understand that she didn't have a real home. She'd go back to the Benchley School or wherever her father was currently hanging out and he would be blotto and she'd end up taking care of him. There are some people in this world who, no matter what, always end up taking care of everyone else.

No, she said, that wasn't it (explaining in a voice that didn't sound like her voice but was thin and tired), only sometimes lately she would get depressed and didn't know why, or maybe she was just tired and then got depressed. Anyway, she was no doubt just momentarily down. She felt guilty moving them out of the small affordable house into the large unaffordable one. Though the truth was, her mother's death had made the down payment possible.

I asked if she had gotten to see her mother before she died.

"Nope," she said. "I never did. She never came back to the States. When she died, she was living alone in Paris, not in what you'd call the grand style. When I finally saw her there, she was this little heap of bones, and I said to myself, so this is the monster you hated all those years. Of course, I hadn't seen her since I was eight. The funny thing is—this is irony for you—what's left of my inheritance from my mother is paying for my father's nursing home. He's completely *non compos* now. Frankly, I am hoping that he will painlessly expire real soon, because college tuitions are coming along, and then, believe it or not, your friend Morgan has a special plan for her future. She is gonna rewrite her act." She grinned at me. "You'll never guess what the rewrite is going to be."

"Let's see," I said. "What would I do if I were you? Open up a riding academy?"

"I knew you'd think something like that. You are many miles off base, my friend. I am going to go to graduate school and get a Ph.D."

"You are? What in?"

This time she looked annoyed. "In English, you zombie. You were the one who kept telling me how smart I was."

"But what are you going to do with the degree after you get it?"

"I'm not sure. Maybe I won't even finish. I just want to get started on something. I have all these incredible plans, and they change somewhat from day to day. I could teach—usually on Mondays I feel like teaching, but sometime during the middle of the week I switch direction and think I'd like to try publishing. I don't mean working a nine to five in the city, only something small—at least I'll start small—in the basement. A little press of my own."

"Really?"

"Why not? Oh, well, that's a couple of years off. I have to

get Eddie a little farther along. Meanwhile, what's yours?"

"Mine?"

"Your rewrite. I figure everyone should do a rewrite half-way through life."

I laughed at her. "Oh, maybe I'll get married and have three children."

"Ha," she said, "not likely." She looked down at the table and pushed the coffee mug away with her fingertips. "Anyone who could give up a fella as nice as David."

Then the whole little nighttime three A.M. sequence came roaring back into my head, and I felt my eyes narrow and my face tighten, and I put down my coffee mug and proceeded to vent my awful displeasure.

"God, Iz!" Her thin black brows flew up. "What are you so mad about?"

*Easy now*, I told myself, *stay calm*. "The way you butt *in*, Morgan. Leave off on David, okay? This is my life."

"Listen, Isabel, all I've been trying to do is to point out to you that you have this utterly stupid idea of who you should marry. It's your *idea* of marriage that worries me. Take that Walter, for instance." She rolled her dark eyes. "Man, was he for the birds."

"I know that, that's why I divorced him."

"But why did you marry him?"

"Because he asked me. It was the winter I had pneumonia and I was feeling passive and listless and"—I ducked my head—"lonely. I was afraid I was going to die in my room like an old person, only I was twenty-six."

She shook her head. "But there was nothing there. I mean, there was no spark, no uh . . ."

I said stiffly, "We had many interests in common."

"See," she said, leaning toward me across the table, "*that* is what I mean. That is a bunch of baloney, Isabel. You are seeing life through a haze of Henry James. All that drawing room stuff, all those elegant, deep conversations."

"Listen," I said, "forget the Ph.D. You can't even read, for Christ's sake. Henry James was a realist. If you look at his characters closely . . ."

She held up a hand. "Maybe, okay, it wasn't Henry's fault, maybe it was only your parents. Somehow I think they gave you some real screwball notions. You always did think they had this wonderful marriage and you had to do it all over again."

I looked at her, startled. Had I ever told her that? Maybe so, maybe freshman year when my parents were still married. If I had had that idea once, it was now so long ago it seemed like a whole new thought. "No," I said, "you've got that all wrong."

"Is that so? Well, it seemed to me you were sure they were Meant for Each Other, it was the love story of the century, only it occurred to me right away, the first time I came down to see you in New York, that there was a lot of stuff you were sweeping under the rug. And then junior year the stuff just worked its way out. Remember how you used to come to my room and sit on my floor and stare into space? That was when your father left."

"So?"

"So what's perfect about a marriage like that?"

"They didn't *have* a perfect marriage. I may have told you that, but I certainly never believed it." (Or had I believed it? I couldn't remember.)

"It struck me there was a lot you didn't understand."

"Look, Morgan. My father was weird. He was always weird. He just got weirder as he got older."

"Oh, was that the problem?"

"I don't know what the problem was. I don't think much about my father. I don't care to think about him."

"Why did he leave?"

"I have no idea. The middle-aged crazies, maybe. I told you, I don't care to think about it."

"You mean he just went off by himself?"

"There was another woman involved, but I only saw her

once. Six months later, a year later, I don't know when, she took off. Left him with one jelly glass and a toothbrush. Look. Stop worrying about me, Morgan. I am exceedingly cautious."

"That's why you married someone you didn't love." Morgan reached across the table and laid her hand on mine. "But look, Iz. I just feel with David things are right for you. Maybe you should try again. Maybe you should plunge in. You can't think everything out. That's what you did with Walter, you tried to think it all out. It never works, Iz. Love is completely irrational, so why not go with it?" She smiled.

I removed my hand. I said, "You don't appear to be listening. All along I've been telling you: *I don't love David.* Now do you get it? Anyway, maybe that whole maneuver isn't right for me—marriage, children. Look at my mother. What an instructive lesson in self-sacrifice."

"Oh, your mother," Morgan said dreamily. "I honestly loved your mother."

I sighed and got out a couple of singles to pay my check. Outside, Morgan got in the car and settled herself behind the steering wheel. "Hop in, Iz, my tennis game commences very soon, like in ten minutes. I think we'd better go pick up Lily. She's always late, and if we're late today, we'll have to forfeit and those suckers'll be ahead of us on the tennis ladder. Sit back, Isabel, and relax. I am going to drive across town like the very devil."

# 12

Morgan's big gold air-conditioned wagon glided across town as coolly and silently as a capsule floating through space, and I imagined a book published in the year 3500 A.D. purporting to describe domestic life in the latter part of the twentieth century.

"In fact, social status in ancient Sumi depended not upon money or heredity or familial ties but upon proficiency in games, the rules of which are unfortunately not yet clear to us. We do know, however, that the status of members of the Club was openly defined in a hierarchical arrangement called the Tennis Ladder. From the vantage point of this disturbed and tumultuous thirty-sixth century, life in ancient Sumi seems ideally tranquil with a large measure of domestic stability."

Isabel the Archeologist looked out the car window—tranquil, ancient Sumi floated by, littered with artifactual misinformation. In that peaceful-looking little white clapboard house a man is beating his wife in the soundproof basement, and in the fieldstone house next door a woman sprinkles cyanide on her husband's Sunday morning French toast.

We had turned into a narrow, overgrown, rutted dirt road.

"Damn!" Morgan said. "This road is a bitch. What was it you just said?" Raspberry canes clawed at us as we passed, and on both sides of the car steamy, junglelike tangles of vegetation rose up under trees covered with vines.

"I was asking about Paul Caron. Wasn't he kind of, uh, young to just pass out of the picture?"

Morgan stopped the car. The Webbers had hacked a clearing in the New Jersey jungle and built a glass-and-cedar-sided house in the middle of it, but the trees in the glen were so tall and the foliage so thick that in deep midsummer they had to keep their living room lights on—the living room was lit up like a jeweler's showcase. Morgan briefly tapped the horn. Inside, a light blinked twice in answer.

"He was thirty-eight. He died of a heart attack."

"Thirty-eight! My, that does give one pause."

"It was sad. Paul had a lot to live for. He was bright and he had something a lot of men don't have or lose pretty fast—he had real emotional warmth." She tapped the horn again. "Come *on*, Lily."

"What was he like? He seems to have fascinated everyone."

"Oh, I don't know about 'fascinated' . . . there were lots of people who didn't like Paul. Maybe they were envious. He was divorced and he had enough money to live an interesting life. Paul and Douglas got to be good friends. I was glad to see that, because you know Douglas . . ." She glanced at me briefly. "He doesn't make friends easily. He never does try to fit in. Anyway, they used to go down to the shore together and go sailing. I suppose, in a way, we adopted Paul. He'd had such a bad time, and he had these two kids, Claire and Jason, who used to come stay with him on school vacations. God knows where their mother was. Running around Europe, I guess."

Lily opened the car door. She had on a tennis dress that had strawberries embroidered along the hem, and she carried a little red cloth purse, shaped like a strawberry. She said, "Whatever are you two talkin' about? You look so serious."

"Paul Caron," I said.

"Oh, my," Lily said. I slid over as she got in. She slammed the door and stuck her tennis racquet between her lightly freckled knees. "Well, ah liked Paul all right and thought he was innerestin', even if he was Jewish."

I sniggered and looked at Morgan. "Ah, Morgo," I said, "you left out an innerestin' fact. Now it all makes sense. He didn't die of a heart attack, he committed suicide because he couldn't get into the Club."

"Okay," Morgan said to me menacingly, "that is *it*. He was a *friend* of ours, do you get that? Jesus, Iz, when you get defensive, you *stomp* on people."

"Innyway," Lily said, "he was *in* the Club. Morgan and Douglas sponsored him."

Morgan's mouth turned up sarcastically. "We have a number of Jewish families in the Club."

"We do?" Lily said, arching her neat reddish brows and leaning forward slightly to look at Morgan. "Who?"

"Well," Morgan said, "the Schindlers and the Gordons."

"The Gordons!" Lily said. "You mean to tell me Flashy Gordon's Jewish? Why, ah never! He looks just like Prince Philip."

Morgan grunted, whammed the car into reverse, and gunned it forward, raising enough dust to cover Oklahoma twice over. Galumphing back down the dirt road, I remarked on how everyone in the U.S. was getting to look so much like the British Royal Family, as if we'd cracked the Windsors' genetic code. Lily narrowed her amber eyes at me but settled back without comment until Morgan asked after her husband. Thus commenced a long harangue about how he had been up all night pukin', and she should sure enough jes' get out, he was gonna drive her nuts an' drive the kids nuts, an' she hated the boys growin' up that way, seein' their father dead drunk all the time. But what was she gonna do? She couldn't go back home now, she didn't partic'ly like it down home anymore, she had grown past bridge luncheons, and her fam-lee all lived in different parts of the country an' her friends were scattered an' she loved New York, except of course—she looked at me out of the corner of her eye—"for the Jews." She jes' didn't think she could take so many Jews, you know, all in one bunch like that.

Actually, when I am in the South, I have the same uneasy feeling about southerners, but I am far too polite to say so.

After the match, Morgan drove me back to Margaret Allen's. She and Lily had beaten the other team, but her black hair hung limp over her ears, and although her face was shiny with sweat, she was shivering. I asked if she felt all right. "Yeah," she said, "only I'm draggin' and now I have to go back home to that hideous mess. I'd ask you for lunch, but I doubt we have any food around. Wanna come for a drink at four? I know I can put my hands on some booze. Ask Margaret, too. She hasn't seen the house yet, either."

She waved, and the station wagon slipped backward out of the driveway. Going up the porch steps, I saw there was a note labeled *Isabel* stuck to the screen door with two Band-Aids. I zipped it off. *David called,* it said inside, *will you call him, you know where.* I crumpled up the note and stuffed it into my shirt pocket. Upstairs in the guest room there was another folded slip of paper stuck into the mahogany frame of the mirror. Note number two said, *Joan T. called. Has possible apt. Call her at once.*

I smiled and dialed. Good old reliable Joan! Talking to her on the telephone, I knew that the apartment was going to work out. One of the film editors at WJVB-TV was going to Paris for two years and needed someone to sublet. I was excited. In fact, I was sick of free-floating and wanted a little place of my own with a bed, a bureau, a desk, a window, a stove. I was sick of being the Eternal Guest. When I was little, didn't I play house like the other little girls? Two chairs and a quilt and a dark, close space all my own? I was sick of (to tell the truth) traveling. I had lied to Morgan. I was absolutely ripe for a rewrite, an Act II of my own, with all its ropes and sandbags and a pair of firmly muscled masculine arms tugging away at the strings of my preposterously overinflated heart. The problem was, I hadn't completed Act I yet, and time—time on its ten-speed bike—was whizzing by.

I packed and called a cab and left a note for Margaret asking her to tell Morgan that I wouldn't be there for cocktails. Just as I was leaving (the taxi humming throatily outside) the telephone rang. My ESP said: David. I ignored it and went out the door, the little jingle following me like a curse. No doubt David had wheedled the Allens' number out of Joan. Joan, too, was on his side. Poor David. I thought that if he wanted to spend his life tracking me down, it was his business, but it seemed like a god-awful waste of time.

# 13

I met him—he reminded me of this later—first at a cocktail party at the Thistles'. Joan's house in Rye, New York, is smallish but with a large living room that was, late that fall day, far too crowded. It was one of those parties during which you smile a lot and energetically nod and can't hear a word, and besides this it was very warm—the Thistles had a picturesque fire roaring away in the fireplace, but the flue wasn't drawing well, and the room was full of woodsmoke as well as cigarette smoke, and someone had opened a window for air, which air zoomed through the room in an icy swath right toward me. I sneezed. He told me later he had lent me his handkerchief. I didn't remember.

The next place I met David was at the Frick Museum in New York. Walter and I had been divorced just over a year, and I had had a couple of dates, but nothing outstanding, and maybe for this reason was feeling a little depressed. Anyway, it was a Thursday, and I didn't feel like going to work and I didn't. I put on my jeans and tucked them into a pair of tall leather boots—it was snowing outside—and put on a heavy brown sweater and a tweed jacket and wound a long wool scarf around my neck and put on my down ski mittens and set out across town for the Frick. I felt very stylish in my new boots but discovered after just half a block that they were going to be too tight at the heel. By the time I got to the museum, I was limping badly. There was a bench in the anteroom, but when I sat down and took my weight off the bad foot, it hurt even more. I sat for a while recovering my strength, then got up and limped over to the pictures I wanted to see—the Bouchers, and the Vermeer that is in the hall over the table with the lamp. All the while I looked at this painting, I was conscious of the pain in my foot. The pleasures of the aesthetic state are incompatible with the presence of weeping blisters.

I felt cranky and began to focus on negatives: Why is it all Vermeer's women have that same secretive, dull, cowlike look, half-sleepy, half-sly? Brain-damaged Dutch domesticity. I was beginning to actively dislike the lady in the painting, and I stepped back for a longer-range view and against someone. It gave me an awful start. New York is full of people ready to rub up against one but not usually at the Frick. I turned my head.

"Oh, hi," he said, "how are you?"

"Just fine," I said and politely stepped aside so he, too, could view the painting.

"How've you been?" he said.

"I have this blister on my foot," I said, looking at him ironically.

"Oh, really?" he said. "Would you like me to look at it?"

Just my luck, I thought. Go to the Frick and meet a foot freak.

He went on good-naturedly, "You don't remember me, do you?"

"No," I said.

"David Parminter. We met at the Thistles'."

"We did?"

"Yes. Two years ago last fall."

"I don't remember."

"I was the one with the striped crimson tie."

"You were? Did you go to Harvard?"

"No."

"Oh. No, I don't remember."

"I lent you my handkerchief. You said you would mail it back to me, but you never did."

"I took your handkerchief? Me? Are you sure it was me? Why would I forget a thing like that?" Stunned silence. There seemed nothing left to say. It occurred to me that he might have made this all up, so I smiled (not too winningly) and said,

"Well . . ." and raised my hand in a semaphore of good-bye. I stepped briskly away for at least a foot of carpeted Frick floor when I felt a compelling tug at my vocal cords. My scarf. He was standing on its fringed end.

"God! I'm sorry! Are you all right?" He shuffled his feet in a hasty little ballet, and I tried to tweak the scarf away, but he had danced himself onto another fringed corner.

"Listen," I said, "could you just, uh, lift your left foot?"

"What?" He looked at me, dazed. I wondered how the Thistles had met such a dumb guy and decided he was not Joan's friend but Stuart's. "Oh! Oh, my *foot*. Gosh, I . . ."

"Thanks."

"Are you hungry?"

"What?"

"Would you like some lunch?"

"Lunch?"

"Yes."

"It's only eleven thirty."

"It is?" Hands in raincoat pockets, he swiveled around, looking for a clock. "Well, I'll be damned. I ate early this morning, coming down on the plane. I don't live in New York, you see, I come down a couple of days a week on business."

Uh-huh. What else is new? The city was positively aswarm with men who came down "two days" on "business." I said I wasn't really hungry, did not smile, nodded my head courteously, and strode—limping—toward the door. He was right behind me.

"Thing really hurts, doesn't it?"

Gritted teeth: "Yes."

"Let me at least get you a cab."

"I can manage."

"I'll tell you what, I'll drop you off."

"Oh, really . . ."

"No trouble, no trouble at all. God, it's cold out here. I'll bet all the blood in your boot has turned to slush. Here, take my arm. I know, I know, you can manage. You can drop the arm at the curb."

He was squarely built, compact rather than fat, and of medium height. He had dark-brown hair and steady dark-brown eyes and very white skin. His face was square and kind and outwardly amiable, and I saw instantly that he was a plodder, a workhorse who would provide decently for a wife and kids, who would, after ten years of marriage, if all went well, come home in the evening and put his feet up and fall asleep in front of the TV with a drink in his hand. He would, if all went well, be very faithful to his wife and never regret it until after his prostatectomy. He would himself be inclined to prudence but be good-naturedly indulgent to the wife, who would steer him into large mortgages, private school tuitions, and expensive vacations, which (she would tell him) were a necessity because he worked so hard. I felt instantly secure with him (his type never gets divorced), so I took his arm. At the curb he hailed a cab.

Giving the driver my address, I felt pale; my foot throbbed as if it were oozing marrow. Parminter sat back with one arm up on the cab's seat and cheerfully said that I looked awful. He would be glad to take me to lunch. I demurred. He insisted. Demurred again.

Well, how about this? he countered. What if he cooked lunch for me? I was suspicious, of course, but I noticed that under his plaid-lined raincoat, under his plaid sports coat, he had on a white shirt, just an ordinary businessman's white shirt. My throat felt dry, I felt a treacherous ache—the beginning of lust—like the pressure of a finger on that spot just above the tailbone.

I had for some time now been having a mysterious fantasy about men's white shirts. In my mind's mini-film it was snowing or raining outside, and I was in my apartment with a man who had on a striped tie and a white shirt, not a sleazy nylon thing or vicuna or Viyella or flannel but an ordinary, everyday kind of white business shirt, Van Heusen will do, with a longish pointed collar not buttoned down, not of oxford cloth but a shirt that has been moderately starched and has a swift, crackling glaze, and I was—heh, heh—unbuttoning that shirt very slowly, having started (to make it easier) with the middle chest button, advancing thence upward, then down again, until at last I was lifting (with gentle tugs) the tails of this shirt very delicately out of whoever's pants. I felt faint. The cab stopped. He paid. Square, clean-nailed, competent hands flipped open a very full wallet and slid out a bill. We went up the elevator of my building. He said, as we came through the door of my apartment, "Oh, nice place," though my decorative furnishings were rather spare. "Let's get that boot right off." I sat down, he knelt and tugged. The boot came off. He looked inside and whistled. "Awful. What a mess. You must buy your boots two sizes too small."

I muttered, "They were on sale."

"Some bargain. You better go wash off that foot. What do you want for lunch?"

"Oh, look," I said, "please. I usually just have yogurt. Don't fuss."

"I don't plan to. Go wash off your foot. Hey, listen to me. That just goes to show you. My mother was a Seventh-day Adventist."

My responses were dulled by pain. I went into the bathroom, took off my jeans and panty hose, and ran water into the tub. I sat on the edge of the tub and planted both feet in the water. The right, blistered foot stung. Childishly, I wanted to cry. And what was I doing with this stranger in my apartment? Even well-dressed strangers strangle women with their own panty hose and hack them into parts and stuff the parts into the building's incinerator, just down the hall.

He called out, "You have here, let's see, Campbell's onion soup. You want that?" I could hear him in my kitchenette, opening and closing doors. I had trusted him at once. How inane.

"Fine," I said.

"What?"

"Fine!"

"Good, and now for the entree . . ." He opened the re-frigerator door. Moment of silence. Closed it again. "So. The soup stands alone. I see you're a lady who eats out a lot. What happened to that tall, thin fella, the one who had hair like duck down?"

"Who?"

"Tall, thin, blond, bland. Still married to him?"

"No."

I stood up and put on Walter's long bathrobe. I had given it to him one year as a Christmas present. It was a terry-cloth robe of multicolored stripes, and when he opened the box on Christmas morning, he said, "Good God, the coat of many colors. It must be in your genes." It was the only thing he left behind when we broke up.

"What happened?"

"We got divorced. I don't understand what your mother has to do with feet."

"What?"

"You said something about feet, then something about your mother."

"Oh. She was a Seventh-day Adventist." I was standing in the kitchenette doorway. He had taken off his raincoat and sports coat and in the fluorescent glow of the kitchenette his ordinary white businessman's shirt had a delicate lavender sheen. "They wash feet."

"They do?"

"Yes. As Christ did in the Bible." He was stirring the onion soup with a fork but quickly shut off the burner as it began to bubble. He placed the pan on the back of the stove and turned toward me, leaning a little forward, with his left hand (knuckles folded under) resting on my kitchen table, as if he were in a business meeting about to make a speech.

He said, "I'm married and have been for nineteen years. I

have three children. I know you're not going to believe this, but I've never been unfaithful to my wife."

I was standing a few feet away from him with my back to the table, and now I put my hand on the table, as if for support. I looked at the floor. I said in a voice that came out a mumble, "Why wouldn't I believe you?"

I thought it was going to be so easy, but some sort of lump had appeared inside my throat, as if I had mumps. I told myself that no doubt I was getting a cold. I think I knew at once that he would love me and I would only like him, and it would be difficult all the way around, as these things usually are, but I never led him on and I never pretended to feelings I didn't have. I suppose I knew right away that his wife, whose name was Louise, would appear one day and at first be very rational, and later cry, and I would sit looking out the window and she would tell me about their youngest son, who was retarded, and I knew she would say, as she did, that she felt I was without morality, just one of those selfish people who have to have everything and don't care how much pain they inflict, and I didn't even love him, did I? Well, did I?

I liked him very much and trusted him, and it was snowing outside, and my foot hurt and my throat ached, and I thought resentfully, *The hell with it. Let him worry about his wife, I'm entitled to some comfort in this world.* But I couldn't somehow raise my head, and when he moved the two steps to kiss me, he put his hands on my hips and pressed me back against the table, and I leaned back on my right hand, which rested on the table, which table, I usually succeeded in remembering, had a very weak leg, only now I had forgotten, and it began to topple, and I turned sideways, hoping to catch it, and lost my balance, and he, trying to catch both of us, got tangled up with my leg, and we—he, the table, and I—all fell in a heap, suddenly sideways, and the thud, reverberating up the kitchen wall, jiggled a sugar bowl that sat on the unsteady wall shelf, and the bowl leaped up, and while we were lying there on the floor in a kind of dazed pile of bruised hips and legs and elbows, the sugar bowl fell and, tumbling downward, hit the corner of the uptilted table and, in a parody of blessing, showered us with sugar, then, descending, hit my other, up-stuck hipbone. I moaned.

"Oh, God," he said in a terrified voice, "are you all right?"

I sighed and lay there in the glistening sugar. In the light of the kitchen, it was festively pink, like the cotton candy you get at carnivals. I extended my arm and rested my head upon it and looked out the window. What else could possibly happen? He sighed and lay down on his side, and for a moment we lay there, a foot apart, looking upward and out. It was snowing heavily now, great curved flakes that did not dance straight down but whirled in loops, flew bravely up, fell down at last. My mother used to say, *"Man muss die Feste feiern wie sie fallen."* Rough translation: Seize the day. Lying there watching the silent snow fall, I thought, *I should lose eight pounds,* and then thought, lazily, that his wife was no doubt a fat frump. She wasn't. She was dark-eyed and beautiful, and her illness had kept her slender, but she was nervous and so was ill or maybe nervous because of the illness. The day she came to see me, she wore a wheat-colored cashmere knit dress and gold scallop shell earrings. I had on my jeans and a plaid flannel shirt. She made me feel awkward and big-shouldered, as gawky as I'd felt in the fourth grade when I was the tallest girl in the class and last in the playground line. I never grew after the fourth grade, and although I am five five and weigh a hundred and nineteen, I think of myself as large. I sat with my arm up on the chair's back and looked out the window and listened and smoked, and I imagined she was wondering what he saw in me. It was raining that day. She sat with her knees placed exactly together. She had gone to Wellesley. She tore a Kleenex to shreds as she talked. The next day I bought an airline ticket to Russia. I had long wanted to go to Russia.

He said, "Do you believe in love at first sight?"

I didn't look at him. I said, "No."

He said (as if he hadn't heard me—is love deaf as well as

blind?), "I saw you across the room and I wanted to love you."

I didn't lead him on or pretend to feelings I didn't have. Maybe I hoped I would have some feelings. He was, at any rate, a very nice man.

Joan Thistle called that very night.

"I can't talk," I said, "there's someone here."

"Who?" she said. "Anyone I know?"

"David Parminter."

Next to me on the bed David groaned and put a pillow over his face.

"Oh, yeah?" Joan said. "Really! I was saving him for me. Do you always go to bed on first dates?"

"It was snowing."

"Oh, of *course,* how obtuse of me, I'd forgotten. Are you planning to grace us with your presence in the office tomorrow, or do you expect to just lie around and . . . wait, there are kids in this room, I can't talk."

"I'll be there. What did old Magoo have to say about the Planned Parenthood P.S.A.?"

"He hated it, natch. He says it's tasteless and inappropriate. How is . . ." Her voice abruptly swerved from the phone and grew higher in pitch: "Hey, wait a minute, where are you going? Where? Listen, drive carefully and don't"—slam of background door in Rye, New York—"drink anything. Damn those kids," Joan said, her voice swinging back to me. "They don't mean to be rude, I guess. What's he like?"

"Who? Magoo?"

"No, you know who."

"Do you mean in bed?"

David groaned.

"Oh, shit, Isabel!" Joan said. "Will you stop being such a smart-ass? He seems like such a nice man."

"Yes. How did you meet him?"

"His kid goes to our kid's school. In fact, his Phil is our

Peter's roommate. Then we met David one Parents' Day Weekend, and David and Stuart got to talking, and it turned out that David knew Stuart's brother, who's a proctologist in Boston."

"A what?"

"Oh, for . . . I'll explain later."

David, meanwhile, had turned over, reached across me, and was removing the telephone from my hand.

"Good-bye," I said. "I have to hang up now."

"Ask him," Joan screamed as the phone went down, "if he has a friend."

David said, "That was a very tactless thing to do. Is this your way of saying you don't want to see me again?"

"No," I said. "Joan won't say anything."

"What about Stuart? Maybe he'll say something."

"Joan doesn't talk to Stuart."

He was lying on his side, his head held up on his hand. He dropped his eyes. "Oh. I didn't guess that. I thought they were happy together."

I said, "They're happy, they're together, they're just not happy together. Do you have a friend? Joan's awfully nice."

"Not one I can name at the moment."

"That's too bad," I said. "It's not that I feel responsible for Joan, it's just that she doesn't have good taste in men. One of these days she's going to get into serious trouble."

"I'm sorry. I like Joan. You're right, she is a nice person."

"Yes," I said.

"So am I." He said it forlornly, and I thought then how maybe he knew this about himself: that much of his trouble in life came from being too nice. "Let's go get something to eat. What kind of food do you like?"

"Don't care," I said. It was true. I am not a gourmet. I am fussy only about three kinds of food: bread, apples, and coffee. I once brought home from Bloomingdale's five different types of coffee makers so that I could determine which one made the best coffee. I ended up taking them all back and getting a little old-fashioned perk pot from the five-and-dime. I like almost any kind of bread except what Italians eat for breakfast, and I like New York State apples best. When I was a kid, my parents used to rent a summer house upstate on a lake in the Adirondacks, and driving back to the city in early September, we'd stop in the upper Hudson Valley to buy the season's first apples. My mother would say, "Cold Winters Make the Best Apples." Sounds like the title of a book, doesn't it? I have written two brisk little novels, neither one of which I like or ever hope to read again. TV isn't my occupation, either, it's what I do because I need the money. Then, when I first met David, I had two goals, or whatever you want to call them: I wanted to write a book I liked, and I wanted to fall in love. I was getting old and had never been in love. I had this pain all the time, under my clavicles, and I would cry suddenly in strange places. I had loved my parents and many of my friends but had never been deeply in love with a man. I was unfortunately so constituted that I knew it would have to be a man.

I had spent a good part of my life hearing about love and reading about love until I had come to believe that maybe the inability to fall in love was hereditary, that it arrived on the same gene that made me nearsighted and gave me broad shoulders or brown hair. I was luckily past that stage where I had to spend a great deal of time watching my friends be in love. My friends that fell in love now tended to keep it quiet until divorced, but for years before this I was condemned to listen to everyone's tale of love, smiling wanly, gamely nodding, when inside, of course, my heart felt shrunk or withered, tight as a clenched fist. Or had it withered years before? Had it dried up due to a childhood disease, the way a friend of mine lost her hearing in one ear, from mumps? Was my heart muscle scarred from some incident I couldn't remember, the way scarlet fever used to fray the heart's living tissue?

I had spent a lot of bucks on a psychoanalyst, hoping to find out why I had never loved a man. (He was pale, and his black suits smelled musty, but he had a wonderful long, sad face with hooded eyes, like a Spaniard.) I came out of the whole thing much poorer, with a vague sense of myself as a ball of twine endlessly twisted and knotted. My conclusion: the hell with this. We are what we are. I'm not omitting here a chance for change, but I think we all have several personae, and the fascinating maze of my own personality had some time back begun to pall. Meanwhile no lover had appeared. I had the odd idea that if I found someone to love deeply, I might write a book I liked, but I knew pretty quick that he wouldn't be David. Still, I never led him on or pretended to feelings I didn't have. It was Morgan who, with typical common sense, summed up my problem some time later from her hospital bed: "Isabel," she said, "you are just too picky." Then the nurse came in to start a new IV.

# II

## World Series Time

# 1

So I took the apartment on Charles Street and set down new roots in my back-half parlor floor with built-in kitchenette. The room was tall-ceilinged and sunny with a charming little red marble fireplace. Long windows overlooked a small city garden, where a mossy brick path ambled crookedly between ivy beds and around a large birdbath. This facility attracted a number of city sparrows. When I first heard the precise figure of the rent, I swooned and leaned dizzily against a long window and, without meaning to, pushed it all the way open, and in the dim green jungle outside a bird was happily singing, and I sighed and straightened up and said, "I'll take it."

The garden was tended by Miss Potter-Pryce-Jones and Miss Pennington, who together had the basement–through. First thing every morning, before the dew was off the ivy, Miss Pennington, with a red bandanna tied around her head, would come out and sweep up ailanthus leaves. I would stand at a long window drinking my coffee, and she would look up and shout, "These trees have a dirty habit!"

Miss Potter-Pryce-Jones was an architect who worked for the city housing authority, and Miss Pennington stayed home and wrote history books for children: *A Princess of Aquitaine,* et cetera. Miss Pennington was tall and thin with a beaked nose and springy white hair that was cut short and parted, 1920s style, in the middle. Miss Potter-Pryce-Jones was smaller and tanned and muscular and wore her hair in a circlet of Roman ringlets pasted against her forehead. She liked to stroll around the garden in fatigue boots, battle jacket, and hard hat. She told me one day (hallooing from the island) that she and her "part-ner" used to have a dog, a Pomeranian, but it had died and . . . she pointed wordlessly to the spot at her feet.

I fell in love with my new home at once and felt at ease there. In every place I have lived there has been a whole cycle of sounds to adjust to, most of them unpleasant: not just the traffic pattern outside the windows or the usual creaks and faucet drips, but the neighbor's cat that yowls every one A.M. and the Swiss insomniac above you who paces his uncarpeted floor every night in hobnailed boots. My new apartment had prettier sounds than most. There was a Morton, L.T.V., who lived on the top floor of the building and played the oboe darkly, beauti-fully, so that every evening at seven, while I sat with my glass of white wine, a rope of iridescent silk would unwind some-where above me and meander across the courtyard and sinu-ously glide into my window. There was a silvery tintinnabulat-ing bell that belonged to a slit-eyed yellow tiger cat who strode up and down the brick paths of the garden looking for game, and the comical, jeering *preep preep* of a largish sparrow who liked to sit on the edge of the birdbath and taunt the cat. I got to know this nervy sparrow and used to toss him broken-up bits of Ritz cracker spread with peanut butter. This annoyed Miss Potter-Pryce-Jones, who did not enjoy cleaning the mess out of the birdbath and who thought the crumbs drew rodents to the yard. Unmoved, I continued my evil practices and never let on who the culprit was.

I think I was happier there than I'd ever been. The weather early that fall was beautiful. I bought an old quilt (appliquéd in red and green in the President's Wreath pattern) and threw it over the greasy threadbare upholstery of my rented Hide-A-Bed sofa. I bought an old oak table and placed it at the windows. I bought a large pot of red geraniums and put it on a white plate on the oak table.

I spent my weekends reading and washing my hair, visiting health food stores and eating salads. I lost five pounds and felt pleased with myself. I walked a lot and took showers and had clean thoughts. I did not see David, I did not see David. I was leading an orderly, stable, pleasing existence but often felt sad in the evening: I knew it couldn't last. Like the hero of a famous Henry James story (was his name Marcher? yes, Marcher), I sensed catastrophe coming . . . but how? and when? I felt like an athlete in training for a terrible endurance contest, a marathon of the head and heart that would make me or break me. My forebodings often come true. I have wonderful ESP.

When Joan Thistle called one Saturday morning in October, I was standing on a ladder with the paint roller in my hand while WQXR played *Moments Musicaux*. Da da da de *da*! Da da da de *dah*! I was painting the walls light yellow.

"Here I am," Joan said after I picked up the telephone, "Joan Thistle, your friendly procurer. How about dinner in Rye tonight? I know a swell fella. You can stay over later if you want."

"Let's get one thing straight," I said. "If he's married, forget it. I hate these scenes with the wife."

"No, no. Getting divorced. Already in the process. Been through the girlie circuit, looking to settle down. Height, five ten. Weight, one seventy. Two children in college. Well-off, sort of. That is, for the moment."

"What's his IQ?" I asked sarcastically.

"A hundred and thirty."

"Did he tell you that or did you guess?"

"I guessed. You know I don't believe in the validity of IQ tests."

"What's his name?"

"Oh, uh, I forget."

"Joan!"

"It's . . . uh . . . you'll find out when you get here!"

"Joan! It's Parminter, isn't it? What are you *doing*, Joan?"

"He's getting divorced, Isabel. Does that mean nothing to you? He wants to marry you."

"Will you leave me alone? I told you, just leave me alone!"

So that when the telephone rang again immediately after I'd hung up, I put down the roller and the pan full of yellow paint and grimly went to the jingling thing and squatted (I hadn't yet bought a table for it) and lifted the receiver and said, "No, Joan. I said, *no*. N.O. You don't understand. I think he's a very nice man, that is all," there ensued an awkward silence broken by a deep half-laugh, and a voice said, "Isabel, this is Douglas Whiteside."

"Oh," I said, then stupidly, "Hi!"

"I'm calling to ask you a favor. Morgan's had to go into the hospital, and I've got to go to Boston on family business. You know I wouldn't ask you this if I hadn't tried everything else—I called Family Service and I tried a local employment agency, and there's just nothing in the way of someone suitable to stay here for a week with the kids. Do you think you could do it? I understand that it's asking a lot, but I'm more or less desperate. I would hope, at least, that the kids won't be trouble-some. Sarah's fifteen, and Tess is thirteen and very helpful. Eddie's only eleven, but he's never presented a problem that I can think of."

"I know," I said, confused. "I know how old they are."

"Is this at all possible for you? I realize how inconvenient it will be—having to commute back and forth."

"Oh, it's not that, it's ... what's wrong with Morgan?"

There was a silence. "Hasn't she told you?"

"I haven't talked to her since the first week in September. She said she felt tired, that's all. She said she thought she was just turning into a crock, she knew there was nothing wrong."

"She has leukemia." His voice was dry and spare saying this, and at the same time dullish, like a piece of metal that has been hammered repeatedly. I couldn't answer at all. After a moment I cleared my throat and said, "What kind of leukemia?" I knew there were different kinds and one meant several years, and one didn't.

"Acute myelocytic leukemia."

"Is that ..."

"It couldn't be worse. A year, more or less."

"Ah." It was a pain I felt, like a blow to the diaphragm that made me gasp.

"I'm sorry to have to tell you like this. I thought you knew."

"No."

"She had several weeks of extensive chemotherapy in the hospital. She came home and seemed to be doing well, but suddenly developed an infection."

"I see. Yes, of course I'll come. When do you want me?"

"Can you come on Monday, after work?"

"Yes, but I doubt I can get there much before six or six-thirty."

"That's fine, that's fine. You see," he blurted, "I wouldn't ask you to do this at all, but I don't feel I can leave Sarah alone with the others at this stage. She needs some adult supervision."

"Yes."

"Many thanks, Isabel."

"Of course."

"I think the house is in fairly good order. I'll shop today for groceries. If you need anything else while you're here, you can charge it. There's a small grocery downtown where we have an account—he delivers, too. The major problem is a car—the station wagon's in the shop. I'll leave some cash for taxis in the desk in my study, at the back of the middle drawer. And"—his voice fumbled—"I don't know what else to say."

"There's nothing to say. I'll be there."

"Thank you," he said, and then there was a long, sustained pause, as if neither one of us had the power, imagination, or energy to hang up, until at last I did, saying politely, "Good-bye," but putting the receiver down in a kind of sloppy two-part motion so that it made a click-clack. My hands were sweaty and cold.

I sat down on the floor. I had painted only one wall of the apartment and saw now it was the wrong color, a deeper yellow than the delicately effervescent, pale sunlit shade I'd thought of, a fatty overweening yellow that smacked of bad things: cowardice, illness, leukocytes, death. I knew almost nothing about leukemia. I imagined a leukemia victim as simply becoming paler and paler, fading away into a wisp of yellowish, papery protoplasm. Three of my better friends had already died—one of diabetes, one of melanoma, one of lymphosarcoma. My chest felt tight, and in the silence of my room I heard a funny noise—my own harsh breathing: I was panting. Inside the cage of my ribs my heart kept desperately pumping away—bump, bump—as if to reassure me that it was still there, that physically, at least, it was performing its duties on a regular basis. That even if it couldn't love, it could at least squeeze the blood in great shuddering spurts back through the arteries.

"Children, let us think of the heart as a little pump! Let us think of the brain as a marvelous teeny computer. Are not our bodies wonderful? Let us praise the Creator who has bestowed on us these wonderful machines! Keep them pure and clean and out of trouble and your machine will give you valuable service." Our minister's speech to us, one day in confirmation class. He loved to make little speeches. His rosy cheeks shone as if greased with lamb fat. His little gold-rimmed spectacles twinkled. He never stopped smiling. When he sat in a chair, his skinny black-clad knees moved apart to make room for the great black-vest-covered paunch that hung down between, shaped like the thorax of an insect. He wore a heavy, round gold wedding band on one hand and a ring of the Masonic order—it had a pale amethyst stone—on the other. He loved to call the girls into his study for "private talks" (God knows why, there wasn't a Lolita in the crowd—a doughier, lumpier bunch would be hard to imagine), and on the way out he would somehow, somewhere, pat us, oh, just an ordinary fumbling little pat that no doubt was meant to be on your shoulder and missed, or maybe he did mean to take your elbow and grabbed your—oh, nothing that amounted to anything, by no means reportable. Besides, who would have believed it? The *minister*? O. T. Arbutus, D.D.?

When I was in college, a scandal occurred. Dr. Arbutus was accused of trying to rape a fourteen-year-old. Oh, the ironies of fate—he didn't deserve it. Even far away in Massachusetts I had heard about Pamela and her straight but twitchy hips. Good-bye, Dr. Arbutus! Good-bye wonderful little machines!

We are bags of guts and pus after all, and it's a wonder that we live as long as we do. Only sometimes one longs to howl. I wanted suddenly, heart-sinkingly, to see David. Not fair, I said to myself, don't use people that way. Still, I wanted to sit on his lap and put my arm around his neck and lean my head against his and cry.

So now I spoke sternly to myself: *You know, Isabel, if you go out to Joan's tonight, you will end up in the sack together, and that would be a very bad mistake. Leave him alone, Isabel. He will find someone else.*

I decided to stop painting—this was clearly the wrong yellow—and I put on a jacket and went for a long walk. I walked uptown, and then I went to see a double feature at the Regency, *The Tales of Hoffmann* and *The Red Shoes*. I hate the part in *The Red Shoes* where she is lying there a-bleeding, her legs crushed, and she whimpers, "Take off the Red Shoes." I want to throw eggs and tomatoes and yell, "Leave 'em on, stupid!" What else is there?

Afterward I had a hamburger in a coffee shop. The fry cook, who was black, asked me for a date. I shook my head. Sorry, I said, I was off men. He laughed, throwing his head back. His white teeth made a perfect gleaming arch like a miniature Japanese bridge over a curving pink fauvist river. His teeth were strong, shiny, immaculate, musical-looking. They looked as if, tapping them with a wooden chopstick, you might extract musical sounds. "Thas aw raht, lady," he told me. "Doan feel bad. You look lak a lonely lady, thas all."

That's me, all right. The lonely lady. But let's not make too much of this. When surveyed, 92.9 percent of the American population said they had been lonely at one time or another.

Married people get lonely, too. You think when you're a kid you're going to meet some person and fall in love and stop being lonely, but that's not the way it works. I was never lonelier than when I was married to Walter. I didn't want to marry David and end up lonely again.

# 2

Most days of that week, when I stepped out of the Summerville train station, Lily Webber would be there waiting for me, always in a tennis dress, leaning against the side of the dented Mercedes with folded arms and downcast fiery head.

"Get on in," she said to me on Monday in her low voice. "Ah'll drive you to the Whitesides'. Ah am between car pools. Put your suitcase in the ba-yuck, why don't you."

The back seemed full-up already. Goggles and flippers in various sizes lay on the floor; a large blue iron casserole sat tipped into the seat, its belly protruding, its cover tilted. Fanned out on the seat next to the casserole was a slither of plastic-covered library books.

I said, getting in, "You read a lot, don't you?"

"Some," she said and started the car.

"Do you have any favorite writers?"

She glanced at me, amused. "Why, no," she said, "ah read mainly comic strips." She turned her eyes to the road again. "Why is it New Yorkers think anyone outside the city cain't even spell? People in this town read a whole lot."

"Do they?"

"Town supports two bookstores. That's pretty good for a small town."

"Yes, it is."

"Down home nobody too masch reads books. When we were kids in high school, Donal' an' me, we used to read books together. You b'lieve that? We used to neck an' read books. A course ah never let on to mah friends how much ah read, it would a ruined me. Ah met Donal' at the public library. It was his spring vacation. He was writin' a paper on Sidney Lanier. Know who he was?"

"Yes. Well, vaguely."

"Uh-huh. Well, Donal' was goin' to school up north an' ah was impressed outta mah mind. He was handsome then, too—tall, skinny kid with blond hair cut short and parted jes' so. I fell crazy in love at sixteen. I'll tell you who we used to read then: John Crowe Ransom and Robert Penn Warren. Eudora Welty was about mah favorite. She unnerstands *foibles*."

I laughed. She slowed down and made a turn onto a wide, pleasantly shaded street that had no sidewalks and as many potholes as a back road in the country—obviously one of the most prestigious streets in town. There is generally (I have found) a suburban antipathy to sidewalks. "Ah have read your book," she said. "Not the first one, but the secon', ah forget its name."

I braced myself but grinned. "Did you like it?"

She turned into a gravel driveway and stopped the car, ducked her head, and gave me a look out of the corner of her amber eyes. "Yeah," she said, "ah did. But ah thought *somethin' was missin'*. Tha-ut casserole is for you all. Put it in a moderate oven for half an hour. It's kielbasy. Ah simply adore kielbasy. Trina gave me the recipe."

I hopped out and lugged the casserole and my suitcase out of the back.

"Thanks so much for everything," I said. "You're terrific to do this."

She looked up at me out of the car window. "Once ah broke mah ankle, an' every day for a month Morgan picked up the twins an' took 'em to school for me."

"How do you think she is?" I asked, at last.

"She's cheerful an' tryin' not to worry anyone. She doesn' feel all that bad an' maybe doesn' b'lieve it yet."

"I'm having trouble with that myself."

"Yeah," Lily said. "Good luck, now. Everyone uses the kitchen do-ah ovah they-uh. Call if you need anythin', hear?"

I stood in the driveway with my suitcase and the blue iron pot at my feet as she backed out and, like a true genie, disappeared in a puff of smoke.

One of the things I know about myself is this—that a small but insistent part of me craves this other life, this old ivy-draped house hidden behind tall trees, standing as if it had always stood there, deep in green lawns, amid lush gardens, with the squareness and simplicity of a house in a little girl's sampler. Four high chimneys, steep-pitched roof, shutters, fanlights. If you stood at Morgan's front door and looked through a sidelight—"Hello!" —you'd be able to see clear through the house and out the back door—"Good-bye!"—a scheme as simple and direct as life itself. The house was built of rosy brick, and a long aqua pool reclined in front of it, so that it seemed to be always placidly admiring itself. A couple of gold maple leaves and a giant pink plastic ball floated slowly around the pool in a clockwise direction.

I strolled around to the back gardens. A chorus of cheerful country noises—insects, birds—hovered benignantly in the air and mingled with the voices that you could not hear but that seemed at any moment about to waft out of an open window or to meet you—oops! sorry!—coming around a corner. But the gardens were a disappointment: they were overgrown, choked with weeds. Near a tall paling fence staked tomato plants looking like scraggly Christmas trees still bore rotting yellowish globes of fruit. Marigolds leaned upon each other like rows of broken soldiers limping home, and here and there a rusted zinnia thrust up out of a clump of tall coarse grass. In the herb garden giant bushes of rank tansy had sprung up, crowding out the other plants and filling the air with their evil smell. There was something unwholesome and desolated about this garden, and I remembered, with a sudden shiver, that in the nineteenth century tansy leaves were crumbled and sprinkled on grave clothes.

I went in the fanlighted back door and saw at once that Sister Chaos had come and unpacked her bag stuffed with rust, mildew, moth. Half a stiff sandwich lay on the hall table, and on every windowsill was a small collection of soft-drink cans. Cartons of books were everywhere; paintings leaned against the walls as if hiding their heads in mourning. In the living room the furniture stood awkwardly on the bare wood floor, as dazed as if the moving men had just left.

I got my suitcase and took it upstairs, hoping that the guest room, at least, would be neat and bright. But I wasn't exactly a guest, and the bedroom doors that opened on both sides of the long, straight hall disclosed blasted landscapes—smelly clothes, flung books, tossed sneakers, dumped towels. At the end of the hall was a closed door to what I still (faintly, foolishly) hoped was a clean room and a bed made up for me, but when I opened the door, I saw that this was obviously the master bedroom—two intertwined bodies lay on the large bed, both barefoot but otherwise clothed in jeans and T-shirts and as fast asleep as Brüderlein and Schwesterlein in the old Grimm's fairy tale my mother used to read to me at bedtime. One of the bodies was male and new to me, the other belonged to Sarah Whiteside. On the nightstand next to the bed a silver porringer, an old-fashioned baby's dish, held a couple of butts. The air in the room was sweetish with pot.

I stood staring at the kids on the bed. Suddenly Sarah sat up and returned my stare. She was a tawny, rosy fifteen-year-old with dark blond hair and green eyes. She said to me, "What the hell do you think you're doing?"

The boy groaned and rolled over and opened his eyes.

I said, "Come right downstairs, will you, Sarah? I'll be in the kitchen." I closed the bedroom door behind me. My head had begun to hurt.

Downstairs I saw from the kitchen window that Tess Whiteside had arrived—in jeans and riding boots, a riding helmet swinging from her wrist. Hands passed a pile of school books to her through the open window of a station wagon. She was a tall, thin thirteen-year-old with her mother's black hair. Tess and I had always been good friends. When she came into the kitchen, she shrieked, "Isabel!", threw down her books and put her arms around me.

Sarah appeared in the doorway, still barefoot, still scowling.

"Hi," I said to her brightly. "Do you think you could help me clean up the kitchen? And maybe you could make a salad for dinner."

The front door slammed—her boyfriend leaving, I guessed —and Sarah looked at me steadily, resentfully. Eddie Whiteside appeared behind his sister and said, "Jeez, Sarah, will ya move your giant butt?"

"Hi, Eddie," I said. "Do you remember me?"

He looked at me indifferently. "No," he said. He was a thin, pale, dark-haired child with dark circles under his eyes.

"I'm Isabel," I said.

"Yeah, my dad said you were coming."

"We haven't seen each other for a couple of years."

"Where's Mom?" he asked Sarah.

"You dope," she said, looking down at him, "she's in the hospital."

"Oh, yeah," Eddie said and yawned and scratched his chest through his T-shirt. "I forgot."

"You watch too much TV," Tess said to Eddie. "It's corroding your brain."

"You should talk," Eddie said to Tess.

"She's right, you little jerk," Sarah said. "All you do is watch TV."

"You should talk!" Eddie said to Sarah.

"Well, let's get organized for dinner," I said. "Mrs. Webber has made us a casserole."

"Can't we have McDonald's?" Eddie said.

"I won't be having dinner," Sarah said. "I'm dieting." And she turned and walked away.

"Hey, wait a minute," I called after her. "Sarah? Come back here please, I really need your help."

"I'm not supposed to help with meals," Sarah said, staring at me over her shoulder. "I'm in charge of the laundry and the dusting and the vacuuming and every other goddam fucking thing."

"Ya fucking haven't done it though," Eddie said loudly.

"Sarah," I said, trying out my whine, "please stay and help. I have no idea where anything is."

"I'll help," Tess said and put her arm around my waist. She had her mother's dark eyes, but white and rose skin. "We don't need Sarah, Isabel. She's just an immature fifteen-year-old baby. Besides, she's probably still high. I'll bet she was upstairs with Larry, smoking pot. Sarah the pothead!" she called out to Sarah, who was padding away through the dining room. "Sarah the waste-o!" Sarah did not look one bit wasted to me. In fact, she was more stacked than her mother, and although her legs were long, the thighs were so filled out that you could see pale ovals at the backs of her blue jeans, where skin had rubbed fabric.

"She's a bitch," Tess said cheerfully and leaned her head against my shoulder. "We don't need her."

"She hardly does anything," Eddie complained. "All she does is smooch around with Larry and go to parties and talk on the telephone."

"Tomorrow," Tess said, "I have a field hockey game after school, and then I have swim team practice at the YW with only an hour in between. How'm I going to get from one thing to another, Isabel? See, my mom always picked me up. Do you think you can pick me up?"

"Wait a minute," Eddie said to Tess, "I got a midget league football practice all the way across town, and my bike's got a flat tire, so she's gonna have to drive me. The coach gets

101

really mad if we're late, and I've been late twice before this month, and he said if it happened again he'd take me out of the game next Sunday."

From some other part of the house a stereo started a wave of music with a beat that seemed to thud inside my stomach and the telephone rang and the Irish setter, who had so happily watched all these proceedings with nothing more than a wagging tail, suddenly gulped three times and vomited.

"Oh, yetch!" said Tess. "Look! He must have eaten a bird!"

I answered the telephone. It was Douglas Whiteside calling from Boston. He wanted to know how everything was.

# 3

I had forgotten (had I ever known?) how self-centered children are. We ate dinner in the kitchen, Tess and Eddie saying not one word about their mother but chattering incessantly about school, friends, games, and TV programs. I wasn't hungry and sat at the table with them, twirling a glass of white wine from a jug of Gallo chablis I had found in the refrigerator. Sarah broodingly stayed in her room until we were almost through, and then, still barefoot, came into the kitchen, opened the refrigerator door, took out a carton of yogurt, yanked open a drawer, took out a teaspoon, and left. I thought to myself how clever she was—she had gotten caught and had made me feel guilty.

Eddie lifted his head and, looking from me to Tess, said humorously, "Shitty Sarah."

"Don't say that," I said. He tilted his head and looked at me with interest.

"Why not?" he asked.

"Because," I said firmly, though it didn't seem like a very complete answer. I turned to Tess. "What's Sarah's boyfriend like?"

Tess wrinkled up her nose. "He's really dumb. I don't know why she wants to go out with such a stupid kid."

"He's not dumb," Eddie said. "He's a good basketball player and a good football player. He's a nice guy, and he's going to show me how to throw passes if I teach him to ice-skate."

"Do you like to ice-skate?" I asked Eddie.

Tess rolled her black eyes. "*He* plays *ice* hockey. That's all he *thinks* about is ice hockey."

"What position do you play, Eddie?"

"Right wing!" he said. "I love to score those goals, man!" He jumped out of his chair and wound up and swung the invisible stick forward for a slap shot: "Wham!". . . and another, "Wham!" and a third time for a very rapid hat trick: "Wham-o!" and the puck sailed through the black kitchen window and out through black time. How many years ago, I thought, while Tess neatly stacked the dishwasher, October then, too, when I'd been sitting tailor-style on the grass of the Little Quad with a book open in my lap, and Morgan had dropped down beside me, still in her gym shirt and skirt, exuding an odor of sunshine, damp grass, and sweat. She had lain back on her elbows and squinted up at the sun. "God, Iz, we had the most exciting game ever. You know Jane Parker? That redhead in Gillette? We worked out a terrific play, passed to each other twice, then she did this marvelous backhand shot and I saw it was just going to go wide of the goal and I somehow made it up there in time and kind of reached over and tapped it in. Hot dog! Right past the goalie and both defensemen. Incredible. It was the most glorious feeling, so neat, like solving a math problem."

I said that I did not like math.

She laughed. "And you don't like sports, either. Honestly, Isabel, I know you could be a terrific athlete."

I groaned.

"Come on," she said, jumping up. "I'll show you how to stick handle."

"Oh, please."

"No, seriously. Come on, that's it, stand up. Look at those shoulders, you were obviously meant to play hockey. Now. Put one hand here, and the other here—that's right. Say, you catch on fast. I am placing the little ball right here, see? Right here on the grass? Now all you have to do is make contact between the..."

I swept the stick back, then forward again, and to my surprise the ball lifted up off the ground and flew in a beautifully high arc down toward the end of the Quad, where, unfortunately, a window seemed about to—yes—receive it. There was a two-part sound: first the main ear-shattering crash and then, almost as an afterthought, a delicate tinkle.

"Hmm," Morgan said. She was standing cigar-store-Indian-style, with one hand shading her eyes. A very white startled face appeared at the broken window and then disappeared. Heads now appeared in many windows. "Go, Morgo," someone shouted from the third floor. In an inconceivably short space of time a stout figure in a plaid kilt and British walking shoes—the kind with floppy, fringed tongues—came stumbling across the grass. Mrs. Lipton, our housemother, was a purple-faced, chain-smoking woman who was a widow and wore her black hair with bangs cut too short. Thus our nickname for her—"No-Bang" Lipton.

"Oh, Morgan, Morgan," she said hoarsely, stopping a second to cough while the smoke from her cigarette curled up between her fingers, "how could you, my dear? This is absurd, absurd. I will have to take away your privileges this weekend."

"It was me, Mrs. Lipton," I said.

"You!" She narrowed lusterless eyes at me. I knew Mrs. Lipton didn't like me. She liked the healthy, hockey-playing, student-government, judicial-council, Christian Association type, and I was the dormitory malcontent who regularly slept through chapel and had complained at house meeting that I thought house meetings were silly. I had instantly, as a reward, been elected to a committee, a responsibility which I declined, and which had prompted a twenty-minute speech at the dinner table the next night on our responsibilities in a Democratic community. Mrs. Lipton had been a government major at Vassar.

"So!" she said. "You!" She took a long drag on her butt and sensuously, pleasurably let the smoke unwind out of her purple lips while she looked at me with a gloating expression. What was it going to be? The rack? The wheel? Maybe she could hire two elephants—Rudyard Kipling could ride one and Somerset Maugham the other, and they would joggle off toward where the sun never sets or rises with my poor irresponsible, undemocratic body between them. My soul would expire like a puff of smoke, and out of this cloud a tiny cherub would appear trailing a banner with this message: *She was uncooperative and would not play field hockey.*

"I am afraid," said Lipton, and took another cruel, gloating drag on her Caporal, imported from the U.K., "this means three weekends, Schliemann. Let's make it the reception desk, shall we?"

There was a strong echo effect in the Little Quad, so that despite Lipton's hoarseness, these words ricocheted off the walls like cannonballs. She had outdone herself. Three weekends. Wow! I had been so busy watching Lipton I had forgotten we were standing on what amounted to a little grassy stage and that hanging out of windows all around us were galleries of eager college-girl spectators, waiting for justice to be done. Did anyone hiss or boo at my public execution? No, from all around there was clapping and cheering, and later only Morgan and little Nancy Prior with her dingy hair and snuffle came up to me and said, Gee, too bad.

Later that night, after Tess and Eddie had gone to bed, I called Joan Thistle. She'd been out of the office that day, on location.

"Isabel," she said, "you are truly a beast. David was so

*nice.* He is so warm and sensitive and likable. What is *wrong* with you, anyway? We had the nicest, quietest, pleasantest time on Saturday. I think I'm in love with him."

"Fantastic," I said briskly. "Much happiness. Listen, Joan, I am not coming in tomorrow."

"Why not?"

"Because, Joan, I'm out here in New Jersey at my friend Morgan's house, and everything is kind of a mess. The house is a mess and the kids, too. I just thought I'd hang in here and kind of get things organized. And besides, I want to see Morgan."

"Where is she?"

"She's in the hospital."

"What's the matter with her?"

"She has leukemia."

"Oh. Oh, God."

"So could you handle everything tomorrow? Don't forget to call up Sandy Evans and make sure she remembers we've got Studio 3 next Tuesday at ten o'clock."

"I know, I know, I'm your boss, remember? Are you there all alone? Is her husband there?"

"No, he's in Boston. Listen, Joan, I need a little advice here. The kids—Tess and Eddie, they're all right, but Sarah, the fifteen-year-old, is going to be work. I walked in, and she was on her mother's bed with her boyfriend. They'd obviously just had a pot party. I mean, how do I handle this? We didn't have pot when I was fifteen."

"Clothes on or off?"

"On, but still. They were both o-u-t."

"You threw him out, of course, and then you told her that she wasn't going to see him for a while."

"Jesus, I'm only here until Friday."

"What kind of kid is she?"

"She used to be, well, lovable. Just a very nice little girl. She has changed, I guess."

"Apparently so. Well, be tough."

"I'm not her mother."

"Look, Isabel, if her father trusted her, he would have left her in charge and not asked you. I mean, at fifteen she should be capable of managing things for a few days. Obviously she's not trustworthy, and he knows it. Isabel? David's going to be in New York all next week."

"Not with me, he's not."

"Oh, you fool," she snapped. "Who do you think you're going to find? I can't figure you out. You must have a terribly high opinion of yourself."

"Aw shit," I said and hung up. It was ten P.M. I turned on the kitchen radio and decided to scrub the floor. I was in a limegreen slosh of Mr. Clean when the telephone rang.

"I'm sorry," Joan said abruptly. "I'm jealous, that's all. It's your life."

"Yes," I said.

"Good luck, and if there's anything I can do . . ."

We hung up simultaneously this time. I mopped up the floor and rinsed out the bucket. It was 10:35. I felt horribly tired. I put the mop and bucket away in the broom closet, and when I turned around, Tess was standing in the kitchen doorway. She had on a long, pale-pink nightgown with puffed sleeves. She was standing still, her arms stiff at her sides, looking at me with wide-open black eyes.

"Hey, Tess," I said. "You ought to be asleep, kiddo. A growing woman needs her beauty sleep."

She stared at me. "Is she going to die?" she said. "Is my mother going to die?" When I put my arms around her, she was perfectly rigid, and then suddenly she crumbled and her head fell on my shoulder. She began to cry—very dry, adult sobs. I didn't know what to answer and so I said nothing but kept my arms around her for a long time.

At eight o'clock, the next morning, after the kids were gone, I put on a pair of old pants and began to clean. My mother used to say there were two kinds of clean—Irish clean and German clean. Irish clean, she would explain disdainfully, was neat on the surface—"picked up"; but German clean (her face would break into a radiant Teutonic smile) was "clean all the way through!" We had always, when I was growing up, lived in a clutter of books and papers. Things were not always "picked up," but by God! underneath, it was all shiny-bright. Blood tells. If I have enough time, I don't mind cleaning. It's not that I care how clean things are, but I do like to scrub with vigor, especially if things are really grungy, as they certainly were here.

My poor friend! This sorrowful, dirty house! Morgan's houses had always been clean, if not neat—she lived with a lot of human content. There was always, of course, a great deal of athletic equipment everywhere, and clumsily formed pink pottery ashtrays, a Laura Ingalls Wilder book sticking out from beneath a seat cushion, a magazine left face down on a sofa, and a friendly dog lying in a patch of sunlight—that sort of thing. But Morgan's new house depressed me, not just because it was dusty and grimy and smelled bad, but because it obviously hadn't become more than a long, elegant box in which to store people and furniture.

I remembered how surprised I'd been the first time I came out to Summerville to visit Morgan. The Whitesides were living in a small rented house then, on the other side of town. I suppose I'd expected just a bigger, more cluttered version of the little college room we had shared for nearly two years. Instead, everything was neatly, thoughtfully, prettily put together, and the furniture was polished, and the silver was polished, and it turned out that we liked the same colors—yellows and greens, not too much blue, maybe because for two years we had looked at those morose blue dormitory walls. Even in that little rented house there was lots of sunlight and plants and good cheer.

In the living room I put an old scratched Beatles album on the stereo and dusted furniture and moldings to it. I vacuumed around Rusty the setter, who lazily lifted his tail in greeting, and at eleven, just as I'd finished, the telephone rang.

"Hi, Isabel? This is Trina Pratt. How are you? How's everything going? I called you at work in New York, but they said you were out here. Is everything all right? Listen, last night I got the strangest urge to bake, I don't know why. Isn't that odd? At eleven I wasn't at all sleepy, so instead of going to bed, I went into the kitchen and baked three pies. Isn't that crazy?" Her shrill voice suddenly dropped into a throaty undertone. "If I stay married to Ralph much longer, I'll have to open a bakery. Anyway"—her voice rose again—"I thought I'd drop off a pie for you and the kids. You have a choice of apple or pear—take the apple, it's a whole lot better. How's it all going?"

Fine, I said, except, oh, Sarah was being a little, uh, difficult.

"Oh, I bet. Douglas is nuts to stick you with Sarah. He ought to be there himself. Honestly, sometimes I do think he's the world's most impossible man."

"It's not really his fault, Trina. He had to go to Boston, and he couldn't get anyone to stay."

"Yeah, well, let me tell you, Sarah's got a lot of problems. She's been going through a bad time. For a while there I thought that kid was going right down the drain. I think maybe lately she's improved somewhat, thank God. You should have seen the boyfriend she had this past summer, one of the truly worst kids in town. Hey, a customer. I've got to go. I'll see you later. Been to the hospital yet?"

I said that I hadn't had time, but I was planning to go soon.

"Brace yourself," she said and hung up. I put down the telephone and stood looking around the living room. It was now dusted and smelled of lemon furniture polish, but everything still looked ill at ease. Standing there, I saw that the sofa belonged against the long wall and the loveseats should be facing each other in front of the fireplace, but no, of course I wouldn't change a thing. I suddenly had a scary thought. I knew I had come a different route through life, and it had always seemed to me that Morgan was a kind of alter ego—she supplied the flowers and children I didn't have. Now this alter ego was disintegrating, and in an odd way I seemed to be wanting to pick up the pieces. At that moment I saw something in myself I didn't much like, and I went upstairs to get dressed for a visit to the hospital.

# 4

My friend Fran Beyer, a classmate from my Miss Blanchard school days, died of melanoma at Memorial Sloan-Kettering. Alison Stilwell, an ex-roommate of mine from early working days in New York, died of lymphosarcoma in Greenwich, Connecticut. Margie Stern, a diabetic who had worked with Joan and me, had had first a toe, then a foot, then a leg amputated up to the knee. I had visited Margie several times and kept trying not to notice the growing blank space under the white blanket cover, but two months later she died anyway.

I myself hadn't been in a hospital except for appendicitis when I was nine and a day trip a few years ago. A week after Walter and I separated, I found out that I was pregnant. I never even seriously considered having the baby. I think a kid should have a father—even a poor father is better than none—and besides, I was supporting myself and I didn't want to have a kid and have to drop if off full time at some day-care center when it was four weeks old. I know sometimes it has to be that way, but I guess for myself, since I had the choice, I didn't want to do that. That was three years ago; I was thirty-three then. It's all right for me the way it is now. I am not very maternal, I guess, not a natural mother. I don't often think about it, only sometimes I wonder what the baby might have looked like. Say! It might have looked like Walter.

"Hey you," Morgan said, sitting up a little in bed. This was hard for her to manage—her left wrist was taped to a burbling

IV. "God, you're a peach to do this. How are the kids? Is Sarah behaving herself?"

Already she was much changed. She was thinner, and there were brown circles under her eyes, and her black hair looked stringy and dull. She had on a yellow bed jacket that made her skin look even more sallow.

"Everything's just fine," I said. I bent and kissed her cheek and patted her thin arm. In August she had been tanned, but now she was simply yellowish, and the dark down on her arms stood out clearly. The bed jacket had silly clown ruffles on the collar and satin ribbons tied in bows down the front. "Where'd you get that thing?"

"This?" She looked down and picked up a ribbon between two fingers. "Douglas got it for me. Awful, isn't it? I can't believe he picked it out, it's not my type."

"It is sort of totally not you."

"On the other hand," she said, "I have changed. I'm not the same person anymore." She looked away and shrugged. "Do you know what I am now? I'm a full-time sick person."

"Oh, Morgan."

"No, it's true. Being sick is a whole career. You get up in the morning and you think about your red blood cells and if you feel tired, which is all the time, only sometimes it's worse than others, then you have to go in and get your cells checked. All I've done since August is have naps and get my red blood cells checked. Sometimes I go to bed right after dinner. It's a lovely life. Sleeping Beauty, that's me, but I don't think my prince is ever coming. How is Sarah? Is my daughter giving you a hard time?"

I pulled a chair up to the side of the bed and sat down, but before I could say anything, Morgan put her head back on the pillow and closed her eyes. Her eyelids looked as shiny and purple as the skin of an eggplant.

"She's going to kill me," Morgan said and then opened her eyes again. "She used to be a wonderful kid, and then all of a sudden everything changed. I don't know whose fault it was, or if it *was* anyone's fault. I don't know why he came to town—we were all so stupidly happy until he came. He changed everything, everybody. I told Douglas to leave her alone. I kept saying, 'Just leave her alone.' He hit Sarah once—I couldn't stand to see that. He'd never done that before. I'd never seen him hit one of our kids before. Oh, don't look so surprised. You didn't really think we always just sailed along on a sea of bliss. And it wasn't his fault, it was my fault. Sometimes I think I deserve this."

I was puzzled and couldn't follow. I said softly, "I don't understand."

"I deserve this," she said again, turning her face away. "I am being punished and I deserve to be."

"Oh, come on," I said. "For what? My God, Morgo, you can't think of it that way. If you think of it like that, you'll give in."

She rolled her head around on the pillow. "You see, I've got an infection. Septicemia. That's blood poisoning. My blood is poisoned. I am being punished. That's what you have to be careful of, is infection. Because the drugs wipe out your own antibodies. The drugs kill the cancer cells and the good cells at the same time and then you have nothing left. To fight with. How is Eddie?"

I said that he was fine. I said that he had told me about playing hockey, and then I asked her if she remembered the time I had broken the window in the Little Quad. She smiled and looked away, then said that Eddie had a hockey practice Thursday and asked if I could check on his transportation. "Is it Thursday? Yes, I think it's Thursday. He was Margaret's lover, I think. Where is Margaret? She said she'd come today. I've asked her to paint my portrait. I want there to be something when I die."

She was frowning and moving her head from side to side. I could see that she was feverish—when I put my hand on her arm, her skin felt hot, and dry, and I had the strange idea that if I wanted to, I could simply crumble her in my fist, the way you do a dead leaf. She shook my hand off. "Don't," she said. "Awful. Where've you been? You didn't bring your paints."

She said this staring past me toward Margaret, who had come in the door and was standing at the foot of the bed.

"Now, Morgan," Margaret said, "you know we talked about it and decided we wouldn't do it here. This isn't the right place. We'll wait until you get home and I'll paint you in that green dress you like so much."

"Yes, that's right," Morgan said. "Not here. In my house. I wore that dress to the Christmas dance. Is it true, Margaret? I don't know if it's true. I shouldn't have told her. I'm sorry. What about Douglas? I don't know. I don't know anything." Her black eyes filled with tears and she lay straight back, exhausted. A nurse came in dragging a cart full of clinking medications. We left.

We were silent going down in the elevator. We went through the hospital lobby, past the gift shop and the coffee shop and the florist shop bright with pots of yellow chrysanthemums and arrangements of autumn leaves. We went through the heavy glass doors, where a workman was slowly polishing the doors' brass trim and humming to himself.

"Morning," he said. We nodded.

"What was it she told you?" Margaret asked, looking at me with a crooked smile, narrowing her eyes against the sun.

"I'm not sure," I said. "She wasn't making much sense."

Margaret reached into her purse, took out a pair of sunglasses, and slipped them on. "How did you get here?"

"I took a cab."

"I'll give you a ride home." Walking toward the parking lot, I, too, put on sunglasses, as if the bright October air were too clear, too revealing. In the car, at a stoplight, Margaret said, "Aggressive chemotherapy."

I looked at her curiously.

"That's what it's called—the treatment they're giving her. That's all there is."

I asked, "Does it work?"

She shrugged. "It buys time. The trade-off is that you spend the time being sick."

"Not much of a trade-off," I said.

"That's all there is." For the rest of the ride neither one of us said a word.

In the Whitesides' house I had chosen for myself a small room over the kitchen that must have been meant for maid's quarters. I had moved out the cartons that were full of old curtains and draperies and swept out the corners and put a bunch of marigolds from the garden in a little bowl on the dresser. The room suited me. It had two small dormer windows and a closet fit for a midget, but it had all other essentials: a narrow iron bed, an old bureau with a cracked top (and one leg propped by a matchbook), a chair, a reading lamp. One dormer window had a view of the slate tiles of the garage roof. The other view was better—down below I could see the back garden still rustily blooming.

I have a feeling about myself that is not sad, only resigned —that I will end my life somewhere as an old lady in a similar room, all alone. I suppose in essence I am a person who doesn't need a lot. I need a room of my own, a decent bed, a desk, a lamp, a chair. It would be nice to have someone to eat dinner with and sleep with, but there is something inside me that has always been resigned to the ultimate aloneness, maybe because I was an only child. In our family we were great respecters of privacy. A shut door was a shut door, and no one opened anyone else's mail. You had a right to your own thoughts, too. No one pried. I was taught when very small that it was wrong to ask personal questions, so that afternoon when I decided to clean up the kids' rooms, I did so uneasily, feeling that even a kid—most of all a kid—has the right to a private space. *Well,* I thought, *I just won't look too hard,* though God knows what I expected to find. *Playboy* under Eddie's mattress? A diary in Tess's desk?

I smiled when I saw in Tess's white-painted bookcase the same teenage sex manual my mother had given me, now in its tenth edition. In Sarah's room, the room of an eighteenth-century maiden, with a canopied bed and cross-stitch samplers on the wall, I looked with distaste at the mess. A small wing chair was covered with dirty clothes. Dirty clothes were everywhere. She had a Queen Anne dressing table all her own—it was a clutter of makeup, creams, used Kleenex, spilled powder, cotton balls, a box of OB's, acne lotions. She had enough makeup to rig out a Forty-second Street prostitute, which I suddenly wondered if she had become: in the center of the table was an open box of condoms, one of the more reliable brands, and I stared at it with a feeling somewhere between disbelief and despair. I had gathered all her dirty clothes into one large heap and now nervously redistributed them, sprinkling them here and there, trying to make the room look as it had before. Should I tell her father when he came home? Of course I should. Or should I? Sarah was only fifteen. And condoms; why condoms? I wondered. The pill or something else might imply parental approval. Condoms make you think she's outfitting an army. Maybe she is bluffing. Maybe she just wants attention. Oh, hell. I went downstairs.

Sarah had come in from school and was sitting in the study, one leg slung over a chair, talking on the telephone. She had on brown cord pants and had taken off her healthful Dr. Scholl's sandals. (Jesus, these kids worry so much about their *feet*.) As she talked, she was engaged in picking up a pencil by flexing and curling her bare toes. She looked at me, smiled, hung up.

"Hi, Isabel," she said ringingly. "Gosh, you really cleaned, didn't you? Everything looks so nice. It does make me feel bad, I've been meaning to do it for so long. Is there anything I can do? Do you want me to get supper?" She smiled at me sweetly.

"No, thanks," I said. I wanted it to be brisk—it came out cold. She blinked. Her green eyes took on a wary look.

"Maybe," I said, "you could just find out for me who's picking up Tess."

"Oh, sure," she said. "I think it must be Mrs. Pratt's friend,

Mrs. Sullivan." Sarah yawned and suddenly vaulted out of the chair. She stretched overhead, then touched her toes, then swung her arms in a windmill arc.

"I feel so *good*," she said. "I finally got an A from old Melon Head, that's my English teacher, Mr. Malone. And I got an A minus on a history test. That *was* a surprise! I hardly studied. You're awfully intelligent, aren't you, Isabel?"

"I don't know," I said. "I've often wondered."

"My mother thinks you are."

"Your mother is intelligent, too."

"I don't know," she said, still smiling. "Is she?"

"Yes."

"My mother said once she thought you were going to be famous."

"And here I am, just one of the girls."

"No," she said, giving me a hard green stare. "You're really not like the other women." Then she smiled and left the room, flicking out her long mane of hair as she went. *Smart*, I thought. *Oh, smart Sarah*. Clearly, in every way, she was outwitting me.

"The thing I don't like," Joan said the next morning, "is it's got that California attitude—it assumes all the kids are having sex."

"Aren't they?" I asked morosely.

Joan made a face. "Will you let me finish, please?"

"Sorry." We were in a still-darkened viewing room and had just seen a public service film made by a small independent California studio. The subject was teenage pregnancy.

"It assumes all the kids in high school are having sex or are going to have sex, and here, kids, is where to go when the girl gets knocked up. I don't like it."

"What? The film? The attitude? Both?"

"Both. You see, there may be kids who will see this film who aren't having sex, and then they will feel strange and out of it."

"How about the adults who aren't having sex."

"That's your fault and nobody else's."

"I was speaking generally."

"Speak for yourself, Isabel."

"You and Stuart are getting along better, I take it."

"No, but I met a terrific guy last night."

"Oh, yeah? Where?"

"Jeanette Oompala and I had a drink together at Raga, and while we were there, this fella came in who happened to be an old friend of Jeanette's from her student activist days on Morningside Heights. I nearly fell off my chair. Lust hit me right between the eyes."

"Is that where lust hits? Did he fall for you, too?"

"We got along just . . . mmm . . . terribly well. Very well indeed. Enoch's a little young."

"Like twelve?"

"He's thirty-four. What do you think?"

"That sounds young to me. What does he do? Is he married?"

"He's divorced. He's a lawyer—a public defender."

"How sweet."

"Well?"

"Well what?"

"Well what do you think?"

"I think fools rush in."

"Oh, Isabel, do you know what your trouble is? You have always been so careful. Why don't you just go ahead and take a chance once in a while? What's the worst thing that can happen?"

"Death?"

"That is going to happen anyway. Meanwhile, why live as if you're dead?"

I mused out loud, "Why is it everyone feels they have to give me advice? Do I look stupid? Incompetent? What?"

"Unhappy," Joan said agreeably. She stood up and snapped on the viewing room lights. "I think we'll say no on that one. I don't think we should encourage high school sex. Let's go have lunch."

We went down the elevator and out into the brilliant October street. Lately Sixth Avenue has come to resemble a Middle East bazaar. On the sidewalk in front of our building, vendors were hawking wind-up toys, gold chains, umbrellas, Indian jewelry, oriental silk blouses. The smell of food was everywhere. There was shish kebab and pita bread, and a Russian immigrant was selling slices of pizza and sections of his novel, which he had mimeographed himself. All this street life was making me feel queasy and light-headed. When the light said Walk, we swarmed across the street with the rest of the jingling tide.

Why is it that here, in Manhattan, cheek, jowl, and elbow next to variegated humanity, I feel so stunningly unique? Geographic density? An island's poetic compression? Other cities I have lived in not entirely surrounded by water—Baltimore, Washington—with their endless suburbs, broad white highways radiating outward from the heart's coagulated center, the concentric habitable rings gradually growing less dense, lighter, the lots better spaced, the houses wider, brighter, made me feel hopeless and depressed. We went across the plaza and down some steps to the little health-food restaurant we liked. The tables and floors were light Scandinavian wood, the salads smelled and tasted like hay. Oats. Feedbag. Horse. Morgan.

"What's wrong?" Joan asked, looking at me carefully. We are exactly the same height, and often, when we are standing together, she gets me right in the eye.

"I don't know. I feel worried."

"About what?"

"About being here, in New York. Tess didn't feel well this morning. She's upset. More than she'll openly let on."

"What about the boy? What's his name?"

"Eddie. He seems fairly oblivious, but who knows?"

"And the older girl, Sarah?"

I told Joan about the condoms. She shook her head. "Well, at least she's using them . . . hopefully."

"Seriously, didn't you ever have this problem with your kids?"

"My kids?" Joan said. "Are you kidding? They're scared to death of sex. I keep wondering if it's something I've done or the culture has done."

"Or Stuart has done."

"Let's not talk about Stuart, I'm on my lunch hour. Yes, you have got to tell her father."

"Oh, God, oh, God."

"What's the matter?"

"I'm getting stomach cramps just thinking about it. I know he is going to be terribly angry. He's sort of an old-fashioned type, and very puritanical. At least that's the way he's always struck me. It's funny, I guess I really don't know him very well, even after all these years."

"What does he do?"

"He's the headmaster of a private school. Quite a large one."

"At least he's not in public relations. They're the worst. Life becomes total bullshit. After a while, big lies—small lies, it's all the same." We shuffled two steps closer to the hostess in the meek line we were standing in. "The truth is, I'm not brave, Isabel. If I were, I would have taken my chances and left Stuart and his bullshit a long time ago." Joan's face, which is broad and pretty, suddenly drooped. She has round cheekbones and a full mouth and a short, straight nose. Her very white skin is just beginning to show some lines, but her blue eyes are lively—she looks much younger than she is, she *thinks* much younger than she is. Sometimes, in a comic way, she reminds me of my father —her head is so busy her sense of appearance gets skewed. Her pale blond hair tends to stick out frowsily at the sides of her head. Her clothes instinct is a little off, too. She always has on one thing too many, a pin or a belt with a hideous clasp. Today it's a scarf printed in large orange polka dots which rides up out of the neckline of her dress. Then she tucks it down. Then it rides up again. Joan buys all her stuff at sales. This is why nothing fits her well, and consequently she spends a great deal of time straightening and hiking, tugging and pulling.

"Two?" the hostess said. "Two? Are you two, ladies, please?"

We were seated at a table only inches away from another. The girl at the table next to us had a great cloud of dark hair which hung down to candy-striped eyeglass frames. Behind the glasses her mascara had smudged into puddles—she was crying.

"Peggy, aw, Peggy," her friend whispered, glancing at us.

"I'm sorry, I'm sorry," Peggy said and wiped her nose with her wrist before she began crying again. "I didn't mean to break down this way."

"We better go, huh?" her friend said. "Let's leave, okay?"

"Wherever you go these days," Joan said cheerfully after they left, "there is so much human tragedy. What do you think that was? Dumped by a lover? Pregnancy? Abortion? Maybe she'd like a nice safe married lover. I can get Stuart for her wholesale. God, wouldn't that be great, Isabel, if I could pawn off Stuart on somebody else?"

"How do you know he hasn't already thought of that?"

"I'll have the spinach salad," Joan said to the waitress, "with, oh, low-calorie salad dressing. Because," she said to me, "I don't want him to leave until I'm good and ready to get rid of him and I'm not ready yet. And coffee," she said to the waitress, "with Sweet'n Low. And the chocolate cake."

Why was it, I wondered, that every marriage I knew resembled a long war of attrition, a Verdunesque stalemate, a cold war with spies and double agents, or worst of all, the death-like chill of total indifference. Which is how Walter and I ended. Finally we lay side by side on our bookcase-headboard king-size bed like two medieval stone figures from matching sarcophagi. At the end, if he had jumped from the thirtieth floor of the

Empire State Building, I would have shrugged and in perfect serenity stepped over the bleeding parts.

That night in New Jersey, after everyone had gone to bed and even Sarah was more or less safe in her room, I sat down at Douglas's desk in the study and excitedly began writing down ideas for a story in a spiral-bound plastic-covered notebook. The cover of the notebook showed (in various shades of green) a pretty long-haired girl on a surfboard in foaming water. I like the idea of surfing. Sometimes in the past when I have been writing well, I've felt as daring as any surfer, and then there are those long periods of inertia when no big waves come and you lie around sullen and morose, only waiting for that holy moment when you are under the wave again, a wave that is all around you like the translucent sides of a carved jade shell, or perhaps only the calm green light of imagination, "a green thought in a green shade." The desk had upon it a pleasant green-shaded brass lamp, and the circle of light it made in the dark, on the desk, on my own scribbling ringless hand with its bitten cuticles and uneven nails and ink-stained index finger and one small brown spot next to the little finger's knuckle (oh, God, oh, God, an age spot, I am getting old), this circle of light seemed to enclose me, keep me safe. I saw it, the light of my own mind, as a fortress against a black and howling barbarian world.

And indeed, the weather had changed. Outside, a dark autumnal wind was beginning to beat upon the curtainless windows, and I could hear the creak of tree branches and a scrabble somewhere that I took to be twigs scratching glass—oh, light, bright island of sanity! Wasn't I brought up to believe that intellect is almost everything? Goethe! Schiller! "Ach," said my father, "if the Germans had only had one writer in 1932 with the stature of Lessing!"

I stopped writing and lifted my head to listen, but it was only the wind. Then, as suddenly as it had begun, the holy fit passed, and a damp white fog drifted across my brainpan. I put down my pen. I had started writing the story of my seduction at age twenty, but I couldn't seem to get on with it. Couldn't even write a damn story. It was a tired story anyway. How many girls are seduced by older men? It would make your head reel, I guess, if we had statistics, and anyway, it has lately become a question as to who it is gets seduced. These kids seem to know so much. Besides, one can always say no. I, however, said yes. Well, that's not quite right. I don't think I said very much. He did most of the talking, and there were extenuating circumstances. I have never particularly regretted this incident, only now and then I look back on it (and myself at twenty) with humorous curiosity. Why? It didn't wound me for life, it didn't propel me down the path of prostitution or frigidity or ongoing amorous adventures, only I wonder occasionally in passing: Why him?

Hell.

Why anyone?

I snapped the notebook shut and opened the center drawer of the desk to put it away, and a tide of photographs sloshed toward me. I shuffled the pile together and then laid them out on the desk one by one, like a fortune-teller dealing her deck. Squint-eyed, chin in hand, I sat carefully studying them in the light of the green-shaded lamp.

Douglas—a tall, skinny, knob-kneed kid. Towhead slightly tilted, eyes deep in shadow, hands held loosely on hips. Camp shorts and shirt, bulky, falling-down socks, sneakers. Written on the back in rust-colored ink: *Douglas, Chewonki, 1948.*

Douglas—standing, back row of hockey team, helmetless, hair looks white in glare of winter sun. Both gloved hands—one on top of the other—encircling hockey stick.

Douglas—(rare pose!) grinning. In shorts, shirt labeled Exeter. Streaks of dirt under both eyes; lips, although smiling, are cracked and puffy. Gloved hands hold lacrosse stick.

Douglas—serious, stiff as a stick, in morning coat with radiant Morgan, a shiny-faced bride on his arm. He looks straight out at the camera, she looks at him. Her lifted veil forms a huge, filmy halo behind her. I didn't go to the wedding, had the first of my three bouts with pneumonia, so at the last minute Matilda Chessley was basted into my slit-up-the-sides maid-of-honor dress.

Douglas—in sun-speckled garden shade, sitting in a deck chair looking guardedly down at oval, blanketed bundle.

I skimmed the rest of the pile, the only other photograph of interest one of the Whitesides and the Allens together at a picnic table somewhere. Wine bottle on table, paper cups. Jerry Allen in T-shirt stands holding a can of beer, looking (in profile) with tender expression at Morgan, who is also standing, in peasant blouse, holding a food-heaped paper plate in one hand, plastic fork in other. She looks out with tender amusement at the viewer? photographer? Between these two, sitting on a bench, backs to camera, heads tipped together as if they'd been having a deep conversation, then suddenly turned, are (1) Margaret, who has on a gingham sundress and wears her hair in a braid down her back, and (2) Douglas, who looks up at the picture taker as if annoyed, black brows up, forehead in furrows.

Question: Who took the picture?

I turned the snapshot over. It was dated July of three years before, and scrawled on it in pencil: *At Paul's.*

# 5

We had that week the strangest variety of October weather. The blue clarity of Monday and Tuesday passed into the rain and wind of Wednesday night. Thursday morning was clear, chillingly autumnal, lightly brushed with frost. The wind had brought down most of the laggard leaves, and beyond the paling fence I could now for the first time plainly see the Whitesides' neighbor to the south, an eccentric Tudor house with red roof tiles, chimney pots, and half timbers. Men had come to cover the swimming pool with a long piece of bright blue vinyl; silver puddles of rain water lay on the dimpled blue, and yellow leaves lay upon the puddles. Despite its frosty beginning, Thursday grew steadily warmer. It was World Series time, humid and hazy. A smoky purple warmth hung in the air, and New York City (said WQXR) was having an air inversion. On Friday I went to work—Tess was well again—and at six o'clock Lily left me off in the Whitesides' driveway with a fresh-baked coconut cake. A blue Dodge Colt was pulled up in front of the garage. In the kitchen Douglas was sitting at the table, his sleeves rolled up, his necktie off. He was frowning and looking down at an arithmetic workbook, while Eddie (whose dark head was bent and whose shoulders were wearily hunched) scrubbed at the page with the eraser end of a pencil.

"Now you know," Douglas said, his voice a deep, slow rumble, "you can't do that, Eddie. We've already gone over that. What you do to the top, you must do to the bottom." Eddie's black hair was rumpled, and when he looked up at me, his face was pale—the strain of fractions.

"Oh, hi," he said to me indifferently. He didn't need me—he had his father again. He looked down at the book and sighed and stuck the pencil's pink eraser into his nose.

"Here she is!" Douglas said heartily and stood up, noisily knocking the chair back. "You look as if you've survived after all. I wasn't sure you would."

I laughed and said I was fine.

"I understand you had to take some time off from work. I'm sorry, I certainly hadn't meant for that to happen. I hope it didn't upset things for you." He looked down at me, his pale eyes searching mine, and for the first time in our long acquaintance we smiled at each other.

"Not really. When did you get back?"

"My plane got in at two. I went over to the hospital before I came home."

"How's Morgan feeling today?"

"Fine, fine," he said in a voice that was too positive. "She's much better. Going to come home Monday or Tuesday."

"Dad?" Eddie said, looking up. "Dad, it doesn't come *out* right. See, if I do the same to the top and bottom, the answer comes out different than the one at the back of the book."

"Just a minute, Ed, all right?" Douglas frowned at him and then smiled down at me and shrugged. "Traumatic."

I said, "I'm going to wash up, then I'll get us some dinner."

"Ah," he said, "dinner is all taken care of. Eddie and I cooked."

"So I've been displaced!"

"Temporarily laid off," he said. "You'll probably need a vacation after this week."

Eddie yawned and stuck the pencil into his ear and looked out the kitchen window.

"Concentrate!" his father said and lightly rapped the boy's head with his knuckles. Douglas bent to look at the workbook, and I went up the back stairs. I did feel displaced—how strange to be needed one moment, and the next casually discharged. I smiled ruefully to myself, thinking how with men I was always so guarded, so afraid of getting hurt. How could I know that after a week with these kids, who had no blood of mine and weren't even especially dear to me, I would feel so jilted? Fickle kids, I thought to myself and, passing Sarah's bedroom—the same tumult of clothes, books, panty hose, jeans, clogs, jewelry that I had been passing all week—thought with displeasure that sometime I would have to speak to her father.

We ate outside on the wooden picnic table at the back of the house. Supper was sloppy joes fresh from the delicatessen downtown, three layers of rye bread, roast beef, ham, and cheese, all slathered over with a shrimp-colored bath of Russian dressing. Tail swinging, Rusty the setter moved from one to the other of us and occasionally laid a heavy, begging paw across a knee, occasionally a warm prickly chin.

"Delicious!" I said to Eddie. "You are some great cook."

"I think they're awful," Tess said. "Why did you spend money on this revolting stuff?"

"Maybe you shouldn't eat a whole lot," I said to her. I explained to Douglas that she had had an upset stomach.

"That's funny, Tess," he said, "so did I. The minute I got off the plane at Logan Airport, I felt sick."

"Did you see Granpa?" Eddie asked.

"Yes, but he wasn't feeling well, either."

"If I were married to that woman," Tess said, sounding just like her mother, "I'd be sick a lot, too."

"Isabel's okay," Eddie said to his father, "but she's not a very good cook. Can I watch the Series, Dad, just for a while?"

"All right. Got your homework done? Tess? How about you?"

"I've got silly *Latin*. All I do is *Latin*."

The back door banged once, twice. The TV went on in the study, and lamplight filled the window of Tess's room. The sun had set, and the moon had come up—a huge orange disc in a purple sky. *Now,* I thought to myself. Sarah was out, having dinner at a friend's house. How to begin?

"I want to thank you," Douglas said formally, "for coming out on such short notice. I'm terribly sorry you missed two days of work. It doesn't seem quite right for me to ask you to do that."

"You didn't ask me to do that, it just happened."

"I was hoping it would all go smoothly."

"It did go smoothly." *Go on,* I thought, *tell him now.*

But in a sudden confusion of light and sound a car's headlights swung up the drive and into our eyes, and at the same time a car stereo barreled out some sort of violent semimusical blare, and then the car—a white fastback with a dented door—swung around and both the headlights and the music died. I heard Sarah's laugh—it sounded wobbly and too high. She got out of the car looking terribly prim and ladylike. She had on a white pleated skirt, white sandals, and a lacy white short-sleeved sweater, but she wasn't too steady as she walked toward us.

"Daddy!" she said and giggled and bent her head so that her long blond hair fell like a curtain shielding her face. I saw to my surprise that she kissed him full on the mouth. He frowned and turned his head away. The car's stereo started up, its motor raced, and the car roared backward out of the driveway. A stripe of white headlight washed across Douglas's face, bleaching it of color and expression. Sarah laughed and stood there tottering in her high heels.

"Let's go, Sarah," Douglas said. His voice was resigned. He stood up and took her arm; she giggled and leaned against him. They went inside. In a moment more lights went on upstairs, and Douglas did not come back outside. When I went in, he was sitting with Eddie in the library watching the World Series, but his chin was sunk on his chest and his eyes were on the floor.

I took a bath and read for a while. At eleven I switched off my lamp and tried to sleep. Hopeless. I was wide awake. The full moon sent a strip of tinkling silver in through the window; it spilled down the sill, flowed shimmering across the bare wood floor. In it the shadow of a tree branch was very black. The room was too warm. I got up and opened the window and looked out at the silver-coated night. I remembered how, summers when I was a kid, I would get out of bed and stand at the window watching the silvery moonlit water of the lake. It seemed the most beautiful thing in the whole world—the gold moon rising above the mountains, looking down a little smugly, a little contemptuously at its twin in the lake, who lay trapped and helpless in the water. Was Morgan asleep now in her hospital bed, or was she looking at a window full of moonlight? The luminous green numbers on my little travel clock said twelve, and I was no nearer sleep than I'd been an hour before. I got up and without putting on any lights went downstairs in my bare feet to look for some sleep-inducing alcoholic something or other, just a quick little shot of Lethe. There was a brass cart in the living room that had a small supply of glasses and booze, but I realized, coming down into the front hall, that someone was still up. I could hear Eddie's voice—it sounded querulous, old—and then his father's voice, answering. I went softly through the hall and into the living room. In the bright moonlight I found the cart without any trouble—I could, in the brightness, even read the labels. I poured out a shot of Scotch and with a hand cupped over the shot glass, as if it were a burning candle, started back out of the living room. Then I heard Eddie say, "I'm really glad you're home, Dad," and again I had that rueful, vaguely hurt feeling.

"I'm glad to be back, Ed."

"When's Mom coming home? Sunday?" I'd heard him ask this question three times already.

"Probably Monday. Tuesday for sure."

"Is she feeling a whole lot better?"

"Yes, she really is. She'll be better for a while, you know, then she'll probably get sick again. We have to expect that, you know. She'll be sick sometimes and better sometimes. That's the way it's going to be."

I heard a sigh, then the creak of a sofa or chair, and then I heard Eddie ask, "When is she going to die?"

The silence that moved out of the library was so high-pitched, so full of pain that it felt like a sound dense with waves of a very high frequency that I could not hear but could feel. There was no immediate answer, and then Douglas cleared his throat. He said, "Not right away. You'd better go to bed, Eddie. It's awfully late. At least we got the math straight, didn't we?"

"Yeah."

"Sleep late tomorrow morning, will you?"

"Yeah, I will. You too, Dad."

"Thank you. I plan to."

"Night."

"Good night." The stairs creaked. I waited until I heard a

door close upstairs and then went on to the staircase. In the library the sofa sighed, and I stood there waiting, I didn't know quite for what—something, anything, to happen—and then I heard someone saying "uh-huh, uh-huh." Standing there in my bare feet in the middle of the moonlit hall (the sidelights and fanlight full of moon, and moonlight in a fan shape on the floor), I listened; it was such a strange sound. Except for this sound the house was perfectly still; darkness lay in the corners, and the thick, iridescent moonlight came in through uncurtained windows, and Douglas Whiteside, in his handsome walnut-paneled library, in his beautiful house, in a lovely town, in a corner of the world where people count themselves lucky to live, in a very deep shuddering voice that was still somehow quiet, contained, and controlled—"uh-huh, uh-huh, uh-huh"— was crying.

When I got up the next morning—oh, blessed Saturday!— it was late: ten o'clock. Passing Sarah's room, I saw to my surprise that she was vacuuming. "Morning!" she called out with more vigor than she'd shown all week. Downstairs in the laundry room off the kitchen the washer and dryer were sloshing and thumping, and Douglas sat at the table drinking coffee and reading the newspaper.

"Morning," he said.

"Morning," I said. I looked at him and dropped my eyes.

"Coffee's over there on the stove. It's homemade."

"What?"

"I made it from scratch with real coffee, not instant."

"Oh!"

"You look ready to travel."

"I've got to get back today."

"Why not stay and spend the weekend? We could use a sturdy leaf-raker."

"Come now, don't get greedy."

"But we have so many beautiful leaves."

"No chance. I'm in the middle of painting my apartment,

and I want to get it done. It's disorienting to look at one yellow wall."

*Now,* I thought. *Sit down, Isabel, and tell him. You have to do it.* I sat down.

"Douglas," I began. He lifted his eyes. They were very pale gray this morning and red-rimmed, with black circles beneath them. *Oh, dammit,* I thought. *Poor guy. This on top of everything else.* "I want to talk to you about Sarah. There is something I feel I must tell you."

"Why?"

"Why?"

"Yes, why? Why do you feel you must tell me?"

"Because you are her father and . . ."

"Sarah is completely in charge of her own life."

I sat for a moment, thinking. There was a brown stoneware pitcher on the table, and I now made a great deal of pouring milk from it into my coffee, stirring and stirring, lifting the cup. Still too hot. I put the cup down. I said, "Of course she is—isn't everyone? But the point is, she's fifteen, not twenty-one. I think she still needs your support and guidance."

"Which she will doubtless refuse."

"I found a box of condoms on her dresser."

"Yes?"

"I thought you ought to know."

"Now I know. Could I ask why you were in her room?"

"You may certainly ask. After a week of passing that mess I was tempted to pick it up."

"Next time I suggest you close the door."

"Indeed. Oh, I see. You seem more worried about my— what shall I call it, snoopiness? prying?—than you are about Sarah."

"Sarah knows the facts of life, Isabel, and my feeling at this point is that she must proceed on her own. Regardless of what I say, or you say or anyone says, she is going to do what she wants."

"What makes you so sure of that?"

130

"I've been there before." He said this wearily.

"And you're giving up?"

"Not exactly."

"Maybe in a funny way she really is asking for your advice and guidance."

He exploded. I hadn't realized a voice could be so loud. My hands groped upward toward my ears. "Oh, kindly do not come back at me with this ridiculous pseudo-psychological crap. Do you think you know my daughter better than I do? Is that it? I've lived with her for a long time now. You have been here a week."

I said, trying not to show the anger I felt, "I simply thought you ought to know, that's all."

"Thank you." He said this coldly.

"If it's not inconvenient, perhaps you can drive me down to the train station. Or I can call a cab."

"I'll be glad to drive you. Where's your bag?"

"In the hall."

"I'd like to thank you again."

"You are welcome. Is Tess here? I'd like to say good-bye to her."

"I'm afraid she's at a friend's house. I'll tell her good-bye for you."

"And to Eddie, too, please."

"Of course." I stood up and walked through the house. Sarah sat in the living room in one of her more usual poses, one leg over a chair arm. She was reading *People* magazine.

"Good-bye, Sarah," I said.

She glanced up. "Oh," she said, "bye now," and turned a page.

Douglas drove me to the station in the Dodge. We said nothing at all to each other on the way downtown. He stopped the car in front of the station and thanked me again. I nodded to him as he handed me my suitcase, but I couldn't think of anything to say. I guess I wanted to hit him instead.

At home there was a note from David in my mailbox. Like it or not, he was appearing at four, we could at least have dinner together. So we had dinner together, and he stayed the night. It was nice to have someone to eat with and sleep with, but I woke up at four A.M. feeling depressed, angry with him, angrier with myself.

# III

❧ ❧ ❧

# Christmas
# Week

# 1

The rest of the fall was dreary, damp, and gray. New York was as cold as Moscow, and on Sixth Avenue faces had the pinched, paranoid look of inhabitants of a totalitarian state. Christmas was coming (what? again?) and on the telephone Morgan's clear voice had a gay, bell-like ring. She was in remission, and everything was marvelous.

*Remission!* I thought. *Oh, glory, how wonderful.* I had gone to the public library and caught up on my medical reading. This could mean months, maybe a year.

"Look, Iz, why on earth don't you come out for Christmas? I'd really love it, it would be just us. Douglas's brother isn't coming after all."

Because, I said, well, you see, I was going to spend Christmas with Joan Thistle. A lie. Joan hadn't asked me for Christmas yet, and the chances were slight that she would. The Thistles had large Dickensian Christmases which, Joan told me, always ended in three members of the family not speaking to each other until amelioration set in, two weeks before Christmas of the following year.

Joan's mother was senile and according to Joan would sit at the lace- and crystal-bedecked table rubbing sweet potatoes into her white hair while Stuart's mother (who was nine years older) was sharp as a tack and twice as mean. She was lively and bright, but she lovingly told the same family stories over and over. Nevertheless, as Stuart kept pointing out, Liz Thistle still had all her marbles. It was taken by Stuart as a sure sign of inferior genetic material that Joan's mother had declined before her eightieth year. No wonder their eldest son hadn't gotten into Andover.

"Still," Joan said, when Christmas was a week away, "I'd rather watch my mad ancient mother mush up her hair than have to listen to that horrid woman tell about the time Stuart was four and got to downtown Philadelphia all by himself. Do you know that after twenty-five years of marriage she still considers me the kitchen help? If she doesn't like something, she passes her plate down to me and says to one of my kids, 'Have her take this to the kitchen.' *Her!* I'd like to . . . oh, I don't know, I'm so sick of all that fake heartiness and drunken good cheer. On the other hand, strong drink is the only possible way I can get through it. I go from glogg to grog to eggnog with hardly a whimper. Christmas for me is really going to be on the twenty-third. I plan to treat myself to a whole night with Enoch."

I asked her how she was going to manage this, and she said dryly, "Lie, elaborately." Then she said, "Really, Isabel, if you are desperate for company and think you can stand it, you might come out. It should be entertaining, at least from the point of view of a pure outsider." I gracefully declined. It had occurred to me that knowing about Enoch, I'd feel awkward with Stuart. Well, then, said Joan, narrowing her blue eyes, she might very well ask David, and if I didn't mind, now that we'd broken up, she had a lovely friend in Rye who'd been recently widowed. Really, I said sarcastically—named Lucrezia? Then I remonstrated with myself. Why be a dog in the manger? And I consoled myself with the thought that the world is full of people to whom Christmas is an awful burden. Freshman year in college, the night before we left Northampton for Christmas vacation, Morgan and I had lain awake in the dark of our little room, exchanging Christmases. There was the Christmas I had scarlet fever and the Christmas we had Wiener schnitzel because my mother forgot to defrost the turkey. All other Christmases blended into one with mimetic economy: the smell of balsam fir, the smell of orange peel. Morgan had a different approach. She could mark each year of her life with a different place for Christmas. Lying there in the close air of the steam-heated room, with our suitcases all packed and waiting by the door, Morgan told me her "classic eighth Christmas story. This one is so bad you will never believe it."

The Christmas she was eight, they were living (she and her father) in her mother's mother's house on Long Island. It was a long white clapboard house with green shutters, set in a fragrant hemlock grove with fifty other acres of valuable real estate adhering to it. The house was pleasantly old and had low ceilings, a wide staircase in the central hall, oriental rugs, a cook-maid combination, books in the library, flowers on the tables, polished mirrors, everything, of course, but Morgan's mother. They were, as her father said, "in an anomalous position." They were living with the old lady because they were poor, and they were poor because Morgan's father had alienated his most important client by objecting to an affair the client was having with his wife.

And then, at Thanksgiving, her mother "ran off"— actually, said Morgan, it was more of a swift, steady walk—with the client. And so Morgan and her father were in that position, anomalous indeed, of living with the adulteress's mother on the adulteress's mother's money. Oh, well. The old lady hardly knew the difference. She was slaphappy from brunch until bedtime and had long before given up even the pretense of pouring her bourbon into the perfume bottles. She was never quite sure who Morgan was. Some days she thought Morgan was the gardener's daughter and other days she thought Morgan might be her Kitty all over again.

On Christmas day Morgan got out of bed and went downstairs in her long white nightie and bunny slippers with the pink glass eyes (one of the eyes hung on by only a thread). There was a dried-up puddle of throw-up on the stairs. Macy the cook and Eunice the maid had the day off. The house was cold. She went into the living room and plugged in the Christmas tree, which blinked at her, then blazed up. She knelt and shook some boxes wrapped in silver paper and went back upstairs.

Her father was still asleep, his red face speckled with beard, and when she touched his shoulder, he didn't wake up. She went into her grandmother's room. Her grandmother had gone out to a party the night before and lay on the bed still in her mink coat, face down on the quilted gold spread, the black seams of her stockings crookedly working their way up her little stick legs like burrowing worms, one black satin pump dangling from her stiff toes, and one liver-spotted hand, the one with the huge, staring diamond on it, clenched tight around something—a green matchbox that had *Merry Christmas* stamped upon it in silver. Morgan touched the hand, but it was cold, and her grandmother wouldn't let go of the matchbox.

When her father finally did get up, it was two in the afternoon, and then the doctor had to come and the funeral parlor people with their stretcher. Her father built a fire in the fireplace and made her tea and cinnamon toast. He kept saying she had been a wonderful woman. Who? All Morgan remembered of her grandmother was her liver spots, her huge diamond ring, the cigarette perpetually stuck on her lower lip, her wheeze, her cough. Morgan's mother was somewhere in Europe. The old lady had left everything to her prodigal daughter, who never came home for the funeral, and so Morgan and her father had to move. Again.

As for us, we never went anywhere, we never had anyone in, and the little "family circle" (my mother could be dreadfully Dickensian herself) clicked shut on Christmas Eve with the snap of a lock on an eighteen-karat gold bracelet. We followed the German custom of opening presents on Christmas Eve, and since we lived modestly, this was accomplished in about thirty seconds. My father always got a tie, my mother got (from my father) a three-pound box of Whitman's chocolates, and I always got exactly what I asked for, as long as it was under twenty dollars. I knew the next twenty-four hours would be a nightmare of boredom, and so every year I asked for books. I read my way through Christmas and emerged on December 26 feeling headachy but relieved and waiting for nine A.M., the earliest my mother would let me pick up the telephone to call my friends.

By the twenty-first of the current year I still had no plans for Christmas, although I had found out through intricate and delicate questioning that Ginny Little-Fox and Maria Martinez had "no plans" for Christmas, either. Maria was from Chile, and Ginny had grown up on an Indian reservation near Albuquerque, New Mexico. We decided to "get together" and also to ask Ferdie Jones, despite the fact that when he walked by, my hormonal indicators plunged to zero. And indeed, he asked if he could bring "a dear male friend." Why not? We drew straws for the entree, which fell to Ferdie's friend, Guy. Guy decided to do "a classic turkey thing, my dear, with chestnut stuffing in the major cavity and oysters in the crop. This is so exciting!"

It turned out to be one of the best Christmases any of us had ever had. We drank a lot and sang Christmas carols. Guy had brought a dulcimer, and Maria sang for us in Spanish. I went happily, woozily to bed and woke on the twenty-sixth feeling headachy but relieved. The telephone seemed to be ringing. It was . . . who? Margaret Allen. She wanted to know if she could drop by soon. Half an hour later she appeared in pants, cowboy boots, and a little mink jacket. Where had I gotten the idea that she was so Victorian?

# 2

She looked around the apartment with great curiosity, keeping her hands in the pockets of the mink jacket and staring for a long while at my lithograph collection. They were mainly Vuillards that I had bought at Rizzoli's bookstore. For the past couple of years I had been drawn to Vuillard, as at various times I have been drawn to different composers, different authors. Sometimes the stages of my past life seem like layers to me, and I can date the layers pretty handily: "I was twenty then and liked Keats and Mozart"; "I was thirty-four and rediscovering Henry James, Debussy, Vuillard."

I put on the teakettle. Margaret sat down at the square oak table and looked out the long window at the Misses P's winter garden. The birdbath was frozen over, and the cheeky sparrow hadn't come around for a long time. The ivy in the beds looked brown and dead. My mother had never allowed ivy in the house. When I was ten or so, she showed me the Rilke poem on ivy, the type set up so peculiarly on the page. "See," she said, "how it twists? He makes the poem look as ivy grows." And then she frowned and closed the book. "I very much dislike ivy. In Germany it is planted on graves."

"Dreary," Margaret said, looking out. "It's been a dreary winter. Cold without snow, and all this dampness." I had a potted, two-foot-high Christmas tree on the table, a little fir hung with tiny red satin balls. Margaret idly poked one of the balls with a forefinger so that it swung. "I like your place," she said. "It's all your own, isn't it?"

I put a cup of hot tea down in front of her. "Not quite," I said. "I'm only a very enthusiastic sub-lettor. I even painted the walls twice to get the right shade of yellow. Tell me how Summerville is and everyone in it."

"The same. Ralph and Trina are still bickering. Lily is still amusing and amused and still propping up Donald."

"And Morgan? How is she? I talked to her just before Christmas. She sounded so well that it made my Christmas, too."

Margaret shook her head. "She's sick and back in the hospital."

"Oh, no. I thought she was in remission."

"She was, but it didn't last—six weeks was the extent of it. No one seems to know why it happens this way—some people have long remissions, and some don't. Now they've got to do a colostomy."

"Oh, God. Why?"

"She has an ulcerated colon. As I understand it, this is a side effect of the chemotherapy. It's the same problem, has been all along. The chemotherapy wipes out everything—good cells, bad cells, bad bacteria, good bacteria. So then there are gut problems, colonic problems."

I sat down across from her at the table and put my face in my hands. She picked up her teacup and sipped slowly.

"Good tea," she said. She lowered her eyes and raised them. "Now I have to ask you this difficult thing."

I kept my face in my hands and looked at her. I had an idea of what she was going to say, and I began hurriedly, inside, to marshal my arguments: the job, my own life, lie, make up something, a trip, I, too, am sick, anything, anything.

"Isabel, they really need some help, the Whitesides do. The kids are just, oh, falling apart. Douglas tries, but it is an awfully hard job, and he has got to go up to Boston again. There is some sort of family business that he's got to attend to. Morgan asked me to ask you if you would come."

"Then why didn't she call?"

"She went into the hospital very quickly this morning and didn't really have time. I talked to Douglas briefly. I hope you'll understand this—I'd go over myself, but this is a bad time for me. I can't leave my own kids this week. They're home for vacation, and Jerry is leaving next Monday."

"Where is he going?"

141

"He's rented a place in the next town. We're separating."
Her eyes carefully watched me. Her hands, thin, knobby, rough-
skinned at the knuckles, not–well-taken-care-of hands lay on
the table, one up, one facing down, like the plaster casts of
hands used in a nineteenth-century artist's studio. Her hands
turned over and folded together. "So I can't leave home right
now."

"No, I see. I'm sorry."

"It's been coming for a long time, years perhaps. Nevertheless. It's painful. Hard on the children, even though they're not
small anymore. Did you find your divorce . . . painful?"

"We weren't married as long as you were."

"Still . . ."

I smiled. "I missed his record collection and the smell of
his after-shave in the morning."

"You never talk about him."

"I didn't like him. I really have no idea why I got married.
I thought I should try it. I guess that never works."

"No."

"And he liked my writing."

"Oh." She smiled and looked down at the table and
shrugged. "Jerry has never cared much about what I do. He's
always left it alone."

"Well, that was the trouble with Walter. He didn't leave it
alone."

"He read over your shoulder?"

"Yeah."

"I think Jerry liked me best years ago, when I was pregnant and when the kids were little and I would stay home and
bake bread. He doesn't seem like the domestic type, but he is."
She smiled. Her hands folded comfortably together on the table.
She wore no rings. "I bake wonderful bread."

I liked to think of her baking bread, her strong chapped
hands with oil paint under the fingernails, squeezing the dough.
There is such bounce and resistance in a springy, elastic ball of

142

yeast-risen dough. Kneading is hard work. You have to do it for eight to ten minutes usually. Afterward your arms ache.

She went on slowly, "I suppose we just came to a fork in the road. One day I looked around the house and thought, *None of this is me.* It occurred to me that we didn't really have a life together, I had just lived his life for a long time. I saw that if I wanted to paint, it wasn't possible to go on that way. Strange, isn't it?"

I asked her how old she'd been when she'd started painting, and what it was that had made her start. "It seems odd to me, you living up there in the wilderness and turning out to be an artist."

She said, a smile flickering along her lips, "Brownsbridge may not be the center of civilization, but it's not a wilderness, it's a village. And it was my mother, of course. She"—Margaret hesitated—"she never quite fit into Brownsbridge life. She started painting out of boredom, I think. She hadn't had any real training, but she got to be pretty good at it. You know the kind of thing she did: the Adirondacks in fall in yellows and reds, the Adirondacks in winter—bumpy white hills. My father let her paint because it brought in a little money. Mr. Purdy sold her watercolors in his store. He had an old-fashioned general store that sold snowshoes and fishing tackle and garnet rings and moccasins. And there were my mother's paintings up over the cornflakes! Anyway, as soon as I could make a fist, my mother put a crayon into it. We painted together."

"What did your father do?"

"He owned a lumberyard. It burned down very mysteriously one night. Then we moved to a broken-down farm." She turned her head away and shrugged one shoulder. "So you see, what I'm here for is to ask if you could possibly come back out to Summerville, today or tomorrow. I believe Douglas has someone who comes in now to clean, but that's not the point. What they need is a person, some interested person. An anchor. No, that's not quite right. A keel."

"The thing is, you know . . ." I looked out the window. By God, there was that damn sparrow. He was sitting on the edge of the birdbath, flaunting his *preep, preep*. I took a breath and looked at Margaret. "Last time I was out, I had a fight with Douglas. All right, I'll call it a disagreement, though he made me so angry I could have hit him."

She smiled out of the corner of her mouth. "Oh, dear me. What was it about?"

"It was about Sarah. I think he was unfair to me. He made me feel very much in the wrong, and I don't think I deserved it."

Margaret grimaced. "Sarah. Heavens, can't you see? He's just so defensive."

"Well, I don't want to go back to that. It's too ambiguous. And the thing of it is, I myself don't clearly know what to do. I'd always assumed that he was rigid and puritanical. It turned out that, at least with Sarah, he has no rules."

Margaret sat back in her chair. "He's given her up."

"At fifteen?"

"Yes."

"But I can't, you see, deal with her on that basis. That's no basis at all. So I feel . . ." I hesitated and then brought it out firmly. "If I'm to do this again, if I'm to be a keel, then it will have to be on my terms, with my standards and my sense of direction."

"Do you truly have a sense of direction?"

"It's not all mapped out, but it's in my gut. I want permission to use that. Otherwise it would be impossible."

"I will tell him. He'll say fine."

"How do you know?"

"Because he's desperate."

"You don't like Douglas much, do you?"

"It isn't that."

"You don't agree with him?"

"No, it's not that." She pulled gloves out of the pocket of the mink jacket—cheap woolen gloves with fake leather palms sewn in. I'd seen similar gloves at a supermarket spin rack. "So you'll come? I'm asking you not for Douglas, or even the children, but for Morgan."

I nodded: all right, I would. On Tuesday. That was tomorrow.

At the door she said, looking past me, "I have another favor to ask. If you're going to be in Summerville this week, I wonder if I might use your apartment for a few hours in the daytime. Trina Pratt is driving me crazy. She seems to think I need some kind of talk therapy and she's on the phone or at my door endlessly. Then, of course, she talks about *her* problems. It would help if I had some excuse—some other place to go."

This time I looked past her and ducked my head and cleared my throat. "I'm sorry," I said. "I really don't think I could do that. I hope you'll understand."

"Of course," she said lightly, even gaily, and pulled on the cheap wool gloves as I opened the door.


I suppose I could have said yes, but I am fussy about my space. I don't want my drawers poked into, my closets opened. My inner space, too, I like to protect a bit. Which in a sense is what Walter violated. Well. What had I expected? I knew at the time. There were certain unwritten contractual aspects of the marriage that had nothing to do with sex. I hadn't really wanted to go to bed with him. (It is always a mistake, I found out later, to marry someone you don't want to go to bed with.) It is certainly likely that, after all, I was influenced by my parents, in the way Morgan had mentioned. I thought Walter and I could forge a community of interests, that we'd have lots to talk about and all sorts of cultural activities in common.

He was a rising young assistant professor of English literature at Queens College; I was a writer. I had just had my first novel published when we met. He was to be my permanent Guggenheim, a kind of built-in fellowship for whom I would provide dinner and breakfast and a little sex, not necessarily in that order. I was (I didn't clearly understand this at the time) to be the live-in Creative Person. He referred to me occasionally (I found this out later) in his English sections. He told them with dramatic gestures and pauses that I wrote in longhand on blue-lined notebook paper clipped to a clipboard, that I used an old-fashioned fountain pen I had found on the floor of a laundromat on Third Avenue. As our relationship declined (it never really deteriorated, it just *shrank*) he began to make petulant, offhand remarks about Creative Persons, *Wahnsinn,* and *Genie.* He, too, had read Goethe.

Of course I knew there were these unstipulated agreements I was expected to fulfill: appear at faculty parties; look like a Writer; talk like a Writer. But what does a Writer look like? Moreover, when even just one drink slides down this Writer's throat, she becomes cheerful but tongue-tied; two drinks lead to melancholia and impromptu servings of word salad; three drinks to desultory meanness and Walter, ashy pale, trying to get me out the door before I open my mouth one more time.

I became confused. I knew I didn't look like a writer or talk like one and I certainly didn't feel like one: I had thought up my second novel just before we got married, and it wasn't beginning well. It didn't end well, either, and although I worked on it for several years, picking and prodding, shaking and thumping, it remained thoroughly moribund, was all style and no life. I got depressed and quit writing. This made Walter nervous; I wasn't keeping my part of the bargain. He began to refer to me as the Blocked Writer and then mockingly as the Writer Manqué and finally as Isabel Who Used To Write (but doesn't anymore). Things got grim. I started sleeping with a man who never read novels and happened to be Jewish. Like a large floppy moth, the word "Jew" began to appear, clumsily alighting now here, now there, among the dullish flowers of our evening conversations.

I have referred to a significant Christmas and the bathrobe of many colors but did not tell you my revenge: For a year I stuffed Walter with derma. I ran to the public library for *Kosher Home Cooking* and other rule books of the Hebraic sort. I ran to the five-and-dime, bought two sets of pots and two sets of plates, used one set (yellow enamel) for meat and the other set (blue enamel) for milk. This gave Walter much work in the evening, as he was the one who cleaned up after dinner. I considered shaving my head but compromised by cutting my hair in a crew cut and wearing a bandanna everywhere. I cooked borscht and gefilte fish, gorged Walter on nudeln, simmered him tsimmes. Naturally most of his favorite foods were no longer with us. Crab quiche? Ha. Ham steak with Cumberland sauce? Don't be mishugge. My only miscalculation was that our indifferent sex life was actually enhanced by the ten days ritual monthly abstinence, at the end of which pallid Walter was like a roaring bull in a pasture full of cows in estrus, so I quickly dispensed with that one.

Our last awful Christmas day together, his mom and pops came visiting from Wisconsin, along with younger brother Bob, wife Harriet, and their three white-haired children. I had promised an unusual treat, dispensed with turkey and cranberry sauce, served matzo ball soup and pot roast with latkes. Pops, a glum, lanky man of Swedish descent, was as silent as a chess player in an Ingmar Bergman movie. He chewed it all with melancholy detachment and only once during the whole meal raised his pale brows. "No plum puddin'?" he enquired of Walter. Walter vehemently shook his head. "No mince pie, either?" Pops dolefully asked. "Well, how about a Christmas cookie?" None to be had.

"I know whath for dee-thert!" popped up the sweet little four-year-old named Tim. "Idth mar-thee-pan!"

"No, no!" I said. "You all guessed wrong. It's halvah!"

Pops looked up. "Halvah what?" he asked.

I felt so full of good cheer remembering this awful Christmas that I put on my pea coat and went for a long walk. At the Hotel Washington on Lexington Avenue I went into the coffee shop. An elderly man, pink-cheeked, tweed-jacketed, was sitting at the counter drinking tea. A thin elderly woman in a magenta knit dress with rouged cheeks and lovely china-blue eyes came into the shop from the hotel lobby entrance. She sat up on the stool three stools away from Mr. Tweedy. He said, "How are you today, Mrs. Taylor? I thought perhaps you'd be having your tea about this time."

She said to the counterman (arching her neck), "Tea, please, Oliver," and then began playing with the pearls at her throat. Her magenta nail polish matched the dress. "Oh, how are you today, Mr. Albright? How is your arthritis?"

"A little better, thank you," Mr. Albright said. "It's this damp cold we've been having, you know. That's a lovely color dress you're wearing. And what is that perfume you have on? I noticed it the other day."

"Memoire Cherie." She had a voice as faded as an old corsage, but there was something provocative in it, a hint of flicked silk and lace.

"Is that so? My wife used to wear something sweet and spicy, Carnation, perhaps it was."

"I don't like carnations a-tall," said Mrs. Taylor, lifting her pointed chin and looking with her remarkable eyes—did she have on mascara? yes, she did—into the yellowish steamy space above the Formica counter. There was a pause. I could see that Mr. Albright didn't know what to make of this. Was it a rebuff or only a smart challenge, like the coy tap of a folded fan on a wrist? His stern white brows knit as he thought it over.

Oh, how difficult love is, how impossible courtship, how awful to have to play interminable games, to keep up the armor that shields the vulnerable heart. To take a chance. To risk refusal. And what dreadful humiliation if you are serious and the other is not. I didn't want to go to the Whitesides'. There is something I have left out. I gave you only the words, I left out the feelings. I didn't tell you how (sitting there that night in his garden at the picnic table in the lavender dusk, with gold lights going on next door, and a TV blitzing blue images in the study) we sat three feet apart, and I felt short of breath. My heart hurt. The arcs of my nerve endings kept somehow missing, so what I felt in my head was a crosshatch of sizzling gold wires. My speech center seemed short-circuited. I turned mute. When he got up, I felt abandoned. *Come back. Don't leave now.*

I went on sitting there alone after he'd taken Sarah upstairs, and I couldn't move. Later, alone in New York, the habit he had of looking broodingly downward, and the frown lines between his shaggy brows, and his voice, a deep rumble, came back a hundred times. Was this love? It was boring! It was a nuisance! It was impossible! I wanted to see him again and I was afraid to see him again, and Morgan was one of my dearest friends and she was dying.

And I wondered, idly and craftily and coldly—the wolf inside the Little Red Riding Hood get-up—what it would be like to go to bed with her husband. For she was, after all, going to die.


# 3


"Ah, so! There you are! Where have you been, Schliemann? It's Wednesday, remember? Time for our weekly get-together. How come you're so late this morning? Had too much Christmas, hmmm?"

"Aw, gee, boss!" Joan took me by the elbow and steered me toward her office. "I went out to New Jersey last night. Morgan's in the hospital again."

She kicked the door shut. "Sit. You look like hell. Not so terrific, is it, going out there and playing mom?"

"I didn't think it would be."

"Is he any help?"

"You mean Douglas?"

"Who else is there to mean? Yes, of course I mean Douglas. What does he do, come in after you've done all the work, cooked the dinner, spanked the kids and all?"

"He's not there, Joan, he's in Boston. Why would I go out if he were there?"

"I don't know. Am I crazy, or do I detect a change of tone when you talk about this Douglas? I thought you didn't like him. I thought he was such a stick."

"I didn't know him, that's all."

"What's his background?"

"His background?"

"Do you think you could stop doing that, repeating everything? You sound so moronic."

"I'm sorry, I guess I'm really exhausted."

"I see that you are. And you know what else? I think you're a little intrigued with this man, and I think you ought to be careful. You're both awfully vulnerable, you know. Listen, Isabel, this really isn't a good situation for you. Doesn't he have a relative who can come in? Doesn't she? I mean, for one thing, think of the neighbors."

"I do, I am, they're around all the time. They bring desserts and casseroles. Look, I'm not there on a permanent basis, he'll be back on Thursday."

"So what's this man's background? Where'd he go to school? Exeter? God, what a drag. In my next life I'm going to marry a Jewish graduate of a New York City public school. I'm so sick of the eastern WASP chauvinist imperialist culture I'm stuck in. Stuart went to Andover and he thinks life is really a continuation of prep school. And he's right, it is. Every weekend he plays tennis with his boyfriends and then they all drink together."

"At least he doesn't watch girls."

"It would be better for him," Joan said severely, "if he did." She bent her head to her desk and began writing on a pad of legal-sized paper, stopping occasionally to dip her pen into a bottle of ink. I went on sitting inertly, looking at her bulletin board cluttered with tacked-up notices of coming events in the city, happenings about to occur all over New York. Sometimes the very energy that these nine million souls give off seems to seethe around me, makes me feel drained. Life as an endless hassle. Keep your guard up always, or else. It was like being a beekeeper —one moment without your netting and heavy gloves and you're stung to death.

"Oh, fuck," Joan said. She had tipped over the bottle of ink, and ink was running all over her notes. She started mopping up with Kleenex and a grim look.

"Jesus," she said. "I don't know. Christ. Well, fuck it all, anyway."

I sat there dreamily, watching her blot. She tossed the balled-up Kleenex into the wastebasket and looked at her blue-stained fingertips. "Shit," she said. I smiled at her. "Isabel, you egregious zombie, you're no good for anything. You just sit there smiling and let me indelibate myself."

"Indelibate?"

"From indelible."

"Hey, I kind of like that—indelibate. I didn't know you ever used real ink."

"Enoch gave me a Parker pen for Christmas." She picked up a slim silver pen and balanced it delicately between her blue-nailed forefingers. It had her name engraved on the side—Joan Thistle.

"Cute," I said. "What did you give him?"

She moodily stared down at the blue and white mess on her blotter—her ink-stained notes had risen in places and sunk in others, so that they looked like small relief maps. "Well, I didn't want to spend a lot of money."

"It's the thought that counts."

"So I took my grandmother's diamond earrings and had them made into cuff links." She dropped the pen and covered her eyes with one blue-tipped hand.

"Oh, really. Just a cheap little gift." I looked at the half of her face I could see—her short nose, just a little too wide (it was shiny), and her pale, full-lipped mouth. A generous mouth, I thought. "Did he like them?"

"He wouldn't accept them." Her voice sounded dull. Her

stained hand slid down over her mouth, and she looked at me worriedly, like someone about to retch.

"Why not?"

Her hand fell to the desk, as if shot. "I suppose," she said, "you know, the usual reason."

"Like it would be in bad taste?"

"Yes. To accept expensive gifts. From someone you do not love."

"Is that what's wrong with you? You think that?"

"Very possibly."

"Is that what he said, he didn't love you?"

"No."

"Then you don't have to think that, do you?" I said this in a firm voice and for the first time truly understood why physicians lie to terminally ill patients. Don't cut off the lifeline! Never erase hope! I was like the doctor who, despite all the irrefutable clinical evidence, succors the dying woman with, "I don't know." I knew. I had met Enoch at lunch two days before Christmas. Joan, in an orange jersey dress (that was too tight at the bosom and had a tiny eye-shaped hole in the side seam of the bodice), had fluttered and beamed and blushed. Enoch was a wiry six-footer who gave the impression of being much smaller and perhaps for this reason wore a huge blond Afro. He had a thin face, a thin hooked nose. Cold little blue eyes had taken my measure from behind gold-rimmed glasses. He was, Joan had proudly told me, a Sixties Liberal, had years ago marched in Mississippi and registered voters and now, although already meritoriously engaged as a public defender, worked quite a lot for Legal Aid.

As proof of his politics he wore a navy tie adorned with small green spouting whales. If you missed the point, the tie had written across its middle in fine script, *Save the Whales*. He said, throughout lunch, barely a word, controlling Joan—there is no other word for it—with a glance, a gesture, a lift of his wiry blond brows. Joan seemed to be continually searching his face for messages. These signals arrived in a drastically curtailed code. He blinked. He pursed his thin lips. What, after all, is more controlling than silence? I thought he was a cold little snotty bastard and immediately hated him. I was amazed that my friend Joan, a graduate of Radcliffe College (magna cum laude), could fall for such an obvious creep. I thought she had better sense than that.

Joan picked up a pencil, tapped it on the desk, and then snapped it in two. "Listen, why don't you take the rest of the afternoon off? Take the rest of the week off. You're no good to anyone here. Now get out, please, so I can get some work done."

I gathered my things together—my sacklike handbag, my pea coat, my scarf. Before I left the building, I went to the ladies' room. I stared at myself in the dim glass. I looked pale and guilty as hell. Once, when I was three, my mother accused me of tipping over a pot full of flowers. I honestly cannot remember whether I'd done it or not, but when I denied the act, she accused me of lying and teased me all day, saying there was a big invisible *L* on my forehead. I was smart for three—I knew she'd made it up—but I kept running to the mirror just to check. Had Joan made it up? Or could she see an incipient *A* lightly stenciled on my forehead?

It was raining when I left the building. I thought I could always cut my hair into bangs.

# 4

I didn't go right back to Summerville but walked down Fifth Avenue for a while in the cold drizzle, darting through the revolving doors of one store or another to enjoy the post-Christmas *ambience*, a favorite word of the year. In Saks the tiny twinkling chandelier lights were so dim you needed a miner's lamp to see the fancy goods, and the air was so thick with perfume it would have (chirp!) killed the miner's poor canary. The perfume was sprayed by tall emaciated girls with black lacquered hair in black strapless gowns. They wore unabashed grins, and if you made eye contact with any one of them, you were sure to get a dose of Opium full force right in the eyeglasses.

Or perhaps, I thought at the blouse counter, looking around and wiping my glasses on the handy hem of a display garment, what was intended here was a fabled seraglio setting— the colors that predominated were black and gold, with censers swinging and all around me the babble of foreign tongues, so that (to switch fairy tales for a minute) I felt like the little peasant girl in from the country, all boots and babushka and lumpy clothes, and the tall, slender, dark-eyed women who strolled the aisles, glossy fur coats swaying from their shoulders, looked at me amused, condescending—she doesn't know the language! The language was money, the dialect was nuance, so perfectly spoken you never saw green stuff at all, only the delicate exchange of varicolored plastic charge cards.

The rent on my apartment was now so steep that I hadn't bought anything since November, and I desperately needed some good-looking working attire—shirts, skirts, that sort of thing—but right there on the main floor, basking in the pinkish light of a glass case, I saw a blouse of sheer white cotton with a kind of satiny white stripe in it and a very low ruffled vee neck. Ruffles, Isabel? For the office? Not exactly what I needed for a full day at my typewriter, but what the heck. I grandly hailed the salesgirl, pointed, dug out my very own magic plastic chargecoin, and crossed my fingers, hoping that no double-crossing computer would check out Schliemann, I., and find that she was two months behind on her little bill-o. The terminals must have all been asleep that day or maybe sick with a bad case of burned wires, because she handed the bag to me with a smile.

"Thanks," I said.

"*Shto?*" she said.

Nobody in Saks speaks English anymore.

Later, descending the grimy stairs to the PATH tubes, I remonstrated with myself. Why, Isabel, this sudden interest in ruffles and sheer cotton? Sixty-five *bucks*, Isabel, and you will never wear it. And who would care if you did wear it, now that David is out of the picture? You never bought clothes like that for him, did you? In fact, he used to complain that when you went out to dinner with him, you looked slightly butch in your tweed jackets and boots and blue jeans, and a couple of times he had hopefully arrived at your door with dress boxes, once a box from Martha, where you have never shopped, of course, only (with nose and all ten fingers pressed to the window glass) wistfully looked. You lifted the dress out of its rustling tissue paper—a strapless dress of misty sequined blue, a prom dress out of the late fifties. You got it: He wanted you to be his girl, he wanted to rerun the fifties film all over again. You didn't want to hurt his feelings, but you wouldn't take the dress.

Then why, Isabel, I asked myself, as I sat down on the wicker seat of the 4:40 train to Summerville—the heat was off, the lights were off, the air in the train smelled of coal gas—then why, Isabel, this dainty white feminine blouse with its vee to nicely show off your shoulders and bosom and sheer enough to necessitate a whole wardrobe of old-fashioned lacy underthings —slips, camisoles, etc? Let's see (the balky dialogue went on), I could wear with it a black velvet skirt and a black silk cummerbund pulled in tight (the practical, hard-working, level-headed Isabel losing every round to Isabel of the shamelessly beating breast) and pearl earrings, Victorian earrings if I can find them, and . . . Shit! (*Her* voice again, sneering.) Why not a corset? Why not whalebone stays?

The train started with a lurch. A bulge-bottomed lady shopper with many shopping bags and three-drink-luncheon breath collapsed into the seat beside me. "Oops!" she said and sighed. I cringed into my corner, huddled up next to the grimy, streaked window. The train crawled panting through the tunnel and came out into drizzled-over New Jersey: Hoboken, suburban Newark, weeds, tall grass, junk, smoke from a burning dump, a dead car lot with flattened car bodies stacked one on top of the other, rivers full of black sludge, smokestacks, telephone wires, power lines. The lights went on overhead, and the passengers gave a collective sigh and picked up their newspapers, and the heat came on with a hiss, and I closed my eyes. Who is it you're dressing for? asked hardheaded Isabel. And what is it you'll dress Morgan in?

I didn't want to go to Summerville. I wanted to be in my own place with the door firmly shut against the world.

It was one of those sudden attacks of acute memory that appear in your mind first as an annoying glimpse, a bright patch misplaced, jiggled into view perhaps by the lurch of the train shaking up the old neuron-memory bank. And what was it? Where, when was that scrap of sky this exact shade of silk-azure blue, and what torture as the brush of memory slowly, teasingly painted it in again across the rough-textured but absolutely pure white blank between your eyes. Come on, fill it in now, where, when? There, under the bright blue, the brush moves on vertically in swift blue-green strokes—evergreens, standing up on tall hills like the bristles on a boar's back, and then right there, halfway down the mountain, two bright-red strokes—a roof, and then, below, another swift horizontal stroke of wavering dark gold, the beach across the lake. And all at once the picture gets done in a hurry, and there is the blue-green water and the dock and the old rowboat tied up to it and then—but we've left something out: the wooden windowframe of the front parlor window, of the farmhouse we rented from Crazy Mary on Great Sacandaga Lake five miles from Brownsbridge, New York.

*Oh, yes, Margaret, I did know the area, I know it well.*

The house was just a few feet from the lake's rocky beach,

and in back of the house was a very broken-down barn; the main timber of the roof had fallen in, giving the barn a sway-backed look. All around the barn was a meadow and, on the other side of the meadow, the shack where Mary and her cats lived in the summer.

She farmed the fields herself, without benefit of much equipment. I used to see her walking in back of a primitive plow, in a "housedress" of flowered cotton, severely stained under the arms, and white socks rolled into doughnuts around the ankles, and broken-sided white tie shoes. She wore, for plowing, a large brimmed straw hat with a flat crown—it tied under the chin with dirty pink grosgrain ribbons. She carried a willow switch to urge on the horse, an old long-necked brown nag as swaybacked as the barn. One day the horse turned up on our rocky beach, lying on its side, dead. Flies had already gathered in its nostrils and wide-open eyes. My mother came down from the house and stood looking at it, her hands on her hips.

"*Ach, du lieber Gott,*" she said. "Poor beast. Now what to do?" We went together up to the meadow to see Mary. Mary had hitched herself up and, in her broken-sided white shoes, was pulling the plow. Her face, even in the shade of her broad-brimmed hat, was a vivid red. A strand of gray hair hung across her forehead. Her light-blue eyes had a crazed look, and when she saw us coming, she didn't stop but went along pulling, her eyes fixed on some point in the hot blue and gold summer distance. It had rained the night before, a terrible thunderstorm of the kind we often had up there in the mountains, and with every step her white shoes sank to the ankles in ocher mud, and she pulled them up with an effort that made a sucking sound. They emerged the disgusting yellowish color of shit.

"Mary!" my mother shouted at her. "Your horse!"

Mary went right on, not looking at us, pulling.

"Your horse is dead on our beach!"

Mary gazed ahead, as if she herself had become her own spent, sway-backed animal.

*"Verrückt,"* my mother muttered, *"ganz verrückt,"* and looking down, made a face at her mud-caked moccasins.

I got off at the Summerville Station and took a cab to the Whitesides' house and from there drove to the hospital.

# 5

She was indeed going to die; you saw that at once. She lay flat under the snowy white hospital blanket cover with her arms straight down at her sides and her toes turned up and out, as if even the weight of the blanket were too much to bear. The nurse, who looked as buxom and rosy as a fairy tale miller's daughter, cranked up the bed with the vigorous movements of someone churning butter. At length Morgan's head and shoulders appeared. She had no hair. A crisp, clean white scarf had been tied over her head like the scarf of an Orthodox Jewish woman or a Red Cross nurse from some World War II movie.

"Hi!" I said. She opened her eyes slowly with enormous effort. Her skin was drawn so tight on her bones that when she opened her mouth to smile, her teeth seemed huge, like the teeth of a horse. She closed her eyes. She said, "Too tired." I said I understood. I would come back tomorrow. I left immediately, feeling relieved.

Driving back to the Whitesides' house (I was now using their Dodge Colt), I was suddenly overcome with a spasm of nausea. I pulled over into the parking lot next to the Presbyterian church, left the motor running, jumped out, and erped into the frozen bushes. There was a long honk. I was blocking the entrance. I got back in the car, wiping my mouth on the back of my hand. I wanted Morgan back. Not this Morgan

158

(whom I did not know), but the one I had known since college. On this long journey she was making from life into death she was turning into a thing. She would be more herself tomorrow, the nurse had said soothingly. But what was herself? In panic, I couldn't remember. Margaret Allen had said to me on the telephone, "No, I'm not painting her from life—there is hardly any left." I had come to like Margaret's severity. It was cold, spare, dry, honest. Every day of that week, women came to the Whitesides' door with tears trembling in their eyes and casseroles in their hands, or cakes, breads, Jell-O salads. Jell-O salads, can you believe it? Shiny lime green domes that contained bits of carrot and celery and were poisonously tart-sweet.

One night just after Douglas got home, a Mrs. Thaxter came to call. Her face gleamed with moisturizer, and her wet mascaraed eyes narrowed when I opened the door. She said suspiciously, "Are you the housekeeper?" "Yes," I said. She gave me a package wrapped in foil, took off her coat, and then without a word walked into the living room, hands gracefully extended—with her pointed nails, her hands looked like the toothed halves of a cocked steel trap.

"Douglas!" she said. "My dear!"

He was holding a stack of students' term papers and stood looking at her in confusion, as if he couldn't quite place her face or remember her name. I grinned at him from the doorway. He raised his brows at me over her shoulder, meaning, "Come in." I shook my head: no! You're stuck with her! I went out into the kitchen—the housekeeper's domain—and made instant coffee, littered a plate with Christmas cookies, and brought these things in on a tray.

"You!" he said later. "You're a brat." I laughed at him from the kitchen sink. "What's so funny?" Tess asked wanly, coming into the room. Douglas had told me she was often sick now, with nausea and vomiting, while Eddie, who seemed almost bluishly pale, would sit for long, listless hours watching TV without any perceptible reaction. He didn't laugh or smile, he hardly spoke, and when finally you reached him, it was like talking to someone in the final stages of freezing—he would answer slowly, dreamily, lips moving only slightly.

With Sarah, it was plainly war. "You are to be in at ten. Be here!" I said to her again and again. "Come home! I need your help. We need you."

"Jesus Christ," she screamed at me, "nobody needs anybody!"

Oddly, living in Douglas's home that week, I had no desire for him. The images that had plagued me in New York ceased to exist in Summerville. I was tired, there was too much to do and the needs of the children (not their physical needs but their emotional ones) kept me in a state of tension and exhaustion. I foresaw that when he came home we would stay out of each other's way. We would perform an elaborate, courtly dance—stiffly bowing, passing, curtseying. When he was in the kitchen, I would find an excuse to go to the study and when he sat in the living room, I would stay in the kitchen. For those few hours we would spend in the house together, we would act out the exterior aspects of a marriage—the duties, chores, responsibilities —without that bond, that sexual spark which, kindled, makes of long love (if not a roaring blaze) at least a small, companionable fire. I felt with some satisfaction that living in Douglas's house I had abraded his image, scoured him from my mind as if with gritty chlorinated powder.

On Wednesday night I went to bed early but couldn't sleep. It was snowing lightly, nothing serious. I shut off the bedside lamp and looked out into the black-and-white night. Through the little dormer window I could see black branches and the filmy snow coming down like a curtain of lace. I have always loved snow—how it softens the harsh edges of winter and muffles sound. I thought of skiing on deep new snow, fresh powder, remembered in my thighs the ecstatic springiness of it, like leaping from cloud to cloud. And shoveling snow—you go out in a flannel shirt and gloves, it's the oddest sensation, soon you're burning with body heat and your skin feels cool at the same time. I thought, lying there, of a winter years ago when I was in the seventh grade and a terrific snowstorm coated New York City. We had a school holiday, and all the kids on the street built two opposing snow forts, and in the blue shadow of "our" fort, with snowballs plopping all around, Marvin Kessler wiped his snotty nose on his wet wool mitten and suddenly kissed me. He was a year younger than me and stuttered. I was indignant. And later, when I was in my twenties, I remembered putting on a fur hat and huge boots and trudging east down Fiftieth Street after a snowfall—I was with someone, who was it? We were going to the Café Nicholson for dinner. Everyone was walking in the street on snow already chunked up with tread marks, and it was like a holiday—people waved and sang and were as gay as if it were London during the Blitz or a carnival.

I thought, lying there, *When this is over, I'll go skiing again. I'll go to Garmisch or Davos.* I thought of Morgan lying under the blanket cover and wondered if she was looking out the hospital window. Could she see the snow? It was Morgan who taught me to ski. When what is over? What did I mean, over? After she is dead? I thought how much I didn't want her to die.

# 6

On Thursday night when he came back from his trip (and although perhaps I imagined it) his face lit up when he saw me. Then he frowned and set down his suitcase.

"Hello," I said. I was scrubbing a pot at the sink and only half-turned around to glance at him. In the kitchen window I saw his reflection unwind the plaid scarf he wore and lay it on the back of a chair. His reflection looked at me—watched me watch him—and I dropped my eyes. I heard a chair bump on the floor as he sat down.

"How was the trip?" I asked.

"So-so," he said. This time he'd driven up to Boston and back. His face looked gray and his eyes strained, as if he'd stared into oncoming headlights too long. "It was snowing up there. Terrible driving, very slippery. I guess we're due for snow down here too."

"Tomorrow," I said. I felt stupidly happy. I folded the dishtowel and hung it over the towel bar and stood leaning against the sink looking at him. He sat at the table with one arm hooked around the chair and the other sprawled on the tabletop. His hand was large and veined and looked warm.

"Where're the kids?"

"Upstairs. Everyone's all right. Sarah's been . . . fair, maybe a little better. I thought perhaps . . . since I have tomorrow off I could take her shopping. She does need some clothes and then maybe we'd have a chance to talk."

"Fine. Whatever you think." He sighed and suddenly put his face in his hands and rubbed his eyes. "God, what a trip. The car broke down yesterday morning. I had to get a new carburetor in Quincy, Massachusetts. I don't know if you had a chance to see Morgan. I wondered how . . . I stopped by the hospital just now, but she was sleeping."

"I didn't go to the hospital today. I meant to, but things got ahead of me. Eddie had a hockey game and at the last minute his ride got canceled so I had to drive."

"I talked to her on the telephone yesterday. She didn't sound well at all."

"No. I saw her yesterday. She was awfully tired."

He glanced at his watch. "It's too late to go back tonight. I'll go first thing tomorrow."

"How is your grandmother?"

"Still alive," he said. "It's incredible. She had a stroke five months ago and lies there partially paralyzed, not able to speak a word. She can understand everything but pretends not to, of course. Actually, this is just an extension of her life before the stroke. She's always pretended not to understand anything." He smiled wearily. "Maybe that's how she got to be ninety. She's a very self-preserving lady."

"Your father lives in Boston, too, doesn't he?"

"Yes, with his third wife. He's not very well. He's had a couple of major heart attacks, but he spends a remarkable amount of time worrying about Mae."

I sat down at the table across from him. He had on a jacket, a sweater, and a blue button-down-collar shirt that had lost one of its buttons, so that one collar edge peeped up over the sweater's neck. "Why is that?" I asked. "Is she sick, too?"

His tired eyes smiled. "No, but she's twenty years younger than he is. And she manages what's left of the family money."

"Really? Is she good at it?"

"Very good at it. I have an uneasy feeling that someday I'll wake up and find I've been disinherited."

"Can't you do something about it?"

"No, not much."

I looked away. "When I was in college, my father ran off with someone a good bit younger than he was. They never got married though. She just took everything he had and disappeared."

"Is he still alive, your father?"

"I don't know. I've lost track of him. I wanted to lose track of him. Even my memories of him are rather slippery."

"Memory being an imperfect organ," he said and smiled.

I smiled back and said, "And you an historian." But I agreed of course. Mnemosyne is a moody lady and her housekeeping abilities are nil. If only she'd arrange things in orderly layers, neatly classifiable, so that when the bric-a-brac got excavated, things would appear without cracks or missing pieces or forged parts.

He said, "If memory were perfect, my profession would cease to exist."

"Nonsense," I said. "Historians would still be around,

making up their stories about the past, inventing the past and reinventing it."

"Pretty cynical, aren't you? Your father was an historian, was he not?"

Ah, yes, my crazy father and his *magnum opus;* my mother going out to the office every morning, where, for a pittance a week, she typed up ads that came in over the telephone of the German-language newspaper. Hideous, boring work. I said, "He shouldn't have been—he, too, had a bad memory. When my mother died, he didn't remember enough to come to the funeral. All the while she was sick, he never once came to see her." Douglas started and dropped his eyes. I said, "He was no different, I guess, from what he'd always been. Completely self-absorbed and self-centered." I stared down at the table. He looked down at the floor.

He asked, lifting his head, "When are you going back to the city?"

"I'd planned to go back tomorrow."

"I don't like to ask you this, but I wonder if you could possibly stay until Saturday? I don't want to impose on any plans you may have, so stop me if that's the case." I shrugged, watching him. He said, "There's a trustees' luncheon in Far Hills and Eddie's got a hockey game in Newark. I'd be very obliged to you if you could stay until Saturday. Or through the weekend." His eyes searched mine. I looked down at the kitchen table, where his hand lay sprawled, half-open. No doubt he'd forgotten that Saturday was New Year's Eve. Well, what difference did it make? I wasn't engaged for the evening, and neither was he. He turned his hand upon the table and lightly drummed without making a sound. I nodded.

He went off to the living room to do some paperwork. I unloaded the dishwasher and put dishes away. I was on my way upstairs to get a book when the doorbell rang: it was Mrs. Thaxter.

Later, in the kitchen after she'd left, I said to him: "Her fingernails!" He had brought out the coffee tray and was tipping the cups into the sink. "They looked positively dangerous."

"It's the most puzzling thing," he said. "She has wonderful children."

A sharp knock came on the kitchen door. It felt like Mrs. Thaxter reprimanding us. When I turned to see who it was, a face appeared in the window that I couldn't believe. I jumped back like someone surprised by a jack-in-the-box as David opened the door and stuck his head in.

"Hello!" he said brightly. "By God, I found the right house after all. It was a work of art just to find the town. Ah, the wilds of New Jersey! How are you, Isabel? I talked to Joan this morning, and she mentioned you were out here again. And this must be . . ." Slowly Douglas stood up.

"David," I said, "this is Douglas Whiteside. Douglas, this is a friend of mine, David Parminter." Certain forms of civility have clearly been invented to discourage murder. For a nickel I would have taken the bread knife to Parminter. I looked from one to the other. David still stood with his face thrust out of his Black Watch plaid scarf, only now he had shot his right hand forward and was grimly smiling. Douglas looked at the hand (still wrapped in its pigskin glove) and after a long moment brought his own hand out to meet it. *Oh, wonderful,* I thought. *I hope he isn't planning to stay.* But David was already peeling off his gloves and scarf and camel's hair coat and rubbing his hands together and saying, Cold out there, what? By God, he knew we were bound to get some snow. It was obvious he would be with us for an hour, at least.

Cozily, we had drinks together in the living room. Douglas took off his tie, rolled up his sleeves, and built a fire. Eddie came halfway down the stairs, cased the visitor, got introduced, and then hollered up the stairs while I sat there wincing, "Hey, Sare, guess what? Isabel's boyfriend is here." Even the Christmas tree seemed to lean forward a little from its corner, the better to hear us, I guess. It looked stooped and tired, and the loops of its gold tinsel chains were out of sync due to constant swipes from the dog's tail. The dog had also eaten all the gingerbread cookies on the lower branches, so that from the waist down, the tree was hung with a lot of black threads. I could see David looking at them, vaguely perplexed. He sat before the fire, to my left, in a yellow wing chair, his legs crossed, one black-socked ankle planted on his knee. His face, usually so pale and always set in a composed tranquil square, was flushed and elongated. If his jaw had been thrust out any further, it would have snapped.

Douglas sat in the crewel-covered wing chair to my right, sunk far down into it with his legs stretched out and crossed at the ankles. I saw, bemused, that his socks didn't match; neither, for that matter, did the laces of his desert boots. Douglas studied David discreetly from under his eyelids, as if he, Douglas, were a naturalist on an expedition who has possibly just discovered an extraordinary new species of mammal. It occurred to me that David must already have had something to drink before he'd appeared at the kitchen door.

The kids went to bed; David stayed on. Our small talk got smaller and smaller and seemed about to evaporate entirely. I sat before the fire first with my left profile, then with my right turned to the blaze, getting distinct views of both men: David's face seemed to be getting bigger, redder, brighter, as if it were a balloon dangerously expanding, while all of Douglas seemed to be lengthening out, melting longitudinally farther and farther into the shaded recesses of the chair. As if he were the host and obliged to entertain us, David told anecdotes, one after another. I stifled a yawn.

"Isabel and I, you know," David said chattily, half-glancing at me and smiling, "met at the Fick."

Douglas's black brows rose up out of the shadows. "The what?" he asked politely.

I cleared my throat and drew my lips back in a grimace so that I could clearly enunciate the short *i* sound. "David meant" —here I gargled the *r* slightly—"Frick."

"Yes," said David, beaming, "the Frick Museum, in New

York. I stepped on her scarf." He smiled at me fondly. Douglas, looking amazed, raised his chin off his chest. David said, "We've had some marvelous times, eh, Isabel?" I grunted. He commenced to relate at great length and in detail every dinner, luncheon, and breakfast date we had ever had; the week that we spent on Nantucket, when it rained ("Not a hell of a lot to do, you know, in the rain," he said to Douglas and winked); the time that he took me skiing and the snow suddenly melted ("Had to"—he looked modestly downward—"find substitute activities"); and the three days we spent becalmed on his sloop on the Chesapeake Bay.

"You two seem to have had a lot of bad luck," Douglas observed.

"Aha!" David said cheerfully. "It is to our credit that we've been infinitely resourceful. Or should I say . . ."

*Say it,* I thought, *and I will kill you. I will pick up this poker and divide your skull.*

He looked at the floor again. "We know how to make good luck out of bad."

*Jerk!* I thought. *Dope!*

"They were all fun times," said David, then coaxingly to me, "Weren't they, Isabel?"

I refused to answer. David smiled, and I saw him glance at Douglas knowingly. *These moody women,* his glance said. *She's no doubt about to have her period.* To his credit Douglas refused to play coconspirator.

"I understand," David said to Douglas, "that you went to Exeter."

"Who told you that?" I said sharply, swiveling my head around so that David would have the full benefit of my burning glare. He had made it sound as if we sat around together discussing the Whitesides.

"Didn't *you?*" David said innocently.

"No," I said.

He looked puzzled. "Someone must have."

Liar. I knew he'd looked Douglas up. He had a habit of looking up (God knows where) any male I'd ever mentioned in passing so that (at least this was my guess) he could compare backgrounds and incomes to see if he came out ahead.

"My second son," David said, "—by God, Isabel, I almost said my ex-son!—is at Andover."

"Good school," Douglas observed.

"The best," David said, "absolutely the best. Although I unnerstand Exeter is a good school, too, of course. I was reading a report just the other day that pointed out how Andover alumni do better in life, though. More sess'ful, you might say."

· There was a pause. The fire crackled merrily, like the hostess at a dinner party filling in with tremulous, bubbly chatter an ominous preearthquake pause; and indeed, a little area of geologic tension had nicely asserted itself and flowed along the lines of the equilateral triangle the three of us made. Any moment now fisticuffs were likely to erupt.

"More successful," Douglas said, with only a modicum of scorn in his voice, "in *what*?"

"Why, suck-cess-ful," David enunciated carefully, "in a business sense, I suppose. However"—he held up a hand—"I for one am certainly not in agreement with that concept. I for one think it's absolutely ridic'lous to measure se'cess in terms of, let us say, money. I believe it is absolutely 'sential, lau-lau-laudable even, that places like An-dover and Ex'er go on educating would-be artists and writers—who never o' course make a nickel—as well as people, say, in education. People like yourself, who no doubt could have had some highly lucrative c'reer in the business world but gave up their prospects for a greater dedication. The primary purpose of a liberal arts education, is, after all, personal 'fillment. Wouldn't you say?"

Douglas said nothing. He was sitting up straight now, though, hands linked together, body tilted forward. The look on his face was one of wonderment.

"Neither Ex'er or An-dover," David went on, "is primarily orientated to the values of a commercial society—that is, ha, ha—not counting their fund drives. 'Course, achievement counts! I do believe in achievement, don't you? But! Le's not forget personal happiness."

*Oh, God, David,* I prayed, *please do not go on. You are not the cretin you seem. You're embarrassing yourself as well as me.* I could see that already I was beginning to feel waves of underdog tenderness for David and that in another moment Isabel the Sucker for a Man Who Makes an Ass of Himself would be promising to see him next week.

Douglas glanced at his watch. "Guess I'll go on to bed." He stood up. I stood up.

"Me, too," I said promptly and blushed.

"Nice meeting you, uh . . ." I could tell Douglas wasn't going to say David, and he settled at last upon a mumbled "Parminter."

"Same here," said David, who did not get up, perhaps could not. He brightly sat on, as if he were the host and Douglas the guest who was leaving. He held up his glass and waved it at me. "How about 'nother drink?"

"David, it's late and I'm tired. I'm very tired. It was lovely of you to come see me, but completely unnecessary." I stood by his chair looking down at him. He caught my wrist.

"Sit down," he said. "Stay jus' for a while." I heard Douglas's footsteps pause on the carpeted stairs and then go on.

"No," I said, pulling my wrist away. "I am going to go to sleep. Now. You've got to leave."

"Can I see you next week?"

"Oh, look, you know we said . . ."

"What about Thursday? Next Thursday, a week from tonight." Douglas's shadow was moving about at the top of the stairs.

I bent and whispered. "This is silly, you know. What's the point? We went through all this in the fall."

"We have things to discuss."

"Like what?"

"Tell you Thursday."

"All right, but please leave now. I'm too tired to think." I heard a floorboard creak at the top of the stairs, and Douglas moved off. I walked with David to the kitchen door and locked and bolted the door after him. When I went back to the living room to shut off the lights, Douglas was standing there, looking vaguely around.

He fixed me with a raised eyebrow. "I left some papers down here, I think."

"Papers?" I scanned the living room. "What kind of papers?"

"In a long envelope. Papers from a bank."

"Are you coming into money?"

"No, I'm borrowing. So he's the boyfriend."

"No, he is not."

"Why not? I'd take him if I were you. He looks prosperous. Just what every girl wants."

"I'm not a girl, I'm thirty-six, and he's not my boyfriend. David has the habit of persistence. He likes to get what he sets out to get. Underneath that innocuous demeanor lies the shart of a hark." I blinked. Something seemed wrong.

Douglas tilted his head. "For a writer you don't talk so good."

"I drank too much. He makes me nervous."

"He doesn't seem like the sort of person you'd be interested in."

"That shows how little you know me."

"Did he set out to get you?"

"Yes."

"And you let him."

"At the time."

"But he's not what you want."

I glanced uncomfortably away and shrugged. "I guess not."

"What is it you want?" He looked at me shrewdly. I thought the question very bold.

I said sharply, "It's really none of your business."

170

"Oh, you're right," he said calmly. "Sorry. Living with Morgan so long, I've begun to take on some of her more blatant characteristics."

"What is it *you* want. You're obviously not a happy man."

He said sarcastically, "Just now, do you mean?"

"I'm sorry. I didn't mean . . . now. I meant, even before. It was just something I'd observed."

"You really know nothing about my life, before this."

"I don't pretend to. It's just that you didn't seem happy. Haven't seemed happy."

"If I give the impression of being unhappy, I'm sorry. I doubt my life has been happier or less happy than those of the vast majority of my fellow humans. Generally when I'm unhappy, there's a reason. Nothing romantic, just very down-to-earth reasons. You see, Isabel, as your friend Parminter would describe it, I am not a success. I am very broke. As your friend Parminter might say, I don't know where the next nickel is going to come from. I have a ninety-year-old grandmother who won't part with a penny while she's still alive and cannily refuses to die. My father, who is very well off, is completely intimidated by his third wife, who has steadfastly refused her poor, importunate stepson. The only thing I can think of, Isabel, in order to raise some cash right now is to sell this house. But I can't do that to Morgan. It's her house. She bought it with money her mother left her. I won't move her out of it now. So you see, Isabel, I haven't been much of a success. I haven't been a terrific provider, and even here"—he thumped his chest with his fist and his mouth turned up—"I haven't had great success. I am no doubt a flop at personal relations. A failure, I guess, in more ways than one. Do you know what I would very much like to have right now? Something that would make me very happy? Some money. Then I could pay my wife's medical bills. I'd like to be able to do at least that for her."

I was in tears and wasn't sure why. I felt angry as well as touched—I'd hated the way he kept dragging in Parminter, as though the fellow were all my fault. I turned and ran up the stairs, then down the long corridor to my little back room. When I opened the door, the cold made me gasp. The room was the last in the house to warm up, and tonight the heat had apparently bypassed it altogether. It was freezing, and I undressed quickly, with leaden, trembling fingers.

# 7

The next morning I went to the hospital, and to my surprise Morgan was sitting up in bed reading a magazine called *Equus*. She tossed the magazine aside, and it slid off the bedcover and onto the floor. I picked it up. She said, "Where the hell have you been?" A sprig of holly was pinned to the top of her head scarf.

"What do you mean?" I said. "You know where I've been —I've been at your house."

"I mean, where were you yesterday? You could have come to see me yesterday. I was here all alone all day. *Nobody* came, nobody at all. I said to myself, 'They've written me off. They think I'm already dead. They're all at Christmas parties while I . . .' Well, I've got news for you—I am still among the living."

I was alarmed. Her dark eyes looked so hostile.

"And Douglas! Jesus, some husband he is. Why is it whenever I go to the hospital, he goes away? Can you explain that one? What the hell do you think he's been doing up in Boston anyway, looking up old girl friends? Setting up wife number two? God forbid he should have to spend any time staying with his kids. I wonder how she's going to like the house. Whoever she is. It was my money we bought it with, did you know that? Douglas has never earned tidily. We've been sitting around for years waiting for that dried up old mummy of a grandmother of his to die—you should have seen her establishment, Isabel, you wouldn't have believed it. Honest to God, the last of the Independently Wealthy. She'd sit in her carved Jacobean chair in the living room and beckon at you, you know, with a little arthritic, crooked finger, and you'd go up to her, and she would bend forward ever so slightly and remove a hair from the shoulder of your dress. Awful. Awful woman. And what do you think we'd have for dinner? Canned salmon! In cream sauce, with canned peas. Or sometimes finnan haddie. Those old Boston types—they never let go. She's not dead yet, is she? She won't die until I do. She's going to make me go first." Morgan laughed. "The old bitch! I have to hand it to her. She's outlived everybody." She sighed, exhausted. "My kids okay?"

"They seem all right."

"How's Sarah doing? Is she behaving herself?"

"Yes."

She lay back on the pillow, and the white head scarf slipped slightly. When she reached up a hand to straighten it, the plastic ID bracelet fell halfway down her thin arm. "You have no idea what I went through with Sarah. Sometimes I think to myself that she made me sick. I read a magazine article once, and it said that if you get depressed enough, the depression suppresses your antibodies, and then you get cancer. Well, let me tell you, I was depressed. You don't know, you'll never know, what Sarah did to me." Her dark eyes narrowed; the hostile tone was back.

I said, "Oh, a lot of that stuff they publish is just nonsense, Morgan." I contradicted her bravely, hopefully, but it was obvious now that she was angry, and her anger was like a volcano —all that dammed-up magma, sliding along below the ground looking for a weak place, a flaw in the rock striations.

"And Douglas . . . Have you gotten lots of nice casseroles? Honestly, it's funny, isn't it, but I do think they're lined up out there, waiting for me to pop off."

"Morgan, hey, come on. What *is* this?"

"It's true, Isabel, you don't see it, but I know that even some of my best friends . . ." Her eyes filled with tears.

"Listen, you. This is crazy."

"It's true, just look at Trina. She can't wait to get rid of Ralph. Has she brought over her oatmeal bread? And how about her Irish stew? God! And Lily—he's always had a thing for Lily. And Margaret!" Her head fell to the side and tears slid out of her eyes and down her thin sallow cheeks. "Margaret used to be one of my dearest friends, did you know that?"

I reached forward and took her hand. It was as delicately bony as the skeleton of a little bird. "Hey, Mo-Mo, this is really silly."

"Am I going crazy, Iz? I don't know, everything is so shitty. Oh, ha, that's a joke, on account of my new equipment, see?" She peeled back the covers. There she was, her flesh all snapped into a plastic bag. I was afraid I'd be revolted; instead I was fascinated at how cleverly the thing had been done. "Lovely, what? It'll be an interesting experience, having a love life around this thing." She rearranged the covers around herself. "Maybe that's why I'm a little paranoid, see, I don't trust anyone anymore. I don't even know if I trust you."

I weakly smiled. "Me? Oh, you know me, Morgo, the old *femme fatale*."

"I have this feeling they're all pretending and the truth is they can't wait to get rid of me. I'm a drag, Iz. Who wants to think about dying? Everybody's sick of it, *I'm* sick of it. This all lasts so long, it goes on forever. And the money, all these medical bills. Where's he getting the money from? When I ask, he won't tell me. I'm scared to death he's using the kids' money that we saved for college. I get sicker thinking about it, how we're just buying me time, anyhow. I wish I would just go ahead and die." All the while she was talking she gripped my hand. "Oh, I wanted that house so much, for years, did you know? We saved and saved, and every time we made an offer, they upped the price. And then Richard's little boy needed an operation, in fact five of them, he had this kidney problem—Richard? He's Douglas's brother, he's an Episcopal minister, he doesn't make much money—so we lent them the money we'd saved, and of course they're paying it back, but there went our down payment, and then, of all the luck, my mother died. Do you know what I did when I heard? I laughed. I didn't even care that she'd died; when I got that letter saying that she'd left me some money, I thought, *Good, okay—now we're even.* She left me, and now she has made it even. I didn't care beans about her. Why should I? She left me without a thought. I never would leave my kids, no matter what, no matter how bad things were, or how much I loved someone else. Then, for a while I thought, *This is my punishment because I laughed when my mother died.*"

"Shush, Morgo," I said, "you're getting too upset, you'll make yourself sicker. Anyway, that's a bunch of rot, thinking like that. The way you felt about your mother—well, she deserved it, but it has nothing to do with anything." She was sweating. I took a Kleenex from the box on the nightstand and wiped her face. Her white headdress had slipped again—I tried to straighten it.

"Stop," she said crossly, lifted a hand, and slapped at mine. We both sat in silence. She lay staring at the ceiling. She said at last, "You've been a pretty good friend."

"So-so."

"No, you have been. Pretty good. Only I worry about you."

"Morgan's Problem."

"You have this crazy idea of life. You don't know what life is about."

"I doubt that's true."

"Books. They don't tell you anything about life. The nutty way you were brought up. All that music and"—she made a face—"literature. All that reading. God!"

I smiled and shrugged, feeling foolish. "Well, that's what my parents thought was important."

"Literature!" She smiled, but it turned into an angry, twisted expression. "I'll bet you don't really know what it's like."

"What *what's* like?"

She looked at me. There was an unpleasant smile on her face, the dark eyes mean and full of hatred. I took my hand away from hers. My heart bumped. I dreaded what she was going to say. It would be something humiliating, dangerous. "You don't know anything about life, really. You couldn't even keep poor old Walter interested. You've always been such a prude."

I tried to make a joke of it. "Where do you get your information?"

"And your parents, what a riot that was. That wonderful marriage, all those conversations. I saw through that right away. They never slept together. Did they? They never *touched* each other. All they did was *talk*."

I tried to speak calmly, but my throat was swollen with anger and fear. My voice came out a whisper. "You don't know anything about them."

"Ideas!" she said. "And talk!" She laughed harshly. "How mar-velous! What a roar!" Her laugh careened from r to r like a car out of control. Then she abruptly stopped laughing and looked up at the ceiling. "I wonder if you'll ever learn."

I was silent. I sat in the chair with my hands knitted together and kept my eyes fastened on her black ones. I was afraid if I didn't hold on to her eyes I would drown—she would push me under the water and step on my head.

"Someday you'd better learn—it's in the sack, Isabel, that's where it counts. I always kept Douglas very busy. That's how I kept the whole thing going, you see. Sex is where it's at, my friend. Life isn't so complicated. It's not all that stuff you tried to tell me, all those ideas and poetry. Conversations! Companionship! That was some sort of Jewish idea you had. You Jews have always been good at ideas. Oh, it was always you, Isabel Schliemann, Isabel Schliemann"—her voice mimicked someone, a teacher, someone—"who got the prizes. But what else have you had, Isabel?"

I sat up straight and drew a long, deep breath. I wanted to hit her—this poor, sick wretch who was going to die—and I said, slowly, "What is it you're trying to invent, that we weren't friends? That we aren't now? That we never liked each other and we don't now? Sorry, I won't buy it. Sure, okay, you had the friends and the boyfriends, and I had my books and awards. So what? We were friends then, and we're friends now."

She closed her eyes and said deliberately, "I hate you."

It was like a release. I felt everything inside let go. My hands fell apart, I sat back and asked, idly, curiously, "Why?"

"Because," she said, and opened her eyes. They were full of black tears. "I don't want to die. I hate you because you're going to live. Don't you see? I want to live, too. Please go away, okay? Will you just go away?"

I got up and left the room. I felt stiff all over, in every muscle, as if I'd just gone ten rounds, and indeed, I had. I was exhausted and couldn't yet face going back to the house. The Dodge Colt was in the hospital parking lot, and I slowly drove it downtown.

On Main Street the shop windows had that dismal post-holiday look, although the streetlamps were still wrapped in entwining greens and the Christmas trees were still up and lit. It wasn't even New Year's Eve, but everything seemed shoddy and half-price. In the five-and-dime-store window two girls in blue smocks were pasting up a long sign that said January Sale Days. She had no right, no right at all to say that about my parents. After all, they were dead. At least my mother was. I presumed my father was, too. He would be—I stopped near a barbershop; one of the barbers leaned against the door, reading a newspaper —seventy-five. An old man. He hadn't been a good father, he hadn't been a bad father, only always locked up in his own head along with clouds, castles, cuckoos. Once, when I was eight or nine, he had tried to teach me how to play chess, but when I moved the bishop the wrong way, he had knocked all the pieces off the board with the flat of his hand.

Once, after my mother died, I met my father—quite by accident—in Central Park. It was an early spring day. There were chunks of soot-sprinkled ice melting on the muddy grass banks and puddles that reflected the ragged clouds floating off in the sky. Kids were roller-skating that day, the air was full of birds chirping, red balloons rising, the smell of popcorn. Once a year in the spring I try to memorize a new Rilke poem, and I was sitting on a park bench in the sun working on "Einsamkeit."

> ... *und wenn die Menschen, die einander hassen,*
> *in einem Bett zusammen schlafen müssen ...*
>
> (... and when those people who hate each other
> must sleep together in one bed ...)

I was thinking this over when I heard, "Ahem, ahem," and there was my father. He doffed his hat and gave a slight bow. His ruff of orange hair had turned white.

"Good afternoon, Isabel," he said gravely, as if I were only a slight acquaintance instead of his daughter. He had given up the racetrack togs he had worn when with his girl friend and re-verted to clothes I remembered—a jacket suit, brown with a faint gray stripe, and gray plaid pants that used to have a jacket and vest, as well. He asked if he could sit down. "Why not?" I said. "It's a public bench." He sat down and put his hat down beside him. I could see two old ladies one bench away look meaning-fully at each other over their glasses and crocheting.

He craned his neck to look at my book and beamed. "Ah, Rilke, bravo!" he said and then began to recite in a deep voice, "*Reitet der Ritter in schwarzen Stahl hinaus in die rauschende Welt!*" Uh-huh. The good old German knight on a horse. My mother had a picture of my father in full military uniform, circa 1918, peaked helmet and all, on a horse. Only the little eye-glasses he wore then didn't seem terribly Teutonic. "So. At least I gave you a good education, what?" He leaned back against the bench, folded his arms upon his chest, and closing his eyes, tilted his face up to the sun. I thought how like him that was, taking credit for my education, as if he'd single-handedly raised me. Instead, of course, he and his girl friend had run off with my college tuition money.

He asked me what I was doing. I said, turning my head

slightly away from him, that I was teaching English in a girls' private school. He had on a horrid gray shirt two sizes too big for him around the neck. His powder-blue tie was spotted in three places, his brown shoes were scuffed at the toes. My mother wouldn't have let him go out the door like that.

He started talking, rambling on. I didn't pay close attention. I was planning my getaway, what I would say, a crushing remark, perhaps. "She was so gentle for an uneducated person," he said, "so refined. She had a wonderful sensitivity. She wasn't, of course, a very good cook, and her housekeeping left much to be desired. Nevertheless, we had many deep talks and marvelous conversations." I thought he was talking about my mother. He wasn't. He was talking about his girl friend.

I'd seen her one day, an unattractive woman, I thought, with straggly dark hair that was neither black nor red, but both. She had dark skin and brown moles on her face, a long nose, small eyes too close together. I thought she looked a little simple, perhaps even demented. She wore a fringed head scarf and a black cotton skirt that dipped down to her ankles. And sneakers. When I saw her, she was slip-slapping down Third Avenue, smiling to herself. Then I saw my father, coming around the corner. He wore a bright plaid jacket and a hat. He didn't see me. I ducked into a doorway and pretended to be studying names on mailboxes. "Ida, Ida," he called after her, "Ida, you forgot by the butcher's your handbag, *Liebchen,* he telephoned."

"Unfortunately," my father went on now, "America ruined her fine character. She came here a poor, simple girl, and then it began. First with the clothes and cosmetics, then jewelry and nail polish. Perfume, even. High heels and fancy dresses. Gossip magazines she was crazy about." One day, when he had made an appointment with the ophthalmologist, she had come with a hired van and removed everything, even the bed. Now he lived by himself in a rooming house. He wondered if, was it possible, perhaps, could he move in with me? He was so lonely. He wasn't well now. He needed someone to take care of him. He sat up straight and began to cry. He took a crumpled gray handkerchief out of his pants pocket, tipped up his thick black-rimmed glasses, wiped his eyes.

I stood up and walked away.

# 8

I stood at the plate glass window of the country club's warming hut and watched Sarah skate. The plate glass was covered with chicken wire, a precaution against flying hockey pucks, and out in the center of the open rink a pretty fifteen-year-old girl, long gold hair flying, seemed to be trying to fling herself to death on the ice. She had on faded blue jeans, patched at the seat, and a bright-green ski sweater that had a navy blue stripe across the shoulders. After every fall she would sit a minute, dazed, and then get up, thrust a toe pick into the ice, tug the sweater stubbornly downward, and start the movement all over again. It was some sort of jump. She steeply bent her left knee, made an odd yearning upward movement with her arms, flew up, turned in mid-air, and crashed. Ouch. I winced as she fell again. She sat on the ice with her knees apart and pounded her gloved fist upon it. At last she stood up and skated off, clumped up the wooden ramp on her toe picks, opened the door of the shed, and glared at me. "What are you doing here?" she said. "What's going on? I suppose my father sent you snooping after me."

"No, I was going shopping and thought you might like to come."

She shrugged and sat down on the wooden bench under the window, her hands planted on her knees. "I guess I'm not having a very good day. It probably wouldn't be any good for shopping, either."

"What was that thing you were trying to do? It looked complicated."

"It's not. It's just a loop jump, any idiot can do it."

"I certainly couldn't do it."

"You don't figure skate."

"True. Still, I think you must be a pretty good skater. You look right on the ice."

"Baloney! I stink! I'm terrible!"

"If you feel that way, then why go out and torture yourself? Are you doing this for competition, or what?"

"Competition! You're incredible, Isabel. Why would *I* be competing? I'm no good. I can't do anything right."

I sat down on the bench next to her, a polite two feet away. She picked at the skate laces and sent them flying—*whisk! whisk!*—out of the grommets. Her cheeks were pink, her green eyes icy with tears. There was a fieldstone fireplace built into the shed's opposite wall, and now a tall black-haired boy with an acne-scarred face came out of the other room. Looking at Sarah from under his jumbled black eyebrows, he began poking up the fire. He threw in a split log—gray ash flew in all directions. Sarah glanced up, frowned, looked down again. " 'Lo, Sare," he said. The boy's look seemed to crawl feebly across the floor, stop, retreat.

" 'Lo," she mumbled.

"You were pretty good out there."

She bit her lip. "Thanks."

"You gonna be in the show this year?"

"No."

"No? Why not?"

"Oh, for heaven's sake, I'm too old for that kind of thing."

He laughed. "Ha, ha, yeah, I guess you are. You're getting old, all right." He turned his back to us, and the tops of his ears flamed up, bright red. On the walls on both sides of the fireplace were framed photographs of hockey teams and a sign clumsily lettered in red felt-tip pen, *Will thief who took my new Bauer hockey skates return same to locker room, no questions asked.*

"Where were you planning to go shopping?" Sarah asked. She had both skates off and her feet stuck into fur-lined boots.

"I thought we might go to Loehmann's, just to look."

"Loehmann's! I hate that place. All those strange women in their bulges and underwear."

"I just thought we could start there. I know it's not very *luxe* . . . as they say in *Vogue*."

Silence. She looked into space, linked her hands across the back of her neck, and pulled her head up hard, eyes fiercely closed. She let go and pounded her knee with her fist. "Why, why, why can't I do it?"

"Okay," I said, "let's go. You've got to learn when to quit and think about something else. Another day, tomorrow or next week, you'll get up and do it. It'll be a cinch, like finding a little key. The whole thing'll unlock, and you won't even remember how hard it was. Who taught you to skate, your mother?"

"Yes. And Paul."

"Paul?"

She bent and picked up the skates and tied the laces together. "Paul Caron," she said sullenly. "He was a friend of my parents. He died."

"Yes, I've heard of him."

She stood up, slinging the skates over her shoulder, and said in a low voice, "I'm sick of everything. I wish I could go away to school. I'm sick of this awful town and the people in it."

"We can get as far as Loehmann's," I said, "but you'll have to show me how to get there."

She clumped along behind me—she had neglected to zip her boots—and then, as I pushed the door open, she squeezed through ahead of me and said tauntingly over her shoulder, "He taught me lots of things."

I asked absentmindedly (I was looking back at the dark-haired, lanky boy whose glance followed us so wistfully), "Who?"

"Paul," she said. Her green eyes narrowed. She smiled,

knelt, zipped her boots, and skipped off like a naughty kid down the long slope that led to the parking lot. I poked my way carefully down the slope—it was coated with ice, runoff from the ice-grooming machines. When I got to the car, she was sitting in the front seat, slumped down, feet up on the dashboard. I got in and started the Dodge. It always made a terrible racket starting, as if a chunk of metal had been caught in a Mixmaster.

"You don't believe me, do you?" She was teasingly smiling again. Now she had both feet up on the edge of the seat, and sat with her arms wrapped around her legs.

"About what?"

"About me and Paul. You don't believe it, do you? That we got it on together."

"Indeed. When you were how old? Ten?"

"I was thirteen but mature for my age."

I made a disbelieving sound.

"So," she said lightly, "you *don't* believe it."

"I don't believe you were mature for your age."

She laughed. I backed the car out of the lot. "Good for you, Isabel," she said. "You certainly are getting harder to throw. It's not true. I just wanted to shock you. You're always so shockable."

"Ah, but I'm learning," I said.

"Yes," she said, "but no doubt you'll always be a prude. Don't you believe in sex?"

"Not on all occasions."

"Actually," she said, sliding her legs down and stretching them out, "I did try to seduce him, but he wouldn't." I was at the country club gates now, looking to the left for a break in traffic. I swung the car out into the lane, and it roared into second, chuckled into third.

"Actually," she said, linking her hands behind her head and smiling, "that was another lie."

"Don't you ever tell the truth?" I asked.

"What for?" she said. "It's never done me any good." She sat up straight and looked out the window.

I decided that conversation with Sarah was impossible, full of dead ends and blind alleys. On the other hand the very last thing she'd said had sounded true. I glanced at her. Her profile was bleak, a sad little girl, a little old lady. All these guises and disguises she adopted were wearying, but for her as much as for everyone else. How had Morgan, who was so honest and straightforward, produced this baffling child?

A few nights before, Sarah had told me she had no girl friends. She didn't like girls, she said, they were jealous and bitchy. We were alone in the kitchen. She had come downstairs after dinner and picked at the leftover salad. I had asked her if she liked boys. "Some," she'd said, "but I never sleep with boys I like." I had said the first thing that came to mind: "Oh, how sad!" I wondered now if that meant she slept with all the other boys. High school boys? My memories of high school boys made me smile—sweat and acne and fumbles and bubble gum and good Lord, maybe Paul Caron wasn't a bad idea.

"What are you smiling about?" she asked.

"I was thinking about the boys I knew when I was your age."

"Did you date a lot?"

"I had a couple of boyfriends. One boy I liked a whole lot. Then his mother moved, and he disappeared."

"Do you think about him?"

"Yes, I do. Though I don't know why."

"Were you . . ."—she hesitated—"in love with him?"

"That's the really odd thing. I wasn't, and I treated him badly, and now, after all these years, I think of him a lot. My punishment, I guess. I suppose we all tend to do that—revise the past, make a myth out of our own histories. I'll bet if I had a chance to see it happen on some giant movie screen in the sky, it would be horrendously boring. All those dumb dates we had, and God, we were both so serious."

She smiled and shrugged. "Kids are different now. Nobody's serious."

"Really? Oh, we were. We were serious about everything.

That's why it feels so funny—even though we weren't in love—to have someone like that drop out of your life."

"I hate that," she said.

"What?"

"The way people just disappear."

She had directed me to a strange two-lane back road, downtrodden New Jersey country, scrubby woods, miserable dead fields, little houses that looked like converted chicken coops with yards full of old car parts, steel barrels, tires, junk. We passed a fat-fendered Chevrolet painted a gummy pink, sitting wheelless in the frozen mud.

"There was a boy I liked a whole lot in my science class last year. I was good at science, and so was he. We used to do the lab work together, and we had a lot of fun trying to stump each other. I really worked hard for a while. I'd memorize all that stuff, the enzyme processes, you know, and how glucose is converted to fructose, and the part of the year we did astronomy, I did this paper on pulsars. I did a lot of extra work and started reading *Scientific American*. By the end of the year we were neck and neck for the science prize. Then it hit me that if I won it, he wouldn't like me, and worse than that, I wouldn't like him."

"Because you'd won out over him?"

"Yeah. Silly, right? But that's the way I felt."

"What happened?"

"It was weird—I just lost interest. I got a C on the final exam, and he got the prize. Then one night last summer we were in the Napoli, it's this pizza place over on Center Street. I was there with a couple of kids and he was at the next table with this girl, Judy Daley, and he looked over at me and he said to Judy in a loud voice, 'There's the town slut.' You have to turn left down here, at the stop sign."

I came to a stop and made the turn. There was a white clapboard church across the highway, with a gracefully lettered sign that said Hillsdale Presbyterian Church, 1820. I thought life might have been easier for girls in 1820. Maybe, maybe not.

The double bind has always been with us. I said, "That sure is a setup, isn't it? The usual no-win situation. If you don't, you're cold, if you do, you're a slut. Besides, he wouldn't have liked you any better if you'd won the prize."

"I might have liked myself better. I just quit. I seem to quit on a lot of things. Sometimes nothing seems very worthwhile. I don't know what I'm going to do. I sure don't want to get married."

"Why do you say that? Because of one boy?"

"No, because it seems like such a drag. I mean, I don't want to spend my life raising kids. My mother did it, but I wonder if she really liked it. I don't think it turned out to be what she thought."

"Many things don't. There are a lot of boring jobs out there."

"I don't want to have a job, either. At least not a job kind of job. Last year, when I was working hard for the science prize, I really enjoyed it. I always worked hard when I was a little kid. I read a lot and was good at schoolwork, believe it or not."

"I remember you were. What happened?"

"I don't know exactly. Things just started to go downhill. For one thing, my father seemed mad at me all the time. Whatever I did was wrong. It got so even Tess noticed it—not that she didn't enjoy it. And my mother just kept out of the way. She'd walk out of the room."

"When was all this?"

"A couple of years ago, when I was twelve, thirteen. Anyway, it made me feel helpless. Like no one was ever on my side. It made me furious, mad at both of them. I'd do awful things, go pick at my face, or throw things. Once I got a tweezer and started pulling out my pubic hair, one hair at a time."

"Ouch," I said. "Didn't that hurt?"

"I didn't get all that far. Later my father went into another phase—he just ignored me. Wouldn't fight with me, but he wouldn't talk to me much, either. That's when"—she bit her lip—"I started, you know, going out with guys who were older and"—she shrugged—"stuff like that. It's funny, all that time he was yelling so much at me, it was as if he couldn't yell at my mother. They weren't getting along too well at the time."

"Then things got better."

"I don't really know. The trouble with my parents is you can't really tell. I guess my feeling, my honest-to-God gut feeling, is that things weren't really all that terrific, and my mother wanted to buy the new house to sort of, you know, pull it all together again."

"Well," I said, "so it goes. People have ups and downs, even married people. Are you planning to go to college somewhere close by?"

"As far away as I can get, if I can get in somewhere. My marks are pretty bad. Maybe it's too late."

"Oh, wow, why too late? What are you, sixty?"

She shook her head. "No, but it really makes you wonder. I mean, I keep thinking about how just when things were getting better for my mom and dad, you know, when they finally got the house and everything, this happened. Well, heck, it does seem so pointless."

"Tell me what you'd do if you didn't think everything was pointless?"

She turned and laughed at me. "Oh, gosh, I don't know. I'd like to do some sort of biology in college. The life sciences. Maybe medical school, but I don't want to treat sick people. I'd like to do research of some kind."

"Then why not do it?"

"I don't know if I'm smart enough."

"I think you are. You're smart enough to fool me most of the time."

"Fun-ny."

"Serves you right."

"You know, Isabel, my mother really does admire you. When I was small, she'd talk about you all the time. Sometimes I got the feeling that she thought she was, oh, dull."

"Dull? That's incredible. Your mother was more fun than

anybody. She was the kind of person who kept everybody going, you know? I'd be feeling kind of dumpy and down, and she'd walk in and say, 'Okay, snap out of it, we're hitchhiking to New Haven.'"

Sarah's eyes smiled. "My mother was so great when we were small. We really did fantastic fun things. She was always thinking up stuff for us to do. She always wanted me to read, though, maybe because of my dad. She wanted him to be proud of us."

We came to the shopping center, and I pulled into the lot. As we walked to the store the wind blew mashed Dairy Queen cups around our feet. Sarah scuffed along, looking down at the ground, with her gloved hands in her jean pockets. She looked tired, and older than she was.

"What's the matter?" I said. "Do you want to go someplace else?"

"It isn't that," she said. The winter sun came out for a moment and shone in her eyes. "All the time we were talking about my mother . . ."

"Uh-huh."

"We used the past tense. We were talking about her in the past tense."

When we came out, it was snowing, and Sarah hadn't bought a thing.

# 9

I went back to the city on Sunday, a grimly cold New Year's day, and the next Thursday night, exactly on time, David rang the door buzzer. I let him in. He sat down, still with his camel's hair coat on. His brown eyes seemed opaque. He loosely knit his hands across his lap. "And how've you been?" he politely inquired.

"Fine, thanks," I said. He sat looking up and down the yellow walls of my apartment, to see what was new, what was gone.

He said, "You've got a new calendar."

"Yes. It's a new year."

"I mean, it's a different type. Last year it was great masterworks of art, and the year before that, composers. This year it's . . ."—he squinted at the wall over my desk—"*The Classicist's Almanac.* I didn't know you were interested in antiquity."

"It's not mine. I mean, it wasn't mine. The Whitesides had several, and I took it because I didn't have one yet, and sometimes in January it's hard to find calendars." I was nervously babbling.

"How is your friend doing?"

"Only so-so. She's home now. They have a nurse for her, part time."

He sat on the sofa, I sat in a comb-back Windsor chair I had bought on Bleecker Street. It has an uncomfortable high wooden seat, and the carved out depressions have never seemed to fit my lower body. I always meant to make a cushion for it. Sitting there, I was higher up than he, and I felt like a teacher in an old-fashioned country school looking down from her platform at the star pupil: He always arrives early, he gets his work done first, he always gets an A, but she dislikes him anyway. I smiled and leaned back and folded my arms. No good. I felt like a corpse propped up in a coffin. I leaned forward, planted my hands on my knees—the old lumberjack motif. There must be some way to sit. I sat up straight and put my arms on the thin arms of the chair—the electric-chair image came swiftly to mind. Any moment now twenty thousand volts would sizzle me blue.

"And how are you, David?"

"Oh, getting along, getting along. Everything's going well. Business is incredible—just skyrocketing." He smiled at me broadly. I smiled, too. *Go ahead. Tell me about your dough.* "And the kids are well, finally adjusting to the divorce. Except for poor Andrew, of course. And Louise is, well, Louise."

"I'm glad about the kids."

"Sure. Now that there's no point."

"No point?"

"To the divorce."

"David, don't do this. I thought we'd agreed . . ."

"Of course, I'm sorry, sure." He raised one hand, a square, likable hand, honest, capable. "Listen. It just does seem . . ."— said cheerfully, logically—"ridiculous."

"What does?"

"The way you live. I mean, you're going to be thirty-seven in the spring. What I mean to say is, I don't know what the hell you're getting out of your life. You don't particularly like your job and it pays peanuts. You love to travel and you can't. I don't know, by gosh, how you pay your rent."

"I'm getting along. It's nice of you to be concerned."

"And your writing."

"What about it?"

"I thought you were going to work on a book this year."

"I have some ideas."

"Aha. But not written down, am I right? Oh, look, I understand. There's no time, is there? You don't get home until six, six thirty, you're tired. I understand. But it strikes me as ridiculous, Isabel. You like me. I know you like me, and I love you and I can take care of you. You could do whatever you wanted, write, whatever. There's no reason for you to live like this, is there? Unless there's a reason."

"Meaning what?"

"Meaning the usual reason."

I was by this time truly exasperated, and I stood up. "I'll be right back. I'm out of coffee."

"I'll go, sit still."

"No, I'll go, I need the air." I was afraid if I didn't get out I would hit him. I should never have let him in. I did so with the idea that we would be civilized. Civilized! What does it mean? The saber-toothed tiger stuffed into camel's hair. Threaten me and I'll kill you. Back, with a jar of instant coffee in a little paper bag, I felt better, more in control—my cheeks rosy, my temper cooled. He still wore his coat. He had put on the lamp and was calmly reading *The New York Review of Books*. I hadn't read it in months. It piled up next to the sofa, waiting for me, letting me know my mind was shriveling as the pile grew higher.

"Oh, instant?" he asked, surprised, when I took the jar of coffee out of the bag. "What happened to the coffee grinder I gave you?"

I said, "It's at the back of the closet. It broke."

"Really? That soon? Did you save the warranty card? Maybe I should look at it."

"Not right now. It would take me half an hour to find it."

"Oh," he said and looked down at the paper spread out on his lap. "Now here is an interesting article on penology. Have you read it?"

"No."

"I must make a note of this, in case I ever need a good warden." He reached inside his coat and took out a little notebook and a ball-point pen. He frowned, wrote something down on the page, tucked the notebook away, and said, "Why is it you switched to instant?"

"I haven't really switched to instant. I just don't have a coffeepot at the moment."

"You don't? Why not?"

"I took mine out to the Whitesides last week because I don't like theirs. Then I forgot to bring it back with me."

"Really? Left in a hurry, did you? I'll get you a new one tomorrow, have them send it. Better yet, I could drop it off myself. Then take you to dinner."

"David. For heaven's sake."

"It's no trouble, really. I'm going to Bloomingdale's to-morrow anyway."

"You loathe Bloomingdale's."

"I don't mind."

"Don't, okay?"

He folded up *The New York Review* and threw it aside and said, suddenly angry, "That stupid pea jacket you wear! And blue jeans. Why is it you can't dress like a woman? You're thirty-seven years old, Isabel, and you're still wearing jeans."

"I'm not thirty-seven yet, not until May. I *like* jeans."

"After thirty-seven comes forty, my dear. You are behaving in a thoroughly stupid way. I know you, Isabel. I know you want to have children and some sort of life other than . . ." His hand drew a contemptuous circle around my room.

"I don't care! I don't care! Listen, David, we agreed that it was all over. Now, if you can't be pleasant . . ."

"I'm being very pleasant. You're the one whose voice is raised."

It was true, my voice had climbed to a screech. I turned and went to the kitchenette. Hand shaking, I poured boiling water over the freeze-dried grains of something or other, what-ever it was, I didn't care, I didn't care. I started toward him carrying the coffee mug and then noticed that a triangle of white paper stood up out of my desk drawer, a warning pennant that signaled mischief. The drawer was somewhat ajar, as if someone had shut it in haste. I went to the desk, opened the drawer, shoved in the paper, took out a coaster, and placed it under the mug. My statement from Saks, that was all. What was he look-ing for, love letters? I brought the coffee to him and placed it on the table next to the sofa. I didn't sit down. Looking at him—that kind, white-skinned face, and the dark-brown hair so care-fully parted, I felt, one by one, the bars come down on my life—my checkbooks, my bills, my letters—slam! Let me take care of you.

"And," he said, going on with whatever he'd been saying

(I hadn't been listening, adrenaline had surged into my ears), "it suddenly occurred to me that the fellow in your second book" —*here it comes,* I thought; I was still standing up, ready for it—"reminded me a lot of that Whiteside fellow. Just, you know, very generally speaking, he was very much the way you described . . . I can't remember the character's name. What was it?"

"I don't remember." I was still in my pea coat, my hands holding on to the back of the Windsor chair.

"And how is he holding up?"

"Who?"

"Whiteside. Douglas, isn't it?"

"Yes. Well, it's hard."

"Yes. Though they're certainly fortunate, both of them, to have such a good friend in you." I studied him intently. He went on. "The way you go out to care for everything, the kids, the house. The night I came out, I marveled at how domestic the two of you seemed." His eyes were no longer opaque. They seemed instead to have concentrated into two yellow pinpoints of light.

"No one asked you to come out." It was the wrong thing to say.

"Yes, indeed, it's generous of you to give up your time to go out . . ."

"Don't go on, David."

"And a wonderful thing for those kids to see, really."

"What?"

"Their mother in one room dying, and you in the next, screwing their father."

I picked up the wooden chair in both hands and threw it at him. I saw him raise one arm to shield his face, and then, across slats and rungs, I heard something like a roar and he was at me. He wrenched me toward him by the arm and slapped my head. I tried to hit his face. He took me by the bunched-up pea coat and shook me and then, with a look that twisted his face, flung me away, toward the floor. I fell on my shoulder and my cheek.

193

I heard the door slam. I lay on the floor and I heard myself moaning and then I began to cry. I was crying not because I felt bad but because I felt better. I was glad he had hit me, I deserved it. I got up at last and staggered to the bathroom and looked in the cabinet mirror. It was flawed at about where my chin appeared and always made me feel ugly—Isabel of the Giant Jaw. Now I looked ludicrous. There was a lump on my cheekbone the size of a plum; my eyes were puffed and red and I had another bruise I couldn't remember getting on my forehead. I looked like what I felt like—The Old Whore. Something out of Hogarth's Gin Lane. Thirty-six and still screwing around. No. It wasn't like that. I'd slept with Douglas because I loved him.

# 10

Driving home from Loehmann's that Friday with Sarah, I'd skidded once, badly, in the new snow. By Saturday morning when I came downstairs, the house lay in white as if becalmed in a blinding fog. Douglas was standing at the kitchen window (why is it I always see him this way? his back to me, his hands in his pockets), and he said without turning around, "It's not going to let up." He had on a turtleneck and over that a heavy knit sweater of blue-gray wool, the same cool color as his eyes. He glanced at me over his shoulder. "Morristown radio station says the Erie-Lackawanna is an hour behind schedule—there's a tie-up at Newark. You could walk down to the station, anyway, I s'pose. Might take a while for the train to come. Might have to wait a good spell." He was being humorous, this lapse into quaint New England speech.

"You're not going out to Far Hills?"

"Don't see how I can, do you? We could toboggan out of

the drive, but the street hasn't been cleared. They're just starting to work on the roads." Far off in the distance, through the heavy, noise-obliterating snow, there was a deep, sporadic thunder—the plows. "I think what we ought to do is have a snow day. We'll get out there and shovel snow—it'll be good for everybody."

Sarah appeared in the doorway in a long pink bathrobe like an extended sweatshirt, with a hood and side pockets. "Hey, everybody, what great luck! I have a big English test scheduled for Tuesday, but I bet we don't get to have it—old Melon Head lives in the sticks. He'll never make it in."

"I wouldn't count on it," I said. "The roads will be nicely cleared by Tuesday, I'm sure. What're you reading?" She held a book in her hands.

*"The Mystery of Edwin Drood."*

"You're reading that for English class? But Dickens didn't finish it."

"I know," she said, "he died." Her tone was ironic.

"Dammit," Douglas said, "is that the TV on already? Eddie? Hey, Ed, shut that thing off and come in here." He turned to Sarah. "Where's Tess?"

"Still in bed," Sarah said. "She's got another stomachache."

"She can work it off," Douglas said. "We're all going to shovel snow."

"But there's no point in shoveling snow," Sarah said. "It's still coming down."

"It'll be good for all of us," Douglas said. "That is the point."

I, too, understood the point of the day. It was as if we had a silent agreement, Douglas and I, to give the kids a holiday, not just from routine but from the eroding pressures of illness and death. The snow kept falling, and we kept shoveling. We built a large fire in the living room and at lunchtime, standing around the kitchen in our socks, had that old grammar school favorite, canned tomato soup and grilled cheese sandwiches. In the middle of the afternoon Tess and I made taffy and baked apples in foil, right in the fireplace. Suddenly at half past three the snow let up and at four the sun—majestic Apollo—appeared streaming orange and purple drifts of clouds—a fiery chariot, indeed —and rattled off into the west, trailing a spectacular winter sunset that coated the snow pink and left the sky full of tattered festal banners—purple, gray, aqua, salmon. We roasted hot dogs in the fireplace for supper, made popcorn, played Parcheesi, and drank cocoa and Scotch, and the light of the fire kept the winter dark at bay in the corners. Twice that evening I heard Tess laugh, and Sarah, with Noxzema on her face, sat curled up in the chair reading. I wanted to ask Douglas, *Is this what it's like, having a family? Is it always like this?* I had grown up so much by myself. A friend of my mother's once said, "You're really odd people. Evenings you sit all alone in various rooms and read." I had never noticed that until she said so. After the children had gone to bed, I said to Douglas, "Is this what it's usually like?"

He was reading a journal. I turned my head to look at the title. *History*. He said, "Usually when?"

I felt confused. It seemed to me that anything I said would now be tactless. "I meant, is this the way things usually are? With the kids."

"You mean before Morgan got sick?"

"Yes."

He turned a page. "No," he said and went on reading. I got up and took some glasses and plates into the kitchen. I thought I'd gotten used to him, but often he seemed to me the coldest of men. What was it he was thinking about? I'd watch him sometimes out of the corner of my eye. He appeared to be reading, but in fact he was studying the floor. Was he thinking about Morgan, life, death, what? It occurred to me standing there in the kitchen that I'd never heard him laugh. I rinsed the dishes and put them into the dishwasher. He came into the kitchen and filled up the teakettle.

"Like some tea?" he asked. By way, I guess, of apology for being abrupt.

I shook my head no and left the room. I went into the study with a glass of Scotch and settled down on the leather sofa with a paperback book that had lost its cover and was thus stamped on the first page, *Property of Essex Academy*. It was an anthology of short stories, the very same ones I'd read in the eighth grade, "The Lady or the Tiger," "The Diamond Necklace." As if nothing had been written for the past twenty-five years. He came into the library with a steaming mug in his hand that smelled strongly of rum. "Mind if I watch TV?" I stood up. "You don't have to leave," he said.

"I think I'll go play a record," I said.

I went into the living room and looked at their record collection—all the classical records were old, the dog-eared jackets marked *Morgan O'Malley*. They were from Music II, a Listener's Appreciation Course, which Morgan and I had taken together at college. I remembered sitting in the stuffy little listening room in the Music Building charting out the themes of Mozart's Fortieth, and Morgan saying, "Is this the bridge? Wait a minute, no, here's the bridge . . . or is it?" Da da dee, da dee dee, da dee da dum. Funny how Mozart turns some sort of key in me with a terrible wrench. I lay down in front of the fire—da dee dee, da dee dee, da dee da dum—and fell asleep. When I woke up, the room was cold, the fire out except for a glowing red splinter of wood. The stereo had shut itself off. I went to the study—the TV was off but the light still on—to say good night. How carefully, how very carefully we had politely acted out our roles all day. He was sitting in the leather chair with his head back and his eyes closed. He opened his eyes— they were red-rimmed, otherwise as colorless as mirrors.

"What?"

"I said, 'Good night.' "

He stood up and came toward me and took my hand and led me up the stairs. At his room—their room—I shook my head and drew my hand away. He reached for my hand again and firmly took it and led me down the long corridor to the little back room where I slept. He opened the door, closed it behind us, locked it. The room was filled with blue light, and the window mullions were lined with heaped-up snow. We kissed each other with greedy force, the bones of our mouths gnawing. In my mind I saw us as two skulls, two ravenous souls come upon each other in the desert, a cool desert of blue snow, and I had a sudden odd image, as if the crack of yellow light under the door were a shaft of desert sun and the door made of stone. I could hear the excited workmen talking in a language that was written in curlicues, and the door—slowly, slowly—being pushed back, the beetles scattering away from the light. Our clothes fell away at a touch, as if they were ancient bandages, and his skin burned and felt cool all at once. We made love swiftly and silently, and neither one of us said a word. Lying under him, with my arms around him and his face buried in my shoulder, I shifted my hips and turned my face to the window. How blue the snowy night was. It was Sunday morning—*Voskrasenya!*—New Year's day. He moved off me and then turned on his side and tucked me into him sideways. We slept. When he left, I woke up suddenly. I had had a dream that I'd somehow been careening down a deep, treacherous, icy river.

In the morning I got up early and left. I walked to the railroad station, occasionally switching the suitcase from my left hand to my right. The streets were plowed, snowbanks piled high on either side. In my haste I had left behind my electric perk pot and my expensive new blouse, still in its Saks bag in the bottom of the closet. I wore a scarf over my head and boots and with my suitcase in my hand felt like one of those blurred, sad, hurrying figures from a black-and-white newsreel out of the 1940s—Isabel the Refugee. I had managed—at last—to fall in love, and I wearily foresaw that it would be a psychic disaster.

# IV

March
Elegy

# 1

Dear Isabel. How are you today?

Thank you, I am rotten.

Well, sure you are. Of course. And you deserve it.

Go away.

You always thought, didn't you, that you were "basically" a good person, that your instincts were sound. Didn't you?

Yes.

Other people were cruel, indifferent, schizoid, perverted. Other people were corrupt, greedy, cold, lustful. You didn't understand. You thought your instincts were good—then how could evil grow out of what you felt to be so right, like a shadow on the heart's brightness? Do you understand now?

Yes.

And what do you think of yourself now?

Go away.

You fell in love—*Ich liebe dich*—you fell in love and went to bed with your dying friend's husband. She had asked from you some small tasks of friendship—a little kindness, a little care, a little love—a few things she never much had.

It doesn't matter.

No? Why not?

He doesn't love me.

Of course he doesn't. But tell me something, do you feel worse because he doesn't love you or because she is dying? You sit here day after day, sit in the dark with your hands before you on the scarred oak table. You sit here waiting for her to die. Do you think he will call you then? Foolish Isabel. A part of you is waiting for her to die, and a part of you says inside your head, God, no! Come. Get up. Go to bed. Do you have a sleeping pill? There's a good girl. Poor Isabel. *Du Hure.*

I wasn't functioning well, and was deeply depressed. I got up in the morning, put on my clothes, went to work. I felt numb, so passive and unalert that it was a clear wonder to me when I safely arrived uptown—as if I were invisible, I seemed suddenly to attract shoves, pokes, nudges, umbrella stabs, shopping-bag slaps. People seemed not to see me, things (on the other hand) took on a menacing, judgmental air. They *knew.* The door of any conveyance—subway, bus—unfolded in my face with a reptilian hiss; elevators shot past me. At work I locked myself up in my little cubicle, and even Joan stayed away. She looked at me with blue eyes narrowed in anger. She wanted to tell me about her love life—I had turned deaf. I couldn't respond. I sat at my desk shuffling papers with trembling fingers under the faulty fluorescent desk lamp. Every fifteen minutes it would flicker and buzz, and you would have to snap it into obedience with a hard flick. Now I didn't hear—I let it buzz on. Always, about four in the afternoon, I would fall asleep at the desk, my head on my arms, and wake up at five with a painful crick in my neck. At home I sat in the dark at the oak table and looked out at the city lights scattered hopelessly about the courtyard. Lights at the dead end of a tunnel. I started taking Elavil and went around feeling goofy and strung-out, as cheerful as if I were walking a wire high up over the city. Something in the drug made me overreact—I developed a blissful indifference to my own mortality. I gave up Elavil. At home, in bed, I would wake up at three and stay awake until six. I had no interest in food. The brass snap on my jeans hung down below my navel.

Weekends, without another human soul to interrupt my more or less mad reveries, I went from Friday to Monday without speaking, eating, hardly sleeping. I would sit at the oak table, picking at the poor dried geranium leaves or simply staring, thinking and thinking, thoughts going round and round, trying to figure things out. Isabel of the Trained Intellect. Rational Isabel! Hadn't I been taught by my intellectual parents that reason controls emotion? Hadn't I read a thousand copies of *Psychology Today*? I knew if I could think clearly, I could stop deluding myself and end this so-called love I thought I felt for a man who . . . who . . . who . . . My thoughts had begun to stutter. "So you see, Morgan . . ." (Can you believe it? I talked to her every morning at three A.M. after I'd woken up, terrified, from one grisly dream or another.) ". . . see how successful I am. I have gotten prizes. I have written books. The only thing I haven't had is the one thing that matters most." Of course I still had my writing. Or did I?

The sad truth is that all my life I have been a writer. I remember sitting at a little table my parents bought for me when I was three. My mother, hopefully didactic, had pasted decals of the alphabet along the sides of the table. I sat there in my plaid sunsuit surrounded by letters and feeling angry, oh, furiously angry, that I couldn't read the words, didn't know the letters. I thought that someday, in revenge, I would write my own stories. When I was four, Miss Parsley, my kindergarten teacher, printed on the back of my candy-pink report card under *Teacher's Comments* (she had wonderful printing, the backs of the *m*'s and *n*'s ruler straight and the pouter-pigeon chests of these letters dipping in with an artful curve as if corseted), *The class loves to hear Isabel tell stories at story hour.*

And summer camp! Year after year I invented ghost stories—they got gorier as I grew older: heads rolled down stairways, the arteries still spurting blood; forests contained trees full of plucked, watchful eyes. Poe's heart—*thump, thump*—beat within my own.

But to write, don't you see, it's not just the words; first you need images, something beyond the blindingly white blizzard that raged between my ears. And you need feelings. My feelings were dead. Only the words kept coming, the lunatic printer inside my head never let up, his dirty fingernails and ink-smeared pocketed apron, his face with its death-tinge—blue-gray, his mouth full of bad, blackened teeth that grinned at me as he jumbled the type in its racks. Words kept coming: lachrymose, saccharine, carcinogen. Sin-again, vulture, vulpine. Douglas, Doug, dug. Grave, death, glass. Cut, sharp, bleed. Hurt, ache, pain.

. ; I had no feelings. I felt that I was wood—no, clay—and that life was changing, moving, surging all around me, and it left me untouched; that I was no longer living but something old, immutable, an artifact uncovered by some cheery yellow-painted bulldozer or backhoe in some deep, fenced-off hole-in-the-ground in midtown Manhattan—something thrust up through stone and clay and layers of other lifetimes, that I was, however, immensely fragile, and perhaps any second now I would crumble into reddish dust and be borne away by an East River breeze, as the Little Fir Tree in the Hans Christian Andersen story dissolved into smoke and drifted off into the sun. I woke up every morning thinking, *What am I good for?* The uselessness of my life appalled me. I had always thought of love, loving, being in love, as renewal, a resurrection—*Voskrasenya* —of the spirit. I felt dead.

I began to have strange thoughts. I began to imagine if I prayed—I hadn't prayed since I was ten—to some Higher Being, He would—Sydney Carton style—strike me dead and save Morgan. I would even things up! Her life, anyway, was ever so much more productive than mine. I thought of ways of killing myself—the slit-wrist bit, the head in the gas oven. If I tried a gun, I would no doubt fail, as I am hopeless with mechanical objects. I had a terrible dread of fumbling the event and having everyone say later, behind their hands, "She just wanted attention." Besides, down very deep inside me there was a tiny pellet of something, a grain no bigger than a mustard seed, that I pictured as if buried in very dense, solidly frozen earth. It was still alive, a promising bright yellow-green, and I thought that when winter was over, toward the end of March when spring came, it would sprout roots, and a quickening life would thrust up through still-cold clods into lemon-pale sunshine. Poor little seed! I guess you are called "hope," the last little trinket in Pandora's box. It was buried there somewhere inside me, so I didn't kill myself but went on, the robot, the automaton, Igneous Isabel, getting through every day of my so-called life.

# 2

In February a gray cold set in with iron force. It wasn't the sparkling kind of winter cold I remembered from my mythic childhood—no snow, tinkling icicles, brilliant blue winter skies, none of that—only an intensification of the autumn's dampness, a deep cold but snowless, with bitter winds. You felt imprisoned by the cold, it was always there evilly waiting, like an omnipresent secret police, so that as bad as the cold itself, was your fear of it: when you stepped out of the front door, the nerves in your face went numb, as if a strange hand had placed a chloroform-soaked cloth over your nose and mouth.

The cold seeped under storm windows and around heavy double doors. It leaked through light sockets and insidiously worked its way between the bricks of the old building, so that at certain places, if you held up your hand near an exterior wall, you felt the layer of waiting cold. The furnace of our house bellowed and shrieked like a beast being beaten to death in its stall. Mr. Esperanzo, the Super, who lived on the basement level of the house next door with his near-blind wife and two grandchildren (their son had gone back to Puerto Rico and left the children behind) met me every morning with, "Cold, cold!" He wore what looked like a child's discarded down jacket—the knitted wristlets high up on his bony arms—and a navy blue watch cap pulled down to his straggly gray brows. When he hauled the black plastic sacks of garbage out of the basement, he was racked with coughing. He was a tall, very thin old man with olive skin and a crosshatch of wrinkles on the back of his neck. His brown eyes were sad. They seemed to say, "Ah, if I could tell you my troubles."

The Esperanzos kept strange hours—up late at night with the radio blaring Spanish music (all piping horns and castanets) and a frying pan full of sausages, peppers, onions, garlic hissing on the stove. In the morning the children would appear, climbing out of the dark stairwell hand in hand, the boy silent, the girl chattering in Spanish, both bundled up to go to school. They, too, wore funny clothes—clothes that were castoffs no doubt, outlandishly elegant for everyday. The boy was sunk inside a long narrow navy blue coat with brass buttons, and the girl trailed a long green loden cape. The boy had a lovely, full, creamy-skinned face. His sister, whose corkscrew curls bounced just above the collar of her cape, scolded at him in Spanish and tugged at his hand as if he were inanimate, a little kid's pull toy she led by a string.

Other, warmer seasons I used to see them in the park—she on roller skates, stopping every now and then to put her hands on the straight little hips of her blue jeans. Except for the skates she would have stamped her foot. Spanish shot out of her mouth in spurts, as if from a fountain. What a pair—the boy would look at her with long-lashed black eyes, and nothing on his face would move, only the little mirrors in the centers of his dark eyes would tragically lengthen. Five and six years old—temperament and dignity. They went to Puerto Rico for Christmas, and when they came back in February, I gave them the Christmas presents I had bought in the children's shop of Saks Fifth Avenue. For her a little hand-knit cherry-red sweater from Austria, and for him a dark-green turtleneck sweater with a squarish soccer player kicking a squarish ball. I liked the idea that the kids would have new very expensive things to wear, although, of course, they wouldn't know the difference. Mrs. E. accepted the gifts, nodded at me shyly from behind her half-opened door.

When the kids came home from the park—it was a Saturday—they appeared at my door, Mr. Esperanzo behind them, a hand on each shoulder, pushing them forward. Nina said promptly, "Tank you for de nice swe-tor!" She ducked under her grandfather's hand and ran away down the stairs, glancing at me saucily through the banisters. With the knee of his stained work pants the old man nudged Alfonso forward. "Ees nice," the little boy said softly. He looked up at his grandfather for approval. The old man severely nodded, first at the boy, then at me, and took the boy's creamy little round hand into his yellow gnarled one. My heart turned. I closed my apartment door.

How was it I had come to this point in life—living alone without children? I knew I could love children. I ought to have children. My womb ached. My heart hurt. My eyes blurred. I felt a dull pain in the lower right quadrant. The pain grew sharp—tugged—ow! Let go. Cramps. I was getting my period. What for? Like an old woman, I shuffled into the bathroom, opened the medicine cabinet, took out a new box of tampons so lavishly decorated—birds, vines, flowers—you'd have thought it was the casket of jewels Faust gave to Marguerite. In the flawed mirror Isabel of the Giant Jaw looked haggard and homely. When I was twelve and had to get glasses, my mother cried and cried. My father was impatient. Perhaps he felt responsible for this terrible calamity that had befallen me—his nearsightedness passed down to me on a chance bit of protoplasm. Perhaps he wondered why, instead, I hadn't been given his talent for mathematics or his ability to think ahead four moves in a chess game. My mother cried and said in German, her voice muffled by her handkerchief, "But her eyes are her only good feature!" My father said, "*Ach, was!* You're making too much of this. Someone will marry her."

Who?

I tugged apart the brass snap on my jeans—it had embossed letters on it that said YES! Yes, what?—and dropped my jeans and pulled down my blue bikini underpants and, glancing downward, saw, at the hourglass-shaped crotch, that which makes any poor single girl's heart stop, shake, shudder. There was nothing there. Nothing really there, a little spot of something or other that didn't count much and was not even vaguely pink. Jesus Christ. There was nothing there. I pulled up the panties, pulled up the jeans, snapped the YES! button, and sat down on the chenille-covered toilet top. The cramps, meanwhile, had gone away. I took thought in my mind. Let's see, the last time was a Tuesday, no, a Thursday, because Joan and I had gone to the Carnegie Cinema to see a Hitchcock double bill, *Psycho* and *The Thirty-nine Steps,* and when I came home, that was—I started to count, using my fingers. That was—hmm. An awfully long time ago. That was just after Christmas, and now it was, alas, the last week in February.

Wanted:

One kind, loving husband for knocked-up thirty-six-year-old lady. I am not beautiful and I usually wear glasses. My cooking is only so-so. The kid will be a bastard. No. I reject that idea. My child will only lack a live-in father. Forget it, Isabel. On what do you intend to raise and support this child? Remember your more-or-less Protestant childhood. Remember responsibility. Remember middle-classness. Pick up the telephone. Make an appointment at Columbia Presbyterian. Oh, Isabel, all your life you have been so careful. All your life you remembered your mother holding up a forefinger and saying, "With men one rule: *VORSICHTIG.*" Careful! Call up now, my friend. You can't afford a child. It is not your destiny.

# 3

Margaret appeared at my door at ten A.M. I was still in my bathrobe, a red plaid wool that had, like me, seen better days. I had bought it just before I went away to college.

"Hello," she said when I opened the door. "Do you have some free time today? I'm looking for company. I want to go down to SoHo. Goodness, haven't you lost some weight?"

We had coffee and then walked downtown. It was the first Saturday in March, damp, gray, but mild, and the hopeful weather had brought out crowds of people. The sidewalks teemed with walkers and shoppers, skate-boarders, roller-skaters, babies in strollers, elderly couples walking arm in arm. In Washington Square Park a small, wiry bald man with a thin body and surprisingly strong-looking legs skated beautifully, pushing off to the side in an elegant easy rhythm, his hands clasped behind his back. Something about him reminded me of my father—he was cheerful but engrossed, oblivious to the flux of the world, listening only to the headset he was plugged in to. As we walked past, I caught faint drifts of momentous *Eroica*. New York is a wonderful city. Meanwhile Margaret was filling me in on Summerville news.

"She was angry at first," Margaret said, "but she's adjusted. In fact, I think she's very happy about it. It's incredible, they walk around like honeymooners, holding hands. He's nauseatingly solicitous. You'd think they'd never had a kid before." Something inside me ached—Trina Pratt was pregnant. "I don't believe in having a pregnancy to pull things together, but in this case I guess it worked. Or maybe the sex finally worked."

"Something worked," I said. I tried to smile. My face felt stiff. I had a vision of my face as a cut-and-paste job done by an unskilled kindergartner—here a nose, there a tight, tilted mouth, eyes crossed.

"I really thought for a while they were going to get divorced. I can't believe that just having a baby could change things like that." She snapped her fingers at "that," and a boy running past us turned his head, and the setter galloping next to the boy turned his head, too.

"They'll have seven kids," I said. "Think of that. Seven."

"Ralph is interviewing for new jobs, too. He says he wants

to be home more. It's funny"—Margaret smiled—"he's suddenly grown three inches. He doesn't seem little anymore. I like him so much better. He's given up smoking cigars so the smoke won't affect the fetus."

"Thoughtful," I said.

"I always thought he was merely irrelevant, but now he's helping Trina with her store. He sits down, you know, and goes over her books and says sternly to her, 'See here, Mrs. Pratt, you simply have got to do something about your cost run overhead.' She loves it. She turns all pink and bats her eyelashes and says, 'Yes, Ralph.'" We came to a corner and waited for the WALK sign. A small crowd collected around us, waiting for the light to change. The couple next to us looked really down and out, dressed in miscellaneous scraps of clothing—baggy pants, dirty quilted jackets. A baby was strapped papoose-style to its father's back. The baby had a little lacy crocheted cap tied on its head, from which thin wisps of blond hair stuck out. It kept looking up at the sky with mild, curious eyes, as if it had never seen sky before. The couple were talking about food and the conversation was straight out of *Gourmet*. Looking down, I saw they had on matching cowboy boots, hand-tooled, no doubt, at two hundred dollars a boot. It's expensive to look SoHo-down-and-out. I noticed Margaret looking at the couple with interest. We walked across the street.

"Did you see him?" Margaret asked me in a low voice. "He reminded me so much of Jerry. Jerry looked like that when we were young."

"What do you hear from Jerry?" I asked her.

"Nothing," she said. "Nothing at all. Checks come in the mail. It's sometimes strange—we were married for nineteen years. It's as if he'd died."

"It's hard for me to imagine what it's like—getting divorced after nineteen years."

"Oh, it's just as it was before—he was never home much, anyway—but now when I'm bored I have no one but myself to blame. And I can be bored on my own schedule. That's a real

210

advantage. I don't have to spend my life waiting for someone to come home so that we can be bored together."

I smiled and looked away. She never would tell the truth about the past—pretending to have written off nineteen years so lightly, the way a flutter of doves flaps out of a magician's silk handkerchief. Good-bye! With me the past kept continually swimming around in my head, bits and pieces of it bobbing up here and there like the orange peels and orangeade cartons that drift in the wake of pleasure boats. Current events and objects often went unnoticed, while in the white-walled space inside my mind I strung together a personal history out of old loves, old devotions.

At the Castelli Gallery Margaret walked around the tall-ceilinged, airy room looking at the Rauschenbergs with great indifference. I stood in front of each one for a long time. These huge montages, ten feet by ten at least, had been assembled on sheets of hard white plastic. Bits of wallpaper, photos repetitively arranged to resemble filmstrips, solid objects—on one a white plastic propeller, slowly whirling, on another a real, orange life jacket glued to a watery red background. Pictures from World War II and the fifties—a ten-year-old child could have made nothing out of them. They made me want to cry. Each montage seemed utterly dependent on the powers of memory; each object, photo, scrap of cloth so evocative that the plastic walls seemed to represent slices of mind, colossal sections of the brain, a brain more or less my age, with its own melancholy obsessions—life jackets, deserts, tanks, the formative phenomena of my generation.

"Ready?" Margaret said. "I'm starved, let's go get some lunch." We went downstairs, into the damp promising air. A little gust of wind scattered a handful of leaflets around our feet. *Repent!* said the leaflets. We went to the Spring Street Cafe.

"Now you mustn't get just a salad," Margaret said to me. "Really, you don't look at all well. You're not the type to look well thin. I've always thought you were so healthy-looking. You're not doing this on purpose, are you?"

I smiled. Yes! A last-ditch attempt at a modeling career.

We stood in the dim light of the restaurant waiting for the hostess to notice us. It was not overly crowded. An Indian couple sat near the window, under a hanging fern. He in business suit, she in T-shirt, one black braid, red dot on forehead, pink and gold sari. A couple who looked blond and foreign (though I couldn't say why, the international dress code is so much the same these days), and two young men with beautifully waved hair styles looking into each other's eyes over spinach quiche, and a handsome, intelligent-looking middle-aged man talking with great seriousness to a young blond woman.

"What's wrong?" Margaret asked.

"Oh," I said, "ah!" David (was it David? I didn't have on my glasses) had seen me, frowned, looked down, and began stirring his soup. The woman's blond hair was coiled at the nape of her neck. She had on a black knit dress, and her long, lithe back leaned so far across the table toward him that she looked contorted.

"Let's go somewhere else," I whispered. "I feel faint."

"Wait a minute," Margaret said, "here comes the hostess."

"Is next to the window all right?" the girl asked, smiling brassily, as she handed us menus. I sat with my back to David. We ordered white wine. Heel-shaped pieces of rye bread arrived on a plate with a little tub of butter. Margaret sipped the wine and looked at me over the rim of her glass. She had on the long garnet earrings she had worn a hundred years ago, last August at her dinner party. She looked past me, toward David's table.

"You know, I was nineteen when I got married, and crazy in love. That is why"—she bent her head, and the long garnet earrings swung—"it took me years to figure out what Jerry was doing. I couldn't believe that he would go off on a business trip and make love to someone else."

"No," I corrected, "have sex with someone else."

"That's the point," she said. "I didn't think of it that way. I thought of it as making love. Then, after a while it wasn't just business trips, it was right at home, in Summerville. I felt horribly humiliated. Meanwhile, of course, I had been so strict with myself." She looked up at me and smiled sadly. "Maybe I should change."

I said, "Do you have someone to change for?"

"Is that what makes it all right? Having someone to change for?"

I hesitated. She seemed to be asking my opinion on a dangerous and complicated question. She said, "The truth is, after a while you don't care anymore. You don't care what he does or what you do or what anyone does. I suppose that's a lack of morality."

I said, "Or attrition of feeling." I looked past her out the window at the tatterdemalion SoHo crowd drifting by, peppered with occasional flashes of uptown class—gallery-goers. "Jerry was from the South, wasn't he? That always seemed strange to me. He never seemed southern."

"He was from Albion, Georgia, but he went away to school up north when he was nine. His family was Jewish. They were the only Jews in town."

"That must have been difficult for them. *And* him."

"Yes. But I didn't understand that at first. All those little hurts—they come out in funny, indirect ways. I thought Jerry was wonderful. I thought his family was wonderful, too. Look, Isabel. We lived on a broken-down farm. My father never finished high school. Up in Brownsbridge, they thought I was weird because I read books and liked art. And there I was, at nineteen, married to an educated man. Jerry knew about books and music and the theater. When his family sat down to dinner, there were candles and flowers on the table. They had wine with dinner and brandy later. Twice a year his mother flew to New York to buy her clothes. I didn't *care* what religion he was. Anyway, he was totally unreligious to begin with, and he'd made up his mind pretty early that he didn't feel Jewish, so why be Jewish? He dropped out early. It wasn't till later I discovered you couldn't drop out so easily."

The waitress arrived with our salads. We had both ordered

Greek salad—little tucked-up pillows of grape leaves, white cubes of feta cheese, dark, shiny olives. The waitress looked no older than twelve, a skinny little thing with dark circles under her eyes. Dickens would have recognized her. Her wan face reminded me of an old photograph I had seen—the sad picture of a weary little crossing sweeper. Sometimes you wonder if anything changes.

Margaret pushed her plate away and lit a cigarette. "It's getting harder and harder for me to go see Morgan," she said. She drew hard on the cigarette and exhaled. "Before I go, I have a whole ritual. I take a bath and carefully put on my makeup, then I dress, and before I go out the door, I have a glass of sherry. It takes me hours to get ready for a visit that takes ten minutes. And as soon as the visit's over and I'm going out the driveway, I start dreading the next visit." She put her wineglass down, and her dark-blue eyes looked at me from a galaxy away. She leaned forward and put her hand on my arm. "Isabel," she said, "I want you to promise me something."

My stomach fluttered queasily. I knew it had something to do with the Whitesides and Morgan. She looked me straight in the eye and held my hand down on the table, as if it might fly away. "Morgan's terribly sick. She's going to die soon. Will you come out and stay with me, please? When it's time?"

I shivered. "All right," I said and let my eyes drop at last. She released my hand and sat back. "I don't know why," she said absently, "but I'm so scared."

Later, when I got up to go to the ladies' room, I saw that the man wasn't David at all—there was only a small resemblance. David had been so good to me. I missed his firm, pleasant body and his common sense. I had liked his straightforward approach to life, the way he had of enjoying every day for what it could bring. He emerged from the bathroom in the morning with his face scraped pale from the razor and his hair correctly parted. Often, when I'd had too much wine with dinner, we would later make excellent love. Next morning he would bring me my coffee while I lay in bed. I would sit up and pull the blanket over my breasts. I couldn't meet his eyes. I felt ashamed, as if I had gypped him. He was a lovely man, and the sex was all right, too, it was just that the main thing was missing.

In the ladies' room, looking into the dim mirror, I saw that I looked better. It had been good for me to go out with Margaret. There were still blue circles under my eyes, but my skin looked less yellow. Then suddenly, without warning, I was overcome with nausea—perhaps the salad had been too oily—and I threw up into the toilet. I flushed it away and wiped my mouth on a Kleenex and stood leaning dizzily against the scratched, graffitied, paint-chipped toilet door.

# 4

I was sliding past the open door of Joan's office when her hand reached out and fastened on to my arm.

"Aha!" Joan said and drew me to her. Apparently she'd been hiding behind the door waiting for me. She pulled me inside her office and pointed to her guest chair, a tricky number made of black plastic slabs and aluminum tubing. It had lost several major screws and was wrapped at important joints with yards of dried-out, curled-up Scotch tape. I sat down cautiously. She, too, sat down and folded her hands on the desk top and looked at me. She had on a white satin blouse with long flowing sleeves and tightly buttoned cuffs. I wondered which role she was about to take on: boss? friend? patient mentor? Was this going to be, "You are fired," or perhaps a more personal pronouncement: "I am leaving Stuart"?

"Hey, hi," I said weakly.

"Hi yourself," she said. "What's going on, Isabel?"

"What?"

"What's going on? I mean, we do have to have a little communication, don't we, just to get our jobs done. I am tired of finding your door locked and having to write memos." She tilted her head. "Is it you or me, or what?"

"Oh, it's . . . not you, Joan."

"You're sure?"

"Why would it be you?"

She limply dropped her head into her hands. "I don't know. Really, I am getting paranoid. I went into this life-style so blithely, and now I can't sustain it."

"What life-style is that?"

"You know: as adulteress. I wonder how other people carry it off. I wonder what's wrong with me. It isn't as if I had been brought up by a puritan—my mother had one affair after the other." She looked despondently out the window. Joan's office has one window which looks directly out upon a gritty tar-paper roof that is decorated with a silver-hooded air duct. Pigeons stroll about the roof in their rocking seaman's gait, looking about with their bright, stupid eyes.

The clear, gray, lit rectangle of window was the only open space in Joan's office. The walls were lined with temporary-looking metal bookshelves crammed with paperback books, notebooks, telephone books. There was a bulletin board that bristled with tacked-up notices of forthcoming events of interest to public-spirited citizens. There were file cabinets all over the room and metal In and Out baskets, and on top of the file cabinets, accordion files, and manila files waiting to be filed. It seemed a mess, but Joan said that she could lay her hand on anything she wanted in five minutes. No one else knew her system. She had done this on purpose to protect her job. It would take them six months to find things if they fired her. She once told me seriously that the master code to her filing system was described in a little red leather notebook locked in her safe deposit box in a bank in Rye, New York. If she suddenly expired, she had said to me, I was to go to the bank and get out the book. Then I would stand a good chance of getting her job. I didn't want her job but was too polite to tell her so.

"You see," Joan said, sighing and fastening her eyes on me—her eyes were a lighter shade of blue than Margaret's—"it's the guilt thing. The guilt thing is killing me—it's murder. Whenever I go to bed with Stuart, I feel so guilty. Luckily it's not that often."

I looked at her curiously. "How often?" It was out before I knew it. Ha. So Isabel the Writer wasn't totally dead.

"Oh, really," she said crossly, "you don't speak to me for weeks, and then you pry into my sex life."

"I'm sorry," I said, "I wasn't thinking. It just came out."

She frowned. "If I told you how often, you'd say he was physically ill. Anyway, that is incidental. Here is what I have decided. I have got to give up one or the other—Enoch or Stuart. The funny thing is, the less I go to bed with Stuart, the more I enjoy him as a person. We used to go to bed all the time . . ." She looked broodingly down upon the desk. "I mean, you know, have sex, and then we'd have terrible, passionate fights, and there would be scenes and throwing of crockery, things like that. Now that we hardly touch each other, we're so thoughtful and polite and kind. Tell me something. Do you think Stuart *is* physically ill? Or maybe he has a girl friend."

"How would I know?"

"What is your guess? He's forty-eight, not eighty-eight, but you'd never know it."

"Still, he plays a lot of tennis."

"Yes."

"And he jogs, too."

"Yes."

"Then I don't really think he's sick. Would you care if he had a girl friend?"

"Oh, yes!"

"You would?"

"Oh, I'd kill him."

"But why?" I was astounded. The unreasonableness of this amazed me.

"It would denigrate me before my friends."

"But Joan, let's be fairsy-squaresy. Let me point out that you are, uh, fooling around."

"Isabel," Joan said with great dignity, "I am not fooling around. I am not merely entertaining myself. I am trying to enrich my life."

"Aren't we all?"

"But you see," she said, "I can't decide. Should I leave Stuart or Enoch? Enoch is passionate but often unpleasant. Stuart is sexless but great on a winter's evening over Chinese checkers."

"Ah, yes," I said, "the usual breakdown. Security versus adventure. Domesticity versus passion. The old tried-and-true versus forbidden fruits. Maybe you could just retrain Stuart or charge up his battery."

"Maybe I could retrain Enoch."

"Joan, are we being funny or serious? I've lost track."

She looked miserable. "A little of both. Actually I'm nuts about Enoch. I'll never let him get away. If he'd have me, I'd leave Stuart tomorrow." She lowered her eyes and frowned and began to doodle very rapidly with a ball-point pen on a manila envelope. She held her other hand cupped to her ear, as if it ached. "I feel awful—selfish and piggy. It's not as if I've never had love. This is not a once-in-a-lifetime thing. Stuart and I—we were so crazy about each other. We were lucky, too. It lasted for years. We had a wonderful time together."

"What happened?"

"I don't know, exactly. I lost my respect for him. It didn't really happen all at once, but it came clear to me one day during a tennis tournament. There was no linesman for some reason, and I saw Stuart call a ball out that was on the line."

"Oh, but honestly. Couldn't you have been wrong? You might not have seen . . ."

"No, I wasn't wrong. And then I began to notice little things. Our tax return, for example. Donations he'd said we'd made. Well, you see, I'd never really looked at the taxes, not until I got this job. All those old prep school ethics of his, all that stuff he used to harangue the kids with. What hypocrisy! It's not how you play the game at all. He never believed that. Winning is what it's about."

"But this does seem kind of hard, Joan. I mean, one wrong call? And I don't want to dwell on this, but what you are doing is, um, cheating. Right?"

"No, wrong. The worst kind of cheating is when you cheat yourself. So don't tell me about cheating. I made a free decision to sleep with Enoch."

"But you feel guilty, you just said so. So you must have some feeling left for Stuart."

"No," Joan said, "you misunderstood me. I don't feel guilty when I'm with Enoch. I feel guilty when I sleep with Stuart. Because I want to be faithful to Enoch." She lifted her eyes. They were such blue, honest eyes. "Isabel," she said, "do you think I'm a lousy person?"

"No," I said and then hung my head and shrugged. "No lousier than the rest of us."

She said, shaking her head, "There is no one I respect anymore, least of all myself."

I wonder what it is about Stuart Thistle that makes me completely indifferent to him. It's not a lack of physical attributes—he isn't unattractive. He is a well-built man of medium height with a springy walk, a squarish face, black hair, bright blue eyes, healthy pink skin, and a wide, white smile. He smiles too much. Maybe he thinks smiling is part of his job: he is head of public relations for a corporation so large that "you can't go a day without something it makes."

I think sometimes the exterior roles people are forced to assume eventually consume the whole person, and the interior person is lost forever. As I get older, I see how work kills souls:

the constant toadying, the pressure to compromise quality, the jocular defense of the lowest common denominator. In a Byzantine palace atmosphere where smiles and lies abound, how to keep alive the ability to risk and sacrifice? Still, I don't quite believe Joan. Stuart Thistle is not a crook, not yet, not completely, he only lies and, to compensate, tries too hard to give an impression of sincerity. He wants to tell you about his tough inner life, his lonely childhood, his rotten boarding school adolescence. Everything he says is supposed to remind you of a poor little Stuart buried somewhere.

When, after three glasses of wine (we were eating dinner together at Il Cortile down on Mulberry Street, Joan and Stuart and I), Stuart started on the "death of the brother" theme, Joan looked at me with raised penciled brows and a face in which a twitching laugh came and went at the corners of her full, pale mouth.

"I was eleven," Stuart said dramatically, looking deep into my eyes. "My brother meant everything to me. We were alone together so much, you see." Listening, Joan sighed and sat back in her chair, hands still resting lightly on the sloping foot of her wineglass. Her hands are not pretty, too square, broad, blunt-nailed. There was a constant cheerful clatter from the kitchen behind us. Dark-haired young men carried trays full of steaming food out of the swinging doors, calling to each other in Italian.

Joan yawned and looked away, off to the side. Il Cortile is a pretty place with a shiny brown tile floor, many plants, tall stone urns full of flowers—yellow and white chrysanthemums, a few pieces of garden statuary. "Isabel," Joan said, "I am going to the ladies' room. Do you want to come?"

I shook my head, no. I was too tired to get up. I didn't mind sitting there and listening to Stuart's stories. Joan slid around the table and out, her large black satchellike bag swinging into the folds of her black pleated skirt. Stuart stared down at the white-clothed table, then looked up and said, "Isabel, do you know what's wrong with Joan?"

"Wrong?"

"She's so irritable. She's edgy all the time. I've asked her several times to go see a doctor. She says she's in excellent health, yet she's always tired."

"Maybe it's the job. It's a lot of pressure."

"Yes."

"And lack of exercise. Lots of times she doesn't even go out for lunch. Just stays at her desk."

"I'll bet *you* exercise!"

"Me? Oh—heh. Not very often."

"No? You've got a marvelous figure. Did I ever tell you that?"

"I can't recall."

He nodded and looked down at the table. "I hear Parminter's out of the picture."

"What? Oh, yes. We split up."

"Too bad! Grand fella!" I hadn't heard anyone say "grand" like that since I saw an old newsreel clip of FDR on a late-night rerun of *World War II*. Grand!

"Yes," I said, "he was . . . *is* . . . a very nice man. It just wasn't, uh . . ."

"Yes. You know, in my opinion Joan's problems all started with Women's Lib. She was always so content at home. Did a lot in the community, too. Then along came consciousness-raising, and the next thing you know, she was right there next to me on the seven twenty-eight in the morning. Had to start ordering two morning papers, his and her copies of the *Times*. Awful expense. We spend forty dollars a month just on a morning paper. Then the commutation ticket, of course, to say nothing of her new wardrobe. The house has gone to hell—the garden's a shambles."

"Can't you hire someone?"

He waved this away impatiently. "The tax situation is incredibly bad, although Joan somehow fails to recognize that her job has put us in a financial position which, at best, is untenable. Of course, the worst thing, to my mind, is her lack of energy. She's always tired. *Too* tired. I've always admired you, Isabel, and I've always felt there was something a little special between us. Am I right?"

We had finished dinner, but a single slice of Italian bread remained in the basket, and I nervously took this piece of bread and jammed it into my mouth and then, without thinking, took a slug of wine—Orvieto—and did not look in Stuart's direction but, chewing all the while, leaned back in my chair and looked carefully, painfully to the extreme left. We had been seated in a little niche guarded by tall classical columns, around which it was difficult to see. But now, with my neck craned at this extreme angle, I looked out at the crowded restaurant—there is always a crowd there, twenty people or so waiting behind a velvet rope in the vestibule—and saw a profile, a thin hook-nosed face under a blond Afro leaning forward over his arms, which were folded on the tablecloth. The girl across from him, a small, well-rounded specimen of perhaps twenty-eight, had plump, dusky red cheeks, a fall of shining dark hair, large black eyes, and little milk teeth which showed when she laughed—she was laughing. She was wearing a fringed purple shawl. Enoch looked enchanted, dazed. I saw Joan coming back down the corridor from the ladies' room and turned my head back to Stuart.

"Isabel," Stuart said loudly, "if you ever need a friend! I know what it is to be alone in the world."

"Thanks," I said.

Had Joan seen? She came around the column, and as she began to slide in under the tablecloth suddenly seemed to falter, like an old stroke-ridden lady. Her skin was so pale it looked green.

"What's wrong?" Stuart said. "What is it, dear? You look terrible."

Joan said nothing.

"Maybe the scungilli," I said.

She sat staring toward the kitchen with wide-open eyes. She swayed slightly, as if in a trance.

"Joan? Joan? Dear? Do you want to go home?"

She nodded. He was, at once, all action, all solicitude. Hailed the waiter, checked the bill, paid. We departed, he holding tightly on to Joan's elbow as we left. They had their car—as we drove down Broadway I saw Stuart glance at Joan from time to time. She sat so stiffly that whenever the car hit a pothole, her body flew up in the air, as if it were weightless. At my place Stuart stopped the car, left the motor running, lights on, double-parked, and saw me to my door. I quickly got out my key. Not to worry. He was distracted. "I think I'd better take Joan to a good doctor," he said. "She's obviously exhausted. Then, too, I've been thinking we're long overdue for a trip. What do you think? Think she'd like that? Paris? London?"

"Wonderful," I said, "grand idea." I unlocked my door, turned on the lights, looked around. *Alles in Ordnung.* "G'night. Hope she feels better."

He had worn a tweed cap and now, with this in his hand, threw out his arms in a helpless "I don't know" gesture, apologizing for . . . what? Not following through on his proposition? I smiled to myself and shut the door. *Hell,* I thought, *he's not so bad. Poor guy. A decent fella.* I had seen at some point a quiver of light, a spark of quick life there behind the fake-sincere look in his eyes. In truth, he had had a hard life. And what makes us dry up sometimes is not that we don't love, but that no one loves us. Makes us defensive, brittle, evasive, suspicious. Ready to be hurt. I had that with Walter. In a funny way, it was David who saved me. He had made me feel so sheltered. Yet now I remembered his features only vaguely, as if he had happened long ago. Why did I have to love Douglas? It made no sense. I stood there feeling enraged and then, twice, quickly, hit my head against the yellow wall. A madwoman. A baby in its crib. A prisoner. The strongest bars are those we forge ourselves. "Mind-forged manacles." Who said that? I couldn't remember.

# 5

She had been talking a long time; her voice was a dwindling whisper but she wouldn't stop. I was tired but determined to stick it out, listening attentively to whatever she wanted to tell me. At ten P.M. I had primed myself with hot black coffee.

His father, Morgan said, had been a "sporting" type. Like her own father? I asked. Oh, no, not like that. With her father it was a profession, it was how they lived. He—Douglas's father—merely took pleasure in it. She remembered his tattersall vests. He had, always, a ruddy, healthy outdoor look, and although he was almost bald, his head had a strong round shape. He had a fringe of sandy curling hair; and piercing blue eyes; a big chest; and he gave off a scent of fresh, cold air, damp earth, leather, whiskey, only occasionally after-shave—not tobacco, he didn't smoke. He hated illness. He'd come stomping and whistling into the house, calling for the dogs. A hard worker, a shrewd businessman. After dinner he would retire to his study and sit under the beam of a tole lamp on his desk, his pen making a steady *scritch-scritch* as he took notes on long yellow pads of blue-lined paper. He liked women, and when a pretty woman he didn't know came into the room, he had an old-fashioned habit of hooking his thumbs into his vest pockets and rising on his toes, all the while tunelessly whistling under his breath. Once, Morgan said, he had put his hand on her breast. It was done instinctively—the way, perhaps, you pet a soft-looking kitten—and he had drawn his hand away immediately and left the room.

Douglas said the only time he'd ever had a serious disagreement with his father was when he brought home his first real girl friend—he was seventeen, and the girl came for dinner. At the dinner table his father had accused him of scratching the side of the station wagon. Douglas had denied it. His father had told him to go to his room. He had refused. The girl had shriveled between the two of them, looking from one to the other with a pale, scared face. His father had picked up a crystal dish full of pickled crabapples and turned the dish upside down on the tablecloth. Later he had apologized. Aside from this incident, they'd always gotten along well until Mae, his third wife, came along.

His father understood that Douglas wouldn't ever care much about money. Douglas was moody, more of a loner, liked dusty books, scholarship, and arcane subjects that his father had no use for. To twit him, his father used to point to the oil painting over the sideboard in the dining room, where, between tall silver candelabra, a pink-cheeked young man in a black frock coat looked out upon them with black Parker family eyes.

The Parkers, Douglas's mother's family, were full of Boston eccentrics, scholars, writers, ne'er-do-wells, lifelong invalids who died at ninety, ladies of accomplishment, and cranks. Douglas was like the Parkers, but the truth was, his father seemed pleased with his son and proud of him, who could say why? Some lost or suppressed part of himself he thought Douglas represented? Or that sneaking admiration we all have for someone who is so much an opposite—in talents or personality—that their essence seems an infinite mystery and, when linked to you by blood ties, seems that much more astonishing.

Douglas's brother, Richard, was three years younger than Douglas, was sturdy even as a small boy, had his father's round head and piercing blue eyes. For some reason that alternately puzzled Douglas and gladdened his heart, his father did not like little Dickie very much. His father prophesied that Richard would come to no good end, and indeed, he was thrown out of several New England prep schools and finished at a small boarding school in the South. He went to Boston University (not Harvard), met a blind girl there and fell in love with her, finished Phi Beta Kappa, went to Union Theological Seminary, and is currently living in Ladu, Indiana, where he is an Episcopal minister. He married the blind girl, whose name is Alicia, and they have three children. Alicia writes children's books. Douglas's father was always uneasy around Alicia. He was uncomfortable with any ill or handicapped person. When she was thirty, Douglas's mother discovered that the nagging backache she'd put up with for so long was an advanced case of TB of the spine, and Douglas's father began a long affair with a woman down the street. The woman divorced her husband, and after Douglas's mother died, Edmund Whiteside married her.

Laura was a different type—tall, thin, with short dark-brown hair and sad brown eyes. She was a sweet woman who had no children of her own. She was quiet and hesitant in manner and perhaps not very quick-witted.

When Douglas was seventeen, his father fell in love with a college girl who was a swimming instructress at the country club. She was a taut-bottomed, gold-downed bundle of long sleek muscle and coppery hair, and Edmund Whiteside made a perfect fool of himself, and Douglas got a job in town for the summer.

"What's wrong?" Morgan asked.

"Nothing. Go on."

"You started—did you hear something? Is it chilly in here? What time is it?"

"Nearly two. It's awfully late. Are you all right, Morgan, really? Maybe you should sleep."

"Oh, Iz, do you mind this? Don't you remember how, those first few weeks at Smith, we used to stay up late telling each other our lives?" I didn't point out to her it was Douglas's life she was telling me, because I wanted to hear. I was absorbing it, every bit, every word, although I couldn't help wondering why it was Douglas she was telling me about. Still, it was true that in a way his life had been hers for a long time.

"Don't worry," she said, "I'm all right," but there was something stubborn in the way she said it, as if she were indeed in pain but had decided to overlook it. "Where was I?"

"Douglas was seventeen and"—I smiled to myself—"his father fell in love with a college girl."

"Yes," Morgan said and blinked and looked up frowning

226

at the ceiling. The small bedside lamp was on with the shade pulled away at an angle so the light wouldn't hurt her eyes. Their large bedroom had become a hospital room. There was a wheelchair next to the bed and an oxygen unit. A large tray full of medicines sat on top of Douglas's bureau. He had moved into the tiny back bedroom—"my" room—and a nurse had the use of the guest room. Tonight I would sleep in the back bedroom. Douglas's grandmother had died, and he had gone to Boston for the funeral, and I had come out to stay with Morgan through the bitter March night. I prompted: "She was a swimming instructress at the country club."

"Yes," Morgan said. "Then the next year he left Laura for Mae—Mae was his secretary."

That summer Douglas had a job at a cement plant, and when he came home at night, Laura would be sitting alone at the dinner table with her pathetic smile. One hot summer day she dusted the house and hung clean towels in all the bathrooms. Then she cooked dinner, a chicken in white wine casserole, and left it in the oven, with the oven turned to WARM. She got into her car and made the two-hour drive to Wood's Hole, and from there she took the ferry to Nantucket. Astoundingly no one noticed that she'd slipped over the side. In death as in life she seemed to have made an apologetic exit. Her body never turned up. Douglas went on to graduate school, and Mae and his father moved out to Dedham for the summer.

Just after Morgan and Douglas married, they went out to Dedham on the train one weekend—they didn't yet own a car. Mae and Edmund met them at the station. Mae was driving. She had a green scarf tied over her hair, large gold hoop earrings, large sunglasses, a blue chambray shirt which she wore unbuttoned with the tails knotted up under her little round breasts, tight white pants, very high-heeled sandals, and an armful of bracelets. Her arms and face were intensely freckled, her midriff dead white. Pale blue shadows delicately delineated her rib cage.

Douglas's father had bought a new car, an MG of the handsome silver post–World War II A series, and he was sitting in the passenger seat in a beret and sunglasses, sipping a martini. Mae chewed gum. She lifted her sunglasses to her forehead and squinted to get a good look at Douglas. Her eyes were green, sharp as cut glass.

"Well, hi, hon," she said. "Lucky you, you don't look a bit like the old man." Douglas blushed, his father roared. He thought Mae was fantastically funny. He was crazy about her.

On Sunday morning Douglas and Morgan woke up to strange sounds—a series of squeals and high-pitched shrieks, as if a pig were being slaughtered downstairs in the living room. Then the sound—Douglas sat bolt up in bed: were they being attacked by vandals?—of furniture overturned, then a thud of feet on the stairs and the slam of a bedroom door. Someone— his father—pounding on the door. The doorknob noisily rattled, the flat of a hand applied to the doorframe. Bare feet thudding back down the stairs.

A few minutes later, while Morgan was pulling on her jeans, she glanced out the window and saw the top of Douglas's father's head—a glinting dome—appear on a level with the outside sill and then, gradually, the entire head—sparse strands of sandy hair, corrugated forehead, nose with its broken veins, thick sandy brows. This visage looked in upon them, crookedly grinned, and held up one forefinger . . . shhh. He was climbing up the rose trellis. He winked, and moved slowly sideways. The trellis creaked and groaned. Douglas and Morgan heard a roar and a coloratura shriek and, on the other side of the bedroom wall, a solid thump (his father had landed)—then hysterical laughter, as if someone were being tickled to death, followed by silence.

Cautiously they went downstairs. In the living room a table with a potted plant on it had been overturned, and Douglas stoically swept up the dirt and pieces of broken pottery. His brother, Richard, was in the kitchen, sitting at the table, knife and fork in hand, chewing at an enormous stack of pancakes slathered with butter and syrup. Douglas poured out two glasses of orange juice, Morgan poured out two cups of coffee. They politely exchanged beverages and sat down. After several minutes had gone by, Richard raised his bright-blue eyes to the ceiling. "Jesus Christ," he blurted, "all they do is fuck." Then he glanced at Morgan and muttered, "Sorry." Richard blotted his lips on the paper napkin, got up, and took his plate to the sink. He balled up the napkin and sent it (with the motion of a hook shot) into the paper bag full of trash waiting to go out next to the kitchen door. In build he was squarish, like his father, with sandy hair on his chest and in his armpits. He was a junior in college and already beginning to go bald.

"Wanna go to church?" he asked Douglas. Douglas said, "No, thanks."

Richard went up the back stairs two at a time, and soon they could hear the water running through the pipes in the back bathroom. All over the house, Morgan had noticed, were books on blindness—Richard was teaching himself braille—books on the psychology of the blind, books on the physiology of seeing. There were books on Milton—Richard was doing a long term-paper on Milton: "When I consider how my light is spent."

Once in April, just after they'd met, Douglas had driven to Northampton in a borrowed car. He told Morgan that night at dinner that he often dreamed of Laura, his stepmother. In his dreams she was unhappy as ever. It seemed to Douglas that his father had felt nothing when she died; instead, it was he, Douglas, who was haunted, afflicted with guilt, remorse, shame. Once at the dinner table his father had pulled Laura out of her chair by an arm and hit her. It was Richard who had run around the dinner table and bravely started pummeling. Was this why Douglas dreamed about her? Strange—he'd always had an odd sympathy for his father but felt on the other hand that he hadn't protected Laura enough.

"You know," Morgan said in her dim voice, smiling up at

the ceiling, "in one essential way, Douglas was pretty much like his father. I just had to point it out to him. Kind of gently assist him to his goal. So what I did that night was, I leaned against him and I said, 'Do you know something, Douglas? I want very much to sleep with you.'" Morgan smiled. "He looked perfectly blank, as if he'd never heard of it. Actually he was scared. He never had slept with anyone."

She turned her head on the pillow to look at me. I saw suddenly—or thought I saw—why she was telling me all this. She seemed to be flaunting the past—this past in which I had no place, none at all. I felt sick with jealousy. I had no place in his life—not in his past, perhaps not in his future—only this awful present. I said, getting up from the chaise that I'd pulled up close to the bed, "It's late, time to sleep."

She turned her head slightly to look at me. Her face was wizened, her black eyes enormous. Her voice had dwindled until it was barely there, a wisp of smoke, and she motioned me to bend closer so I could hear. She spoke slowly, as if she had thought out everything carefully. She said, "Before Douglas I slept with a few men—it was never anything serious for me and . . . I never felt guilty. But I slept with someone after we were married, too. I fell in love with someone else a few years ago . . . He was totally unlike Douglas, almost an opposite. He was warm and outgoing and he brought out a side of me I'd forgotten existed. He made me feel young and full of hope, like a college girl . . . I liked that person, the person he made me feel . . . At home I was everyone's mother and Douglas's wife, but Paul and I could really talk to each other. When we talked, he made me feel . . . it was an exchange, not just . . . a monologue. In a way, you see, Douglas has always shut me out of a big part of his life. That's the way he is. Paul reminded me of you, Iz. He believed in a part of me nobody else has ever cared about . . . But, you know, he didn't love me . . . That was the awful thing. At first I couldn't believe it—it seemed to me I loved him so much that I could simply make his love exist. But of course it didn't happen and . . . everything here at home went to hell . . .

and although Douglas knew it—not because we ever discussed it, but because he sensed it—it never came up. We didn't talk about it. We kind of just picked up from there and went on. In some ways I am sorry it happened—Douglas and I were never as close again and"—she smiled wearily—"it's so easy, with Douglas, not to be close. Yet it was good for me, too. I think before then I'd been depressed for a long time. Nothing that showed a whole lot, but it was there. After Paul I knew that I could change my life."

"Rewrite your act."

"Yes. You have such a funny look on your face, Isabel."

"I'm so tired, Mo-Mo. You must be beat, too. You've been talking for hours." I stroked her forehead. These last weeks her hair had grown back but, oddly, it had grown in curly. Now that she was going to die, it lay in pretty wispy black curls upon her yellowish forehead.

"Yes, I am tired." She closed her eyes. I turned off the lamp. "Isabel?"

I turned at the door. "Yes?"

"Life has a nasty habit of persisting."

My heart was beating steady and strong. She had given me permission.

# 6

I slept until noon and got out of the bed feeling full of evil vigor. Alive! I was alive and not ill. I was in good health and no doubt would be for a long time. I had a bath, dressed, picked up the little room. Ruthlessly I examined everything that belonged to him. There was a pile of change in a glass ashtray on the top of the bureau, and I picked up the coins and held them tight in my fists. I opened the top drawer of the bureau and put my hands on his folded underclothes. I looked at his shirts—white shirts, starched and pressed and neatly put into the Union Laundry's cellophane wrappers. In the bottom drawer of the bureau there were two sweaters, a blue cardigan and the heavy gray sweater the same no-color as his eyes that he had worn the day it had snowed, the night we made love. He had turned away from me, his long back curved as he bent to pull the sweater off.

I put the sweater into the drawer and went to the closet. Not much there. One gray herringbone tweed jacket with gray suede elbow patches. One pair of navy blue corduroy pants. Because it extended under the eaves of the house the closet was an odd shape—short but deep. I kneeled down and felt with my hands into the corners of the closet, and then crawled under the slanted pine-board ceiling. There was nothing there but dust and what felt like a couple of bobby pins. The Saks bag with my blouse in it was gone.

I backed out of the closet, and squatted, thinking. Had Morgan found the blouse? Had she thrown it out or given it away? I had wanted the blouse to be there, something of mine in his house. Someone knocked on the door. I stood up.

It was the day nurse, Mrs. Kelly. "Good morning," she said brightly, poking her head in. She was a stout, pleasant-looking woman with a broad freckled face. Ginger-colored hair was pinned up under her tall starched cap. "You're Isabel, aren't you," she said, "Mrs. Whiteside's friend. Did she have a bad night? She must have, she's sleeping so well." She glanced at her watch, a large square-shaped face on a thick black strap. "Think I'll let her sleep a bit. I've made a pot of coffee, if you'd like a cup."

I liked Mrs. Kelly's coffee and herself as well. She was one of those down-to-earth people who "have seen it all" and yet manage to retain a core of feeling. She'd been divorced young, raised three children alone, and was going to be married again in three months, "fool that I am," she said with a grin. She had grown fond of Morgan. "Maybe a bad thing in my line of work.

Most would say you ought to shut yourself off somewhat because it does hurt after they go. But they sense it if you do, and then what's the point? Well, she's a lovely woman. Even with her being so sick and all, she tries to spare me difficulties. And Mr. Whiteside's a decent man, too, he is, you can tell right away. He sits with her as much as he can. It's hard to be in his place. When they have a bad day, they often take it out on those around them, 'You never loved me,' that kind of thing. He's patient with her and kind. When they get close to it like that, they feel removed from everyone and scared. A couple of days ago she all of a sudden opened her eyes and said to me, 'Nora, I wish I could make love to my husband one more time.' I put down my knitting and went right over to her and gave her a hug."

The telephone rang. Mrs. Kelly hoisted herself up from the table by pushing on both freckled hands. "Hello?" she said into the telephone, and then formally, "Just one moment, please." She held the telephone out to me. I gave her a questioning look. "It's a Mrs. Allen," she said.

"Hi, Margaret," I said into the telephone. "How are you?" She said she was fine and asked if I could stop by, she had something to show me. When I hung up, I thought how odd it was that Mrs. Kelly, who had been with Morgan several weeks, didn't know Margaret's name. Apparently in all that time Margaret hadn't been to see Morgan, and she obviously hadn't called much, either.

"I'm painting again," she said, and she opened the door wide. I'd never seen Margaret's face this way—lit up; that deep inner flash or dark sparkle had become a light, an illuminating beacon. "You don't know," she said. "God, God, I'm so happy."

We stood in the dark paneled hall that had struck me, when I'd first seen it, as Gothic and gloomy. Now the doors both to the library and the living room had been drawn back, and the light in the hall seemed to softly, mistily rise. I had the feeling that light was pouring down the broad staircase in a pointillist river. She took my hand. "Come see what I've done. I feel like a madwoman, I just can't stop. I started painting two weeks ago —no, three. It was just after I'd seen you, that day we had in SoHo. I came home and"—she stopped and looked into the air and smiled to herself—"I got up the next day and started. Come!"

But I had stopped in amazement at the double doors to the living room. A living room? No one could have lived in it. The entire center of the room had been piled high with furniture, a great jumbled-up mass that seemed to me to resemble a pyre. Tables were heaped on the heart-shaped sofa, and the little bow-legged chairs perched precariously on top of the tables. The old photographs had been taken down from the walls, and even the draperies had been stripped from the windows and lay on top of the mess of sticks like raveled bandages. "My God," I said, "what's happened?"

She laughed. "It's all Jerry's stuff. I'm waiting for him to come get it. Awful of me, isn't it?" She took my hand again and, walking ahead, led me up the broad carpeted staircase. "I have this odd sense of having been reborn. I am an artist again after too long of not knowing who I was, of feeling and being . . . dead." Just past the landing with its tripartite Gothic window, was a large painting—an abstraction of such splendor and gorgeousness that I blinked. She said, "There are more, many more."

We walked down the second-floor hall, passing the pretty guest room I had slept in, and took the stairs to the third floor. Here the staircase was narrower and twisted cruelly, so that you were glad to emerge at last and see on either side long rooms that had once been playrooms for children. They were full of discarded toys and beaten-up furniture but no paints or paintings. "Come," she said impatiently, tugging at my hand. "Not here." She led me around a corner to another staircase. Here at last was the stone tower that, from the outside, resembled a silo. The door to it was open, and a stream of sunlight fell across the bottom steps. I looked up. Waves of color flowed down both sides of the staircase, as if the sunlight were indeed a stream or a river and the pictures hung on the steep plaster walls were brightly flowered river banks. There were pictures of all types hung thickly everywhere—oils, acrylics, crayons, drawings, monotypes, as if all this color had been penned up in the tower, had been locked up there and suddenly, when the door to the tower fell back, had come flooding out—a pure stream of splendid joy.

"But it's incredible," I said. "You couldn't have done all this in three weeks."

"No, not all, some of them I'd had put away, but I've done a lot. I've been in a strange manic phase, not sleeping very much, painting more or less around the clock. I can't tell you what it's like, how lovely it is, how alive it makes you feel. The truth is, in all my life I can't remember being this happy. Not when I was first married, not when the children were born, never."

We were standing on the steps near the tower room. From my uptilted perspective I could see the many-paned tower windows above her and, in the round sunny room that resembled the top of a lighthouse, an easel, a small worktable, rags, stacked canvases, paints.

"Let's go outside," Margaret said. "I want to go sit in the sun and feel the warmth."

In the kitchen we made herb tea and brought our mugs out to the back porch. The March sun wasn't strong—still a pale buttermilk sun—but it fell unfiltered through black leafless branches. Like albinos we sat there blinking and itchy with pallid, upturned winter faces. A damp mold smell came from beneath the grass—you could almost hear the earth groaning as it cracked its tight winter corset, and at the bottom of the porch steps, from under a wooden riser, a solemn procession of ants crept out from the dark to one of their places of work. I half-closed my eyes. Through my lashes I could see Margaret's white profile, her slender neck, and the flaming crown of chestnut hair which the sun had ignited. She had on paint-smeared blue jeans, and a green sweater over a white blouse. My outfit, too, except that my sweater was blue.

"Ah, it's glorious," she said. She stood up and with that same movement I'd remembered Douglas making—hands crossed at the ribbing—stripped off her sweater. Underneath she wore (I recognized it at once) my blouse.

"Hey! Where did you get it? That's my blouse."

She looked down at it in surprise. "This?"

I stared at it, trying to remember precisely. Yes, it was. The same blouse.

She said, "I got it, let's see, at Saks, on sale."

"Really?"

"Yes, really. What's wrong? I got it there the same day we went down to SoHo. Later I went uptown to shop and I saw this."

"Morgan didn't give it to you?"

"Morgan?" She sat down again on the step. "No. I don't understand. Why would Morgan give me a blouse? Why all this fuss?"

"I have a blouse just like that." I corrected myself. "Had."

"You're a spendthrift, then. Even on sale I paid too much for this thing."

I relaxed. My paranoia had whispered to me that Morgan had come upon the blouse and had spitefully given it away, knowing it was mine, knowing, or guessing . . . whatever. "How much did you pay for it?"

"Forty-five."

"Good for you. I spent a whole lot more than that. I left it at Morgan's in a back bedroom closet. Now it's gone."

"Odd. Maybe the cleaning lady? Did you look in Sarah's closet? Lately she's taken to wearing her mother's clothes." She said this wryly and looked away. "Isn't this nice! The daffodils are up in front, did you notice? Doesn't the air smell good? I love that damp spring smell."

"Does the furniture going mean you'll sell the house?"

She locked her fingers around one knee and sat back squinting against the sun, then grinned. This did an astonishing thing to her face—broadened it, showed up her crooked teeth, made you aware of the freckles that ambled across her nose, turned her—*returned* her, rather—into the hoydenish North Country kid who had set traps in the woods with her brother and in the summer sold wild strawberries at the roadside for ten cents a basket. "Oh, no, I'm not going to sell the house yet. I am going to get rid of all this rubbish and make this place my own. Jerry wants the stuff for his place in New York—well, let him have it. Besides"—she shrugged—"I don't have a place to go to."

"Have you started the legal proceedings yet?"

"Ages ago. It's such a bore! I don't think I'm especially greedy, but I expect to get something . . . a pension or whatever you want to call it for all those years I played housekeeper. Eventually I'll sell the house, but not quite yet. The kids need to be here for a while, and so do I. And how is your life? Seen any more of David?"

"No. I do believe he is finally gone for good."

She leaned back on both elbows and stretched her legs down the steps. "And Morgan thought she had you all taken care of."

"Well."

"How is it over there? How is she?"

"All right. We were up almost half the night. She wanted to talk. She's got a nice woman to look after her." I turned my head to the side. "Mrs. Kelly is so—oh—motherly."

She leaned back on her elbows. "Thank God his grandmother finally died. I hope he gets some money out of it. The medical bills are enormous."

I said casually, "How is Douglas, do you know? Has he been holding up?" It seemed such an inane way of putting it—holding up, ramrod backbone, stiff upper lip, all that rot.

She said, "From what I can tell. I've spoken to him on the telephone. Actually, I'm ashamed to say that I've been so much into my painting, everything else has just gone."

"You don't know how Sarah's doing, then?"

"No."

"She's the hard one. I like her in a peculiar way. Not in a maternal way, but more as if she and I were closer in age. She's very intelligent. I enjoy her, but I feel guarded with her at the same time."

"That's smart of you," Margaret said coldly. "She's an extremely mixed-up young lady." She stood up and dusted her hands on her thighs. "It's gritty out here. I must get back to work. Call me if"—she looked at me, and then looked down—"you need anything." She went up the steps and through the back door into the house, leaving me to walk alone down the long gravel drive to the street.

When I got back to the Whitesides', Mrs. Kelly had gone for the day, and Sarah was sitting with her mother. They were laughing about something and stopped abruptly when I came in the room.

"Where have you been?" Morgan asked. She had on a new bed jacket—a pink one that Lily Webber had given her.

"At Margaret's."

She closed her eyes. Her eyelids were shiny and bruised-looking. "Douglas says Margaret's been sick."

"I don't know," I said, "maybe she has, she didn't say."

Sarah sat staring out the window. Her long dark-blond hair was combed into one braid. She had on springtime clothes—a shortsleeved blue sweater and a dark flowered cotton skirt. She looked very pretty, I thought. "Isn't it a beautiful day?" Sarah said and looked at me.

I nodded.

"But the temperature is supposed to drop tonight."

Morgan said in a murmuring voice, "I don't think I can stand the cold much more." Sarah got up to leave the room.

Morgan opened her eyes and looked at her. "Oh, honey," she began.

"Yes?" Sarah said, and her eyebrows peaked worriedly in the center of her forehead. She had Douglas's ragged black brows. "Is there something you want, Mom?"

Morgan closed her eyes. "No," she said, "I just wanted to thank you."

Sarah blinked and frowned and then turned quickly to go out the door.

# 7

The beautiful day had ended in cold and sleet. A fire burned on the Whitesides' living room hearth, but icy rain beat upon the black windows. Sarah sat in the wing chair reading Henry James—*The Wings of the Dove*. Eddie was reading a social studies textbook, Tess was upstairs in her room with the radio turned to WVNJoy, Douglas sat at the desk correcting midterm history exams. His pen made a whispering sound as he wrote in the margins. I was attempting to sew on a button for Douglas— the gray herringbone jacket was down to one—but had already stuck my finger two times. This reminded me of something unpleasant in a fairy tale—spindle, spinning, poison, sleep? Upstairs, Morgan lay sleeping.

"Interminable," Sarah said. Her lips moved around the word, enjoying it. She had both legs—feet in woolly slippers— over one arm of the chair. "This interminable winter," she said, looking at the streaming window. Douglas lifted his head, and we smiled at each other over our glasses. Because of the bad weather I had decided to stay the night.

"Schliemann," Eddie said. "Hey, Isabel, that's you. That's your name. Are you related to this guy?"

"No," I said, "not at all. Are you reading about him?"

"Yeah," Eddie said. "'He was this archaeologist, right? And he had like this one dream; ever since he was a kid he'd wanted to find ancient Troy. Then he grew up and got rich so that he'd have enough money to pay for his expeditions, only at first no one believed him; the other archaeologists thought his ideas were crazy because he decided to use the *Iliad* to help him. They didn't believe the *Iliad* because it was only a story. And anyway, he wasn't a real archaeologist, so they just, you know, laughed at him. But he kept reading and rereading the *Iliad* and used the descriptions in it as clues to where he thought Troy was. Then, when he started digging, he found a city he thought was Homer's Troy, but it wasn't—he hadn't dug deep enough. It turned out there were all these ancient cities—all these Troys—in layers, one on top of the other. The real Troy was there, though, underneath, farther down." Eddie looked at his father shyly. "That's really fascinating, isn't it, Dad?"

"Yes, it is," Douglas said. He had been listening seriously. When Eddie finished, he smiled at him, then sighed and began reading an exam book. "Oh, my God," Douglas said and shook his head. "Listen to this: 'Dear Dr. Whiteside, I would have done better on this exam but I had to go to Florida with my boyfriend. You said in class once that life should be a learning experience and I think I learned a lot in Florida. Yours in faith.' I'll bet she learned a lot," Douglas said. "I like that—'Yours in faith.' She's got wit, anyhow."

"Who was that?" Sarah asked.

"I can't tell you," Douglas said. "All of my students are entitled to anonymity." Sarah got up, silently tiptoed across the room, and tried to peer over her father's shoulder.

"Ah ah ah," Douglas said, slamming a hand down on the exam book, "no fair."

"Your students deserve anonymity," Sarah said, "because they're so awful. I'll bet it was Sue Slater. She's always flirting with the men teachers."

"Was she flirting?" Douglas asked, looking up, wrinkling his brows. His glasses had slipped down his nose. He looked eighty, I thought fondly.

"Of course she's flirting with you, Dad. Can't you see that? Who cares about her and her moronic boyfriend, anyway?"

"I think I'll give her a B—. I was going to give her a C+, but if she's flirting with me, she certainly deserves more. It's a shame she made such a mess of the Treaty of Versailles."

"The Treaty of Versailles!" I said. "I haven't thought of that in years. I wrote a paper on it in college—'Keynes and the Treaty of Versailles.' I can't remember the grade I got, but I had a problem with history courses in college. After a while I just couldn't believe them, they didn't seem true to me."

Douglas began writing again. "History isn't religion," he said dryly. "There is no one truth. The best facts win. Besides, it's obvious that the present always redefines the past."

I said, "But it seems to me that fiction is what really tells the truth."

Sarah said, suddenly looking up, "I understand what's she's saying, Dad. Only fiction is about a different kind of learning. We were talking about that in English class last week. Fiction is about feeling as opposed to intellect."

Douglas raised his brows. "That's very revealing, Sarah. It's my impression you kids think feeling is all that's necessary to existence. None of you bother to *think* anymore."

"You're mixing up what I said, Dad. And I'm not talking about sensations, I'm talking about emotions. Besides, I don't think what you're saying is true. I think kids today have a harder time getting down to real feelings, because everybody tries to act so tough. Underneath maybe they're really scared, but they can't let it show. It's harder for kids today because nobody knows what the rules are, and everybody's rules are different. So everybody's tough and wary."

"Well," Douglas said lightly and turned over another exam book, "as far as rules go, we did try."

Sarah said nothing for a moment, and when she spoke, her voice had become smaller, tremulous. "How come you always have to get instantly personal?"

Douglas said, "I wasn't necessarily being personal."

"Yes, you were," Sarah said. "The truth is, nobody can have any kind of discussion with you because you've got to put them down in some way."

"I was *not* putting you down, Sarah."

"You were, but you don't know it. You put me down all the time. You don't take anything I say seriously."

"That's a lot of nonsense."

"Well, last week I talked to you about going away to boarding school and you said we'd discuss it later, and we never have. That's the way you handle everything. Shove it in a corner somewhere, and it will go away, and you won't have to deal with it."

"All right," Douglas said and put his pen down and sat back in his chair, "let's discuss it now."

"Okay," Sarah said. She sat up straight in her chair with her slippered feet planted firmly in front of her and her hands tightly clasped around the book in her lap. "I want to go away to school next year like I told you last week. I want to get out of here—this town. I'd like a chance to start over again where I don't know anyone. I want to go where I can study hard."

"And there's no boy involved?" Douglas said.

"Oh, Dad, there you go again. You don't believe me, you don't trust me . . ."

"Is there any reason why I should?"

". . . you never give me a chance. Maybe I've changed. Maybe I'm trying to change."

"If you can prove that . . ."

"I am trying to prove it, but I can't do it here in this town, everything's against me."

"All right, let's say that if you can earn part of the tuition money—let's say a quarter of it . . ."

"Oh, please, please, please. You know I can't earn that

much. It's March—even if I quit school now and worked all summer, I wouldn't have that much. The truth is, you really don't want me to go. You don't want me to go and you don't want me to stay here."

"I am entirely indifferent . . ." he began.

Sarah leaped out of the chair. "Yes," she said, "you sure are. You're indifferent all right. You're indifferent to me, and you were indifferent to Mother, too. I wonder if you care about anybody."

Douglas stood up. Sarah stared at him, then hurtled violently toward the stairs. Douglas began filling his pipe with tobacco from the humidor on the desk. His face looked askew—pulled out of place. "You don't know what you're talking about," he said loudly to Sarah, who was running up the stairs.

Eddie looked up from his book. "What a dumb bitch," he said.

Douglas, who was standing only a foot or so away from Eddie's chair, reached out a hand and cuffed him on the head. The boy reared back in surprise and then, quietly, with some dignity, closed his book and went up the stairs, not running, but walking steadily.

Douglas went to the window. He tilted his head and tipped the pipe lighter—the lighter flared up, and a cloud of obscuring gray smoke circled around him.

"I'm not doing very well, am I?" he said. "Seems like we're all out of tune around here."

I began sewing again, poking the needle down through the rough tweed, pulling it through on the other side.

"Is it them," he asked, "or me? I don't know. I thought Sarah and I were doing a little better."

"This, too, will pass," I said. "It's growing pains." I sat in the chair with his jacket on my lap, sending him my thoughts: *Don't be upset. I am here. I love you and want to take care of you.*

I looked up, dazed. It occurred to me that, indeed, what I wanted to do was exactly that—to take care of him, to make myself central to his existence, to be a sort of fulcrum in his life.

"Isabel," he said, "there is something I should have said to you before. I've been thinking about this for a long time, since January. I thought about driving into the city to see you, but the truth is I'm the world's worst coward. I couldn't even call you. I suppose I made drinking an excuse for what happened back in January, and I'm sorry. I want to apologize to you."

I felt stung and then thought (my mind working quickly as ever—quick-witted Isabel), *But, of course, he wants some sort of confirmation from me,* and I said, smiling dimly, dim-witted Isabel, "I didn't exactly scream, did I?"

"Dad?" It was Sarah calling from upstairs.

He ignored her and said, steadily, stubbornly, without looking at me, "I suppose I always thought you were so sophisticated, a city girl with a fast-paced life-style. There was nothing in it, nothing at all. I'm sorry it happened. It was wrong of me."

I shuddered. I felt cleft in two, as if someone had struck me in the chest with an ax.

"Dad!" It was Sarah, calling again. She was on the stairs, bent over, looking down at us from between the banisters. "Can you come upstairs? There's something wrong with Mom. I can't wake her. I think it must be a coma."

He took the stairs two at a time.

He couldn't rouse her. Sarah stood next to the bed with her hands held up to her face. Douglas dialed the town rescue squad and spoke—so crisply I knew that, mentally at least, he must have rehearsed this moment. When he put the receiver down, he said gently to Sarah, "What do you want to do? Do you want to stay here or come to the hospital with me?" I was surprised at how carefully he spoke.

"I'll go," Sarah said. He nodded—I thought he looked relieved—and she left the room to get dressed. He turned to me.

"I don't think there's any point in taking Eddie and Tess. She may not wake up for days."

I thought: *He means she may not wake up at all.*

I stood at the side of the bed looking down at Morgan, feeling numb and horrified. She lay flat on her back, her face looked tiny, except for the eyeballs, prominent in their sunken purple sockets. Her yellow stick arms lay upon the cover. She had always kept her nails short, but during these last weeks of her illness they had grown long and curved, were pitted and ridged, like storm-beaten fragments of mother-of-pearl.

"Perhaps," Douglas said, "you'd better go to bed. I'll call you from the hospital if there's any change."

I left the room, not walking steadily, and as I crept along I kept my hand on the wall for support. As ever, the little back bedroom was frigid—I got into bed with all my clothes on, but I couldn't stop shivering. I curled up into a ball, and after a while fell into black sleep. If there were dreams, I don't remember them. When I woke up, I looked at the green dial of the bedside clock. Two twenty-five. No one had called. I had left the door partially open so that I could hear the telephone. I closed my eyes, and Margaret's sinuous landscapes in all colors—purple, gold, brilliant blues and yellows—floated in front of my closed eyes. I had had a thought about her paintings. It seemed to me that over and over again she was painting the hills that encircled Brownsbridge, New York.

# 8

I was nine the last summer we rented Crazy Mary's house. One hot day near the end of August we drove into the village in our old wrecked-up Plymouth. The village was really nothing more than perhaps twenty white houses set on either side of the main street, a general store, a drugstore, two churches. My father parked the car and went down toward the general store, which had a newsstand—he hated to be without his daily papers—and my mother and I went into the drugstore. She was in such a good mood that I knew for sure she was going to let me have an ice cream cone. The druggist got the things my mother wanted —suntan lotion and citronella—wrapped them in glossy paper, tied a string around them, and then began to scoop out my cone. I didn't like this druggist because he cheated on the cones and, instead of a solid scoop of ice cream, would hand you one that looked perfectly round but had a hollow center. He wore his white druggist's jacket buttoned up tight on his neck. He had watery, pale eyes and a stiff expression. He handed me the cone, and my mother distractedly paid him. She was glancing out the window toward the sidewalk, where some sort of argument had begun. We went outside. A tall man in knee-high leather boots—the old-fashioned kind that laced around studs, then through eyelets—was standing next to our dusty blue car. The man wasn't wearing a uniform but had a sheriff's star pinned to the pocket of his tan shirt.

"See your license, bud," he said to my father. My father turned white and nervously began patting one pocket after another for his wallet. He found the wallet in its accustomed place —the inside breast pocket of his jacket—and began to go through its contents with fumbling fingers. Humiliatingly he dropped the papers on the sidewalk at the feet of the tall man, who stood with his arms folded while my father bent to pick them up. My father straightened up and, flustered, his glasses at the end of his nose, handed over his license and registration. The policeman squinted at the papers.

"What's this here name?" he said. "Schliemann?" He pronounced it slowly, in two distinct syllables. "What's this other name here? Siegfried? What kind of name is that?"

"German," my father said.

"That so? You a German? You don't look German to me. I got to know lotsa Germans. I was over there, coupla years ago, in the army."

A small curious crowd had by this time begun to collect in a ragged circle around the tall man and my father. My mother and I were standing off to the side, still in the shade of the drugstore's awning. A farmer in overalls and visored cap stood next to his son, a boy about my age. They both stood the same way, squint-eyed, watching, weight on one foot, arms folded. Two middle-aged women, one in pin curls, the other in curlers, paused, slack-jawed, in front of the drugstore to see what would happen next. The acid-faced druggist was watching from the cool of his store, pressed against the screen door, one arm up, leaning idly against the doorjamb.

"Well, now, Siggy," the tall man said, "I'll tell you what. You get this car outta the way here, and I'll only give you a ticket for"—he produced a pad of printed stubs from his hip pocket—"ten dollars."

"Ten dollars!" my father said. "But for what?"

"For what? You want to stand back here and look at the way you parked this car? It's four feet away from this curb. Now, I tell you what, Siggy, no real German woulda parked his car like that. No, sir. Because I will tell you something, Siggy, those krauts have a few faults, but they know how to do things. I got a lot of respect for those krauts. When they do something, they do it right. Lookit the way they took care of the Jews. Thorough! Wouldn't you say so, Siggy?"

My father's eyes flashed and his jaw ground, as if he were chewing pure gristle. Then a bleak look came over his face. He dropped his eyes and right there in front of me seemed to shrink or wither. I longed to yell something at the man—bully! stupid hick bully!—but my mother took my arm and firmly pulled me away down the sidewalk, away from the tall man, our car, my father. She walked straight down the street, holding my arm at the elbow, not looking back. I saw over my shoulder that my father was standing dejectedly next to the Plymouth, and the tall man, who had put one booted foot up on the car's fender, was writing out the ticket on his knee. The small ring of idle spectators drifted off. My mother pulled at my arm, marching me along, and in a moment, we were out of the village and walking at the hay-scented side of the highway.

This was a narrow two-lane county highway, with a yellow stripe painted down its center. The shoulder of the road where we walked was perilously uneven, with dribbles of melted tar and broken bits of gravel, asphalt, and rocks. By this time, black-raspberry ice cream had melted all over my fingers. I threw the ice cream cone over the barbed-wire fence to a waiting Holstein, who looked up at me, slowly chewing. My mother said nothing. I heard the old Plymouth come chugging up behind us. My father stopped the car in the dead center of the road, straddling the yellow line, and waited, looking straight ahead. My mother pushed me toward the car. "Get in," she said and opened the door to the front seat—unusual; I always sat in back. She got in beside me. I looked at my father. He was pale, his eyes dark, his face covered with sweat. My mother's face, however, was bright red. Curls of damp gray hair clung to her forehead. She had on a white dress with a print of red and blue seagulls flying upon it, and the vee of her chest was sunburned. A drop of sweat slid off her throat and fell into the deep declivity between her breasts. Neither she nor my father said anything at all.

They said nothing at all to each other for several days. If my mother had something to say to my father, she would say it to me: "Tell your father . . ." And my father had nothing at all to say to my mother, except through me. I didn't much care for this role of emissary or ambassador. I didn't like being in the middle, and for that reason or some other, toward the end of that week I lost my voice. I lay in bed, not upstairs in my bedroom but on an old sofa in the back parlor, where my mother could easily keep an eye on me. I slept and watched the sun and shadows on the ancient, yellowed, garlanded wallpaper, and my mother brought me trays full of fruit juice and fruit—thin slices of cool honeydew melon and golden brown-spotted Bartlett pears, glossy bunches of green grapes, red Delicious apples, thinly sliced—but I couldn't eat. My father came in and sat at the side of my bed and made me say "ahhh." He looked down my throat and felt under my chin with his fingers. He had been a medical orderly in World War I. "Hurt here?" he asked. I shook my head. "Here perhaps?" No, nothing hurt. Only I was tired and I couldn't talk. I slept. When I woke up, my mother and father were standing next to the bed.

"Well?" my mother said briskly. She always got angry when I was sick. "How is it? Can you talk?"

"Say Rumpelstiltskin," my father said. "Can you say that?"

I opened my mouth. "Yes," I said. My mother looked at my father and laughed, showing her dimples and crooked teeth. My father put his hand on my forehead.

"She still has fever," he said. "But you'll be all right, won't you." It wasn't a question, it was a mild command.

"Yes," I said again. My voice sounded deep as a bullfrog's.

They left the room, and I heard them talking about me in German, that rich barbarous language, and the sound of this talking—my father's deep voice, the harsh rolling way he pronounced his r's, and my mother's high, clear voice, and the funny way she had, when happy, of suddenly, funnily dropping the pitch of her voice to tell a story, and my father's baritone chuckle and my mother's laugh, with a beautiful tone like ringing glass—their voices talking to each other on and on blended into a dazzling texture that signified serenity, contentment, harmony. I fell asleep.

And the rhythm of our lives picked up again, closed tight, wove over this shameful, horrifying gap, the flaw in the family fabric. But in small ways and large ways things were different after this time in which we had all betrayed one another. Years later, when I was a sophomore in college and going out with a boy I liked very much, my mother said to me (she was tired, depressed, she stood at the window looking out, smoking), "Don't marry a Jew, Isabel, they're too much trouble."

# 9

Morgan died on March 22, the first day of spring. When she died, she weighed eighty-five pounds, and no one noticed until too late that her wedding ring was gone. She had fiercely refused to give it up, had had it adhesive-taped to her emaciated finger. It had slipped off or been stolen, exactly what no one knew. She had woken up once before she died and said to Douglas, "Thank you for . . ." Then she closed her eyes. All the while she was in a coma he sat at her hospital bed holding her hand. I sat a polite distance away, near the window. Once when I came back from checking the house, Margaret was there. Douglas was sitting in the chair next to Morgan's bed, and Margaret was standing behind him, her hands on his shoulders. She glanced at me briefly when I came in but did not move her hands. Douglas lifted his eyes to me, then dropped them. He had on the gray sweater. He looked exhausted. His pale eyes were bloodshot and red-rimmed, his face was gray. He had a long stipple of ruby scab on his jaw where he had cut himself shaving the day before. He said to Margaret in a low voice, "She's not in pain anymore. There's that, at least." Margaret placed one of her hands on his neck, as if to warm him, and he reached up for her hand and held it in his. I stared at first, not quite comprehending, and then (Why hadn't I seen it? Why hadn't I figured it out?), with a growing sense of—what? shame? anger?—I understood. It was as if a curtain had come down, invisible but absolutely impermeable, wrapping them all around, enclosing them, excluding me, leaving me outside and alone.

Some iron in me, some core of pure loyalty to Morgan, made me firm in my rights and obligations. I stayed in the little back room until after the funeral. I cooked the meals and did the necessary things, not for him, but for Morgan. Douglas's brother came with his blind wife and the children—I managed the household. Margaret stayed away. As soon as the funeral service was over, I packed my bag, put on my raincoat, tied a scarf over my head, and took the train back to the city.

I guess I knew what Joan was going to say before she'd said it. She was standing at her office window. She wouldn't look at me. "I'm sorry," she said, "I just couldn't cover for you anymore, Isabel. You've been out so much. Everyone has noticed. Everyone."

"It's all right."

"What will you do?"

I was sitting in her broken tubular chair. "I don't know," I said dreamily. I giggled. "I'm pregnant."

Her hand flew to her cheek. "Oh, God!" she said. "But you can't keep the baby! How far along are you?"

"Almost three months."

She groaned. "Oh, God, oh, God, you stupid, miserable dope. You utter half-wit."

Then, in the end, she got me an appointment through very good pull and went with me in a cab to the hospital to make sure I'd go through with it. Later she brought me back to my place. I had cramps. She made tea and brought me a cup. I sat at the oak table hunched up and shivering. She took the quilt off my sofa and draped it across my shoulders.

"What about money?" she said, sitting down across from me. "How much money do you have?"

"I don't know, exactly. In the bank I guess about a hundred. Don't worry, I can live on unemployment for a while." My teeth chattered. An arrow of pain in my side lit up briefly like neon, sizzled, went out. What had it pointed to? Nothing.

"There's unemployment insurance, and that's all?"

"Yes."

She shook her head and looked down at the table. "Isabel, I am getting divorced."

I was surprised. I looked up, forgetting my pain.

She smiled like a young girl, eyelids modestly lowered. "I've moved in with Enoch."

"With Enoch? Honestly?" Funny. I thought she was going to say David.

She nodded shyly. "I moved in two weeks ago."

"Gosh, I . . . thought that you'd . . . you know. Stopped seeing each other."

"Because of that girl?" Joan was scornful. "That girl was nothing, a nobody, an office temporary."

"Oh."

"I've already talked to Stuart and seen a lawyer. It was amazing."

"What?"

"He was angry. I was surprised. I didn't think that he cared one way or the other. Except of course now his routine is shot. How do you feel? How's the pain?"

"Okay. Don't worry."

"You are such a Prussian."

I wearily smiled. She looked at her watch. "I have to go."

"Okay."

"Isabel?"

"*What?*"

Silence. Only her worried blue eyes watching me.

"Lookit, Joan, don't feel sorry for me or bad, okay? I am all right. I have my resources." I shivered. "I'll get a little pet. A cat or a dog."

Joan rolled her eyes heavenward and stood up. "Very funny," she said. "Call me if . . ."

"Yes. Will you get the hell out?"

"All *right*."

"Good-*bye*."

The door slammed. I was alone again. That night Sarah called and asked if she could come see me the next day. She said it was her spring vacation. She wanted me to know, I guess, that she wasn't cutting school.

There were mauve patches under her eyes, and she looked thinner. I had made cocoa and cinnamon toast for us, and as if we were little kids, we sat at the oak table, eating greedily, licking cinnamon sugar off our fingers. She said that her father was doing okay, but it had been hard on both of them, cleaning out her mother's things.

Sarah reached around—she had hung her down jacket over the back of the chair—and felt into an inside jacket. She brought out a little wad of folded-over tissue paper and handed it to me.

"What is it?" I asked, unfolding the tissue. It was a pair of long onyx earrings, set in gold. The onyx was carved in a curious shape, like scimitars. Looking at them, I guessed art deco, art moderne. My parents' era. "But I don't have pierced ears."

"You can easily fix that," Sarah said. She leaned over the table, her chin in her hand. "My mother said she wanted you to have them. She said that her mother had left them to her, and *she* got them in Germany one summer. It was a long time ago, before World War II. She thought they'd look nice with your color hair. I don't think she thought of you as all that German, particularly. You were just, you know, Isabel."

I remembered that day in the hospital when Morgan had said so spitefully, "You Jews." I had forgiven her, had put it out of my mind because it was such a fierce aberration, and yet it had seemed sad to me—this serpent lying hidden there, coiled up in a nest of friendship. How infinitely complex love seems, in its tenderness and aggressions.

Sarah looked at me flatly. "She left Mrs. Allen something, too—an opal ring. I tried to talk her out of it."

I said, "Mrs. Allen never wears rings."

"Yeah," Sarah said, "I know. She's at our house all the time now."

I saw that Sarah knew and, in one of those moments of intuition, the still flash of lightning that illumines the dark room you've been stumbling around in, saw that Morgan had known something, too. Had sensed a deep attraction. And that was why she'd sent me to stay with Margaret. She had wanted me to find out. Not about Paul Caron, but about Douglas.

Sarah said, "I really don't like Mrs. Allen much. You never know what she's thinking."

Later, at the door, she said, "You cared for my father, didn't you?" I had no answer. She said, "I could tell. It was on your face, in your eyes." She pulled a white knit angora cap out of her pocket and put it on. The cap came down to her black, straggly brows. It was April 7 and snowing.

Jerry Allen's hair had gone a little gray at the curly edges, but he was otherwise unchanged since I'd last seen him in Summerville more than three years earlier. He has a brown-skinned face, a deep-dented chin, and tilted hazel eyes. I thought he was good-looking and sat there at dinner hoping my hormones would simply take over. Removed from the Summerville setting, he was attractively at ease with himself. He'd come to Morgan's funeral and later called me up. Talking to him on the phone, I'd thought, *Why not?*

"So that," he said, "is the boring story on that." He smiled crookedly, and his face broke into deep dimples.

"Then they're not living together?" I asked.

"My dear," he said mockingly, "in Summerville?" He laughed, showing strong white teeth. "Not even married people live together in Summerville. Good Lord, what would the trustees of Essex Academy say? The trustees, bless their iron-bound souls, would throw old Douglas out faster than you can say *cohabitation*. I doubt old Douglas even stays over." I was irritated by the way he kept saying "old Douglas" and irritated at myself for the way my heart beat when I found out they weren't yet married. I wanted to ask Jerry if he knew how long they'd been lovers, but there was no possible tactful way to ask, and besides, it was doubtful that Jerry would know. My own guess was, not until March, about the time she'd started paint-

254

ing. Or maybe I only wanted to believe that in January, the night of the snow, I hadn't been the basest form of mere convenience. My bad old habit, perhaps: rearranging the props and scenery so the script would read better.

We finished our manicotti, drank more wine, had espresso and zuppa inglese for dessert.

"Sometimes," Jerry said, lighting a cigarillo and leaning back in his chair, "I think if we'd done it differently, it would all have gone better. I had this idea of a life we were going to have—the house, the kids, real friends. I wanted some sort of a normal, orderly, middle-class existence. Stability. Do you follow me? My own family was kind of strange." He raised his hazel eyes. I remembered Margaret telling me how much she had loved his family. "I grew up in a small town in Georgia. My family always seemed so out of it. They were Jewish, the only Jews in town." He added, "I am Jewish," and then said wearily, "I guess. In a way."

We had had a lot to drink. I said, "It's hard. When I was in college..."

I thought for a moment I would tell him: *When I was in college, after half a lifetime of living with a Protestant, my father ran off with a young Jewish woman. In middle age he took up Judaism all over again.*

I didn't get that far. Jerry didn't look interested, only petulant.

"And besides," he said irritably, puffing on his cigarillo, "I doubt they'll be happy together. They're too much alike, too serious, too quiet, too damn WASPy. Would you like some brandy?"

"No, thanks," I said. "Oh, I hate that little niche, WASP. Why can't we forget these absurd categories, they're so boring."

"Because *they* don't," he said, sullenly.

"Anyway," I said, "I'll agree that they're both too quiet. You can't light a fire without a spark."

"My guess is it's an interim thing for them both. I knew

years ago that Douglas was attracted to my wife. *Ex*-wife. One summer we all had a picnic together . . ." His hazel eyes turned vague, and he tipped ash off the cigarillo with a practiced flick of two fingers. "But God, Morgan was marvelous, wasn't she? She had a way of looking at you . . ." He shook his head and smiled.

I said, "I loved that quality of hers, that zest she had for life," and I lifted my head. Across the noisy restaurant someone had struck a wineglass, and the glass had rung out, and in my head I heard Morgan laugh, a peal of bright, ringing joy. I thought how, except in my head, I would never hear her laugh again; she was lost to me forever.

Jerry said, "I do think old Douglas would have been an utter stick if he hadn't been married to Morgan."

I sat back. It was late, I was suddenly tired. "You keep saying *old* Douglas. What's that for? It couldn't be a little residual jealousy?"

He frowned and sat up straight. "No," he said. He hailed the waiter. "Check, please," he said.

He didn't call me again. It was just as well. We would have had an indifferent time of it—something was missing, ingredient X, whatever it is. Not just lack of attraction, but something I felt about his personality. With David I'd always felt in danger somehow, of being . . . engulfed. He was so competent, so managerial. Jerry Allen was a different story. He was charming, he was fun, he was clever—intelligent, even—but everything was right on the surface, while in Douglas there was something deep and strange and unknowable, a reservoir of quiet whose depths it would take a lifetime to plumb.

In September Sarah called me again. She had had a shitty summer but, thank God, was going away to boarding school. Her voice was bitter. Since her mother had died, Margaret had been all over her like a rug.

I said, puzzled, "How come all of you are in each other's hair so much?"

She said, "Didn't Margaret call you? They got married in August. *We* had to move into *her* house. They haven't told a whole lot of people because, you know, let's face it, it looks terrible. My mother hasn't even been dead six months. Oh, Isabel," she burst out, "it's really hideous! You wouldn't recognize Margaret. She's had her hair curled and wears it in a big mop. And my *father* . . . last night at the dinner table he started laughing, and then, as if he suddenly remembered, he stopped. Oh, it's so fake, the whole thing."

I interrupted her and said, lying, that I had to go, someone was ringing my door buzzer. She asked if she could come see me on her school vacations. I said of course and hung up.

I stood for a while at my window. The window was grimy inside and out. I put my fingers on the gritty glass and wrote initials—D.W.—then erased them with my fist.

# V

❧ ❧ ❧

From
Isabel's
Notebook

*March 22*

Morgan dead one year.
"Memory is an imperfect organ," he said.
In fact, the sore place he left on my heart has scabbed over, leaving only the faintest of scars. It's as if I have buried him— he is dead to me—while Morgan seems to grow daily more alive. Inside my head she glows on, stubbornly incandescent. Someday, not quite yet, I'll try to breathe her back into existence.

*April 1*

Continuing with my Proust. From *The Guermantes Way* . . . ". . . the garden where we played in our childhood. There is no need to travel in order to see it again; we must dig down inwardly to discover it . . . a mere excursion does not suffice for a visit to the dead city; excavation is necessary also."

*April 7*

Parents' wedding anniversary.
Dig some more, Isabel. Where is it, the dead city? Or is it a childhood garden, grown over but living still?

My mother stands at the window looking out at the lake. It has suddenly turned cool, as it often does in the Adirondacks after the middle of August, and over a light summer dress she wears a green tweed suit jacket. I have a cold and a fever and am lying on the sofa—a bed improvised in the back parlor of the old farmhouse.

My mother says dully, "I don't know, I don't know," and my father, who is in the room, responds smilingly, encouragingly, "I know, I know, I know." It seems to me there is something apologetic in the way he says this—not for anything specific he has done or not done but for himself—he is apologizing simply for being. I sense this often in things he says or does.

"It was crazy for us to marry," my mother says and hastily wipes her eyes on a balled-up handkerchief. "Always such trouble. It made no sense."

"I know, I know," my father says again.

"Better to stick to your own kind," my mother says. And then sighs. "But what was my own kind? I always read too much, everyone in the village thought I was strange. Ach," she says, "irrational, completely irrational."

"Yes," my father says. Now he takes a voluminous white handkerchief out of his pants pocket and blows his nose.

My mother looks over her shoulder at my father and lowers her eyes. She has beautiful eyes—they are silvery gray, and her lashes and brows are black, and her cheeks at this moment are very pink. "I could have married Karl Otto Herrmann and gone to live in Schweinfurt."

"Ah!" my father says. "The fellow with the . . ." He extends both his hands and in a gliding circular motion describes with them a little round globe—his own stomach is flat. He is thin and wiry.

My mother's mouth goes in and up on one side, making the dimple come out in her cheek. "Schweinfurt! Do you remember the . . ."

"Ha! The Opel! The fall of '32, when we lost our brakes and had to stay . . . what the devil was the name of that place?"

My mother smiles, eyes still lowered, and delicately blushes.

"Gasthaus Zimmermann, don't you remember? And they gave us the room . . ."

"With the broken bed and the cracked blue pitcher!"

"And we had there an unbelievable coincidence—Anna Maria Droeschke, with her sister-in-law's cousin. Her face when we walked into the dining room! All the way from Berlin! I thought she would fall in the soup."

"And he was so, so *obliging*, poor fellow, he couldn't have been nicer, so attentive, bought us all champagne, scared to death."

"But in the end—isn't this odd?—she went with her husband."

"She wasn't Jewish at all, eh?"

"*Keineswegs!* She said she was Jewish, and since she had black hair, they believed her. They both died at Dachau, Frau George told me."

"Unbelievable. Guilt, do you think, perhaps?"

"*Weiss nicht.* Who knows? She always had a fellow on the side, so long as I knew her."

"People are a strange lot, eh? What's that? Did you hear something?"

Outside the windows there is the soft, sliding thud of feet running on grass. My mother turns pale, my father's face turns a dark magenta red. He walks—no, *hurtles* himself—through the house to the kitchen door. I hear the screen door open (*squawk*) and close (*slam*) and hear my father walking back through the house. He enters the room with his pale red eyebrows raised.

"What's this?" my mother asks. My father holds a peck basket of peaches tucked into the crook of his arm, and in his other hand what appears to be a box wrapped in newspaper. It is comb honey still in its slat-sided box, bundled up in the Schenectady *Gazette*.

"Maybe it's a mistake?" my father says.

"Why, I don't know," my mother says. "You saw no one?"

"They'd driven off."

"What a mystery," my mother says. "As I get older I see it so clearly, people are an awful mystery. One never knows, never completely understands. They are terrible, they are wonderful, sometimes all at once."

They went on talking, and I lay with my eyes open, contentedly staring at the ceiling, and then smiled and turned on my side and went to sleep. When I awoke, there was a silence, not the glacial, taut silence of midwinter but a silence that had a thousand sounds in it, chirps, peeps, hums, buzzes, an entire midday meadow at work, the kind of silence that seems to flower, grow swollen and fragrant, pollen-heavy, that has in it drones and the smell of honey, that is lazy and full and complete. In my mind, young as I was, this silence seemed richly sexual, an intricate blending, a matrix out of which came all life, change, hope, happiness. Above my head I heard my mother's low laugh, and the bed creaked as she got up. A moment later she appeared in my doorway, in her blue dressing gown that was loosely tied at the waist. She stood sideways, looking in on me, with one hand laid across her breasts. Then she smiled at me and softly closed the door.